Harriet

Harriet Beecher Stowe
1853 portrait by Alanson Fisher

Harriet

THE LIFE AND WORLD OF HARRIET BEECHER STOWE

NORMA JOHNSTON

FOUR WINDS PRESS ✧ NEW YORK

MAXWELL MACMILLAN CANADA   TORONTO

MAXWELL MACMILLAN INTERNATIONAL

NEW YORK   OXFORD   SINGAPORE   SYDNEY

Four Winds Press
Macmillan Publishing Company
866 Third Avenue
New York, NY 10022
Maxwell Macmillan Canada, Inc.
1200 Eglinton Avenue East
Suite 200
Don Mills, Ontario M3C 3N1
Macmillan Publishing Company is part of the
Maxwell Communication Group of Companies.
First edition
Printed and bound in the United States of America
10   9   8   7   6   5   4   3   2   1
The text of this book is set in ITC Galliard.
Book design by Christy Hale
Library of Congress Cataloging-in-Publication Data
Johnston, Norma.
Harriet : the life and world of Harriet Beecher Stowe / by Norma Johnston.—1st ed.
Includes bibliographical references and index.
ISBN 0-02-747714-2
1. Stowe, Harriet Beecher, 1811–1896—Biography—Juvenile literature.
2. Authors, American—19th century—Biography—Juvenile literature.
3. Abolitionists—United States—Biography—Juvenile literature.
[1. Stowe, Harriet Beecher,—1811–1896.   2. Authors, American.
3. Women—Biography.] I. Title.
PS2956.J64 1994
813'.3—dc20 93-38890
[B]

The photographs and prints on pages 35, 131, 135, 184, 186, 193, 201, 204, and 214
are reproduced courtesy of the Stowe-Day Foundation in Hartford, Connecticut, and
the print on page 16 is reproduced courtesy of the Litchfield Historical Society in
Litchfield, Connecticut.

For my mother,
a daughter of the Puritans

Table of Contents

AUTHOR'S NOTE

*E*very once in a while a book appears that so captures the voice and feel, the fire and fury of its time that it shakes the world, and reverberates on into the future. *Uncle Tom's Cabin* was that book in the United States of the 1850s–1860s. It came out of "nowhere"—the columns of an obscure antislavery weekly—to take on a life of its own. Its author was a small, shy housewife who, herself bewildered by the force of what had flowed through her pen, declared that *God* wrote *Uncle Tom's Cabin;* she only set down the words.

But Harriet Beecher Stowe was no ordinary housewife. She was descended from the staunch Nonconformists who had dared the wild waves during the Great Migration of the 1630s in search of religious freedom; who believed their God-given purpose in life was to be their brothers' keepers and to preach God's will. She was the daughter, wife, and sister of preachers; her father blazed so brightly he put all around him (including his own family) in the shade. She was born a girl, in a time and culture where only boys really mattered because only boys could grow up into ordained ministers. But she was also two things more: a mother who had lost a child, and a born storyteller. It was out of all this that she became a writer . . . became an abolitionist . . . became the author of *Uncle Tom's Cabin*.

The book is still in print today, all over the world. It, and its author, are still subjects of praise, scorn, mockery, and outrage. Far more people know *about* the book than have actually read it. Few people know anything about its author at all.

The first time I "met" Harriet was in 1964—the height of the civil rights movement. I was director of a group of teenagers who used our church stage as a platform from which to speak out on the issues and conflicts of our times. Living in the North, we were very conscious of how easy it was for the adults around us to congratulate themselves that "prejudice doesn't exist up here." We wanted to use the stage to give that complacency a big jolt.

We found a play called *Harriet* by Florence Ryerson and Colin Clements. It was the story of Harriet Beecher Stowe and the writing of *Uncle Tom's Cabin*. I knew that book had been a notorious best-seller that had shocked and shaken up the world. I knew modern readers considered *Uncle Tom's Cabin* "sticky-sentimental" and "goody-goody," and that the depiction of black characters offended many. But I didn't know Harriet herself at all.

I found her in that play (based almost entirely on her own words), in Joanna Johnston's and Forrest Wilson's biographies, in her own writing, and in her heritage—which was one I share. Harriet was a "daughter of the Puritans," and so am I. Being a Puritan—or a Calvinist, as it is usually called today—gives a very particular angle to the way one sees the world, and God, and one's "reason for being." The more I have researched Harriet's heritage, the more I have understood my own.

Harriet Beecher Stowe was a middle-class white Calvinist woman; that was the lens through which she saw the world, and the angle of vision from which she wrote. Actually, she was not always a very good writer, in the literary sense, and she never lived in the slave-owning South. But she could conjure up characters out of visions, memories, and dreams; make them live and breathe and speak and move; make them take over her readers' hearts and minds as they did hers.

She knew the horrors of slavery from having lived in a "border state" and from things told her by people she knew, both black and white, who had had firsthand experience with the "peculiar institution," as it was called. She could make readers *see* mansions and slave shanties; *smell* the salt of the sea and the sweat of aching bodies; *taste* the bitter taste of terror; and *hear* the whistle of the lash. It simply didn't matter whether the phrases in which she did this seemed melodramatic in her time—or ours. People loved *Uncle Tom's Cabin,* laughed at it, or loathed it. What they could *not* do was ignore it. Like Topsy, it "jest growed." Like Dred, the militant slave leader in Harriet Beecher Stowe's other antislavery novel, it stood up and demanded that attention be paid.

As a Calvinist, Harriet had been taught that every human soul was a child of God, regardless of the color of the skin in which it was clothed. As a bereaved mother, she felt a special bond with black women she knew whose children had been torn from them and sold down the river. She was the first to try to write African-American speech as it was then spoken; she didn't always succeed at this, but she tried. She portrayed her African-American characters with respect, and with as much accuracy as the men and women of color whom she knew permitted her to know. As for her white characters—*those* she knew very well indeed. The clergy, the complacent, the unconsciously bigoted, the confused, those who tried to do right but didn't know how—she put them on her pages with stinging accuracy, with affection or outrage, with a saving grace of humor. The only time her perspective seemed to fail her was with those who died young. But death was a constant shadow in those days before modern medicine, and belief in the Wisdom of Innocence and the Angelic Child was a comfort to grieving parents.

Harriet survived it all—parental disappointment that she was a girl; loss of mother and of sons; depression and other physical illnesses; a husband who adored and respected her but could never quite support their growing family. Fame. Vilification (being called a "nigger-lover" and worse). Scandals. The bitter irony of seeing her masterpiece—written to awaken her country to the outrages being perpetrated on African Americans—turned into the "Tom Shows" that degraded Uncle Tom and all of his race. And, in the words she herself quoted from Scripture, she "kept on keeping on"—with faith in God, in humanity, and in the future. With love. And always with a sense of humor.

As a daughter of the Puritans myself, I can understand *why*. As a storyteller, I hope I have been able to show *how*. On the threshold of the twenty-first century, we still have much to learn from *Uncle Tom's Cabin* and from Harriet Beecher Stowe. As the great

African-American poet Paul Laurence Dunbar wrote, *"She told the story. . . ."*

A Word about Language and Race

What is correct or incorrect in spelling, grammar, punctuation, and the meaning of words is *not* fixed and certain. Language is fluid; language evolves. Above all, the meanings and connotations of words are continually evolving. Many words of Harriet Beecher Stowe's day have no meaning to us at all. Many then shocking are nowadays accepted. Many then commonly used are nowadays shocking. What is "proper" (in language and behavior) is constantly changing.

Nowhere is this as true as in the language of race. The "proper" (polite) term in the nineteenth century for persons of African descent was Negro. The word (from the Latin *niger*, meaning "black") has been so debased by derogatory use that it is no longer acceptable at the end of the twentieth century. In writing this biography I was confronted with the dilemma of what term to use instead, and I have chosen to denote the races in what linguistically are parallel terms—*white* and *black*. In world history persons of either (or any color) might be either slave or free. It took the American slave trade to debase the words. . . . It took a war (spurred on by a book) to eliminate slavery in America. . . . It took the civil rights movement to make the word *black* synonymous with *proud*.

A Word about the Beechers and Fame

It is difficult for us today to realize the enormity of the Beecher family's fame. In a time before radio, before motion pictures, before television . . . in a nation still dominated by Puritanism, in which reading novels was suspect and attending theatrical performances was considered by the majority to be sinful or at the very least "not quite nice" . . . authors were major celebrities, and preachers who toured the nation's pulpits and lecture platforms were superstars. In the small towns and cities of America, the church was the center of intellectual and social life, oratory a fine art, and listening to a great speaker was a multisensory, almost multimedia, event.

The Beechers were the greatest of the great. Lyman Beecher and his dazzling son Henry Ward Beecher were the equivalent of the most celebrated televangelists today—national celebrities, national role models, national icons. Harriet Beecher Stowe—the first American superstar woman author, in a day when women were expected to exert their influence only in the home—to her own astonishment (and probably her brothers' chagrin) eclipsed them all. She has gone down in history as "the little lady who wrote the book that made [the] great war." Her fame has outlasted that of all her kin.

I

"Wisht It Had Been a Boy…"

1811; 1630-1799

FROM THE VERY BEGINNING, from her earliest conscious memory, there were some things that small Harriet Beecher just *knew*.

Papa was splendid. Papa was, like the biblical patriarchs, a "giant in the earth." Mama was everything beautiful and good. It was a wonderful thing to be a Beecher. It was also a great responsibility. There were more things in the world than could be seen, heard, tasted, touched, or felt. Slavery was a terrible wrong.

No one told Harriet any of these things; she simply knew them.

There was much that little Hattie *was* told, for the Beechers, one and all, were great talkers. The endless wrangling around the dinner table, as theology was debated and family legends shared, was part of what made being a Beecher so much fun. But life was also, Papa taught, a "vale of tears" through which people muddled their way to (if they were lucky) heaven. People were meant to believe in the God Papa preached about, and—if they were men— to become preachers, too. That was why Papa had made a vow to have many children—so he could raise up sons to preach the word of the Lord. Hattie was a genius, Papa said; it was a shame that she had not been born a boy. Papa *must* be right, Harriet was sure, because after all Papa *was* Lyman Beecher.

"Wisht it had been a boy" was practically the first thing Lyman said when, on the fourteenth of June, in the Year of Our Lord 1811, he reported Harriet's birth to his good friend Judge Tapping Reeve. There were already two girls in the Beechers' crowded parsonage, and three boys also. Pleased as Lyman was to welcome this new daughter he could not help wishing she had been a boy. *That* would have been the crowning touch to this first triumphal year in Litchfield.

Litchfield, Connecticut, in 1810, was the most beautiful, most cultivated little town—a miniature city, really—in New England, possibly in the whole new nation. The distinguished inhabitants of Litchfield had had among them two who were greater than the rest: Judge Tapping Reeve and Revolutionary War Colonel Benjamin Tallmadge. In 1810 there came a third, Rev. Mr. Beecher.

Lyman Beecher at thirty-six was the most famous preacher in New England. In a country that in its Constitution officially separated church and state, Puritanism—or Congregationalism, as it was now called—was Connecticut's official state religion. The Beechers had been among the founding fathers and mothers of New England. Small Harriet Elizabeth Beecher would grow up with family legends as much a part of her daily life as family prayers.

Those "protestant dissenters" who had come to the New World in the 1630s in search of religious freedom had been a special breed. Unlike the Separatists, who had landed at Plymouth Rock in 1620, the dissenters of the Great Migration some ten years later were Puritans. They wanted, not to separate from the Established Church, but to purify it from within. They wanted to found in the New World a New Jerusalem.

They were a strong and rock-ribbed lot, those early Puritans, who saw life as a journey to heaven but were even ready to accept being "damned to the glory of God" if God so chose. They saw being their brothers' keepers as their bounden duty, and made minding each other's business their fine art.

Even among those larger-than-life Puritans, the Beechers were something special. They were the only family, the only dynasty, whose head and original landowner had been a woman.

John and Hannah Beecher were among the fifty men and two hundred women and children who in 1638 sailed from Kent, England, to New England with the Rev. John Davenport and former Deputy-Governor of India (and British Ambassador to Denmark) Theophilus Eaton. It was the most prosperous company of Puritans to emigrate to New England, and it arrived in Boston harbor to find the Massachusetts Bay Colony in an uproar. The strong-minded Anne Hutchinson had dared to challenge Puritan authority, insisting on each person's right to make peace with God based on individual conscience and not on church intervention. For this heresy against Puritan teaching—and for the heresy of daring, as a woman, to preach at all—she was expelled from the colony. She and her followers founded a new settlement in Rhode Island.

The conservative Davenport company also believed in government by God's emissaries, the Puritan clergy. But they had no wish to get involved in Boston's disputations. They sent out a small party led by Theophilus Eaton to look for a place where they could set up their own "Bible Commonwealth." The search party found their "New Haven" at a place the native people called Quinnipiack. Seven of their number, including John Beecher, stayed there to overwinter in a crude log shelter. The winter was harsh, and the men's provisions ridiculously inadequate. When the rest of the Davenport company arrived in the spring, Hannah Beecher found her husband had died and been buried in an unmarked grave.

She was thirty-nine years old, a stranger in a strange land with only her young son, Isaac. A lesser woman might have returned to England, or at least to Boston, or not survived. It was *men*—God-fearing, covenanted Christian men—who headed families and had the right to own property. This was the "natural order" of the time, taken from long-standing interpretation of Scripture.

Women were commonly regarded as "weaker vessels." The description did not fit Hannah Beecher any better than it had fit Anne Hutchinson. Hannah had a lion's heart. More importantly, she had a profession. She was an experienced midwife.

For a colony to take root and thrive in an unknown wilderness, a steady supply of healthy children was an absolute necessity. In this new colony, whose constitution ordered that the word of God should be the only governing rule, and land-owning male church members the only free burgesses eligible to hold office or to vote, the Seven Pillars of the church (Davenport, Eaton, and the five other leaders who made up the governing body of church and state) made the Widow Beecher an enticing offer. If she would stay on as midwife to the colony, the land that would have been allotted to her dead husband would be allotted directly to her, *in her own name*. With that land, and that professional position, came power. Hannah, the matriarch, became a potent legend in the Beecher family history.

The Beechers flourished in the Connecticut wilderness. Like the Hebrew patriarchs, Hannah's Isaac begat John, and John begat Joseph the clockmaker. Joseph begat another Joseph, a giant of a man who could lift a barrel of cider into the air to drink from it and who founded on the family farm a blacksmith shop. His anvil stood upon the stump of the very oak under which the Rev. Mr. Davenport had preached his very first sermon in New Haven.

Joseph the blacksmith fathered Nathaniel, and passed on to him the family farm and occupation. Nathaniel fathered David, who became celebrated throughout the colonies as New Haven's learned blacksmith.

With David Beecher at hammer and anvil, the Beecher smithy became a place where the men of New Haven hammered out ideas and beliefs in the white heat of disputation. David Beecher was a skilled craftsman and great reader, who wore out five wives and sired a flock of children. He welcomed Yale College students into his home as boarders, borrowing their books and class notes so he could "read up" on history, geography, and astronomy. He knew the Bible by heart and could quote Scripture with the best of them. He was a regular advisor to his friend Roger Sherman, member of Congress for Connecticut.

In 1775—the year the first shots of the American Revolution were fired—Esther Lyman Beecher, David's third wife, gave birth to a son with the blue-gray Beecher eyes. The child also inherited the family's fierce intelligence and love of learning. He was baptized and brought up in the stern faith of his forefathers, without ever losing his zest for life or his sense of humor. He was named, after the fashion among New Englanders, for his mother's family: *Lyman Beecher*.

Lyman's mother died of consumption (tuberculosis) two days after giving birth, and he was raised by his aunt and uncle, Lot and Catharine Benton, in Nutplains, Connecticut. His childless uncle set out to train him as heir and eventual owner of the Benton farm. But Lyman, though strong and athletic, was a total failure as a farmer. His mind kept wandering. He had his father's insatiable intellectual curiosity. At last his uncle, facing reality, took Lyman back to New Haven for a family conference. Perhaps young Lyman should attend Yale College? The Bentons would provide the needed clothing (with Aunt Benton doing most of the sewing) if David Beecher could take care of the rest. David approved. Lyman was willing. After two years of advance studying under another uncle who was a clergyman, Lyman entered Yale in 1793. For the eighteen-year-old boy it was a heady and mind-opening experience.

The Beechers and Bentons, true to their heritage, were staunch Calvinists. Yale in the 1790s was presided over by a dedicated skeptic, an admirer of Rousseau, Voltaire, and Tom Paine. Under President Stiles, college life was anything but puritanical. Before Lyman could be led astray, President Stiles was out of office and Dr. Timothy Dwight became president. A follower of the famous Dr. Jonathan Edwards, who had galloped through New England scaring sinners to repentance, Dr. Dwight was a fervent preacher of Calvinist doctrine, and became Lyman's mentor-hero.

The following year Lyman stumbled headlong into the shattering mystical experience the Puritans called "conversion." By that they meant that an intellectual belief in God was converted into a firsthand experience of God's absolute greatness and one's own unworthiness. To Lyman, whose imaginative mind was filled with vivid pictures of Jesus' crucifixion and of sinners writhing in the fires of hell, the terrors of the damned and the joys of the "Elect" were very real. Was he one of the Elect? If so, how should he respond? After a year of spinning between faith and doubt, exhilaration and despair, Lyman found his conviction: He *was* "elected," and therefore he *must* preach.

He threw himself into feverish study of rhetoric and logic, ethics and metaphysics and theology, financing his studies by working as the college butler, selling food and wine and hard liquors to his fellow students. By the time he graduated he was well on his way to becoming the greatest theologian, the greatest preacher, and one of the greatest wits in the new United States of America. He had paid his debts, bought a new suit of clothes, and saved up three hundred dollars on which to set out in the world. He had also had another shattering experience, a very joyous one.

It occurred during his sophomore year at Yale when classmate Benjamin Baldwin took him to pay a call at Castle Ward, the Guilford, Connecticut, home of Revolutionary War hero General Andrew Ward. The general and his aged mother were providing a home for his widowed daughter and her many children. The young men from Yale found the four Foote girls in Castle Ward's old millhouse, spinning. It was an encounter straight out of a fairy tale. Harriet, Roxana, Catherine, and Mary were young, and beautiful, and gifted, and Roxana was the fairest of them all. Lyman took one look at her and fell in love as tumultuously as he had fallen into his conversion.

The cocksure young Lyman had already made up his mind to marry a woman as strong and intelligent as himself. It was his good fortune that his heart had found exactly what his head desired. Roxana had sworn to her sisters that she would wed "only a Sir Charles Grandison," meaning a high-minded gentleman like the hero of the popular romantic novel. She gave her heart to Lyman Beecher, the blacksmith's son.

There was one overwhelming problem. Roxana was Episcopalian, a member of the "popish religion." Was it right for a future Puritan minister to woo and wed a woman not a Calvinist? Even more important, was Roxana one of the Elect? She was a truly good woman, as Lyman rapidly discovered, but was that goodness the result of her having given her heart to God through conversion, or was it only "natural goodness"?

Through two years Lyman wrestled with his soul, his conscience, and his desires. He proposed, and was accepted, without ever voicing his religious qualms to his beloved. At last his Yale graduation approached. Lyman steeled himself to bring up the subject of salvation with Roxana, prepared—if her beliefs were too terribly different from his own—to break off the engagement. Eloquently he laid out before her the Calvinist understanding of God's great plan for humankind's salvation. Before he was finished, Roxana was in a state straight out of one of her romantic novels—tears flowing, bosom heaving, looking impossibly beautiful.

Lyman couldn't bear to tell her, then or ever, that he had been prepared to give her up. Instead he wrote her several long letters, expressing his anguished concern for the state of her soul. He succeeded in throwing her into such alternating ecstasy and gloom that her family feared she was losing her mind. Finally he put her to the ultimate test: Could she, would she rejoice even in being "damned to the glory of God"?

Roxana's reaction was pure outrage. Being "damned" meant being terribly wicked, didn't it? How could someone's being terribly wicked possibly contribute to the glory of God? The very idea was blasphemy!

Lyman was rocked by the response. He found his way back to his orthodox beliefs, but he never brought the subject up with Roxana again. He received his license to preach, and preached his first sermon in the Guilford church with Roxana and Aunt and Uncle Benton in proud attendance. He accepted a call to the Presbyterian Church in East Hampton, Long Island, and sailed off with his horse and saddle, all his worldly possessions in a little white trunk, eager to win souls and to make a home for his future bride.

The story of Lyman and Roxana's courtship became one of the family's cherished legends. None of Lyman's children would be so affected by it as his middle child, Harriet Beecher, who should have been a boy.

II

"I Declare! If I Didn't Switch 'Em an' Scorch 'Em!"

1799–1816

EAST HAMPTON, NEW YORK, in 1799 was a tiny fishing village. Its weathered cottages clustered on the south shore of the narrow land spit at the far end of Long Island, miles from New York City and a world away from Yale's intellectual fervor. The land was flat, and the dark forests that the explorer Henry Hudson had found there in 1609 were long gone. A windmill whirred at each end of the single grass-grown street, and geese wandered up and down. But the church had a bell and clock, finest on the island, and there was a wild beauty in the endless ocean and the white sand beaches that stretched as far as eye could see.

There was much to fuel Lyman Beecher's energy and zeal. The Montauk Indians were being exploited by white rum-sellers; something had to be done about that, and not-yet-baptized Indians converted. There was also a local Infidel Club, made up of skeptics like those Lyman had encountered at Yale. The Infidel Club had recently burned a Bible with full ceremony; that could not be allowed to pass unchallenged! Lyman was delighted to discover that his parish extended well beyond the narrow boundaries of East Hampton. On Sundays, two-horse wagons rattled into town bringing whole families from Wainscott and Three-Mile Harbor; from Amagansett and The Springs and Fireplace; from Freetown, where a small community of free blacks lived. To the people of these isolated little settlements, a day of rousing sermons and sociability was the high point of the week.

Lyman bought a cottage for $800, a princely price for a new preacher whose wages were to be $300 a year, plus firewood. But ministers could count on being beneficiaries of a "donation party" at least once a year, and his fiancée was noted for her artistic handiwork as well as for her intelligence and beauty. On September 18, 1799, Lyman Beecher took Roxana Foote as his wedded wife, to love and to cherish, for richer or poorer, in sickness and in health. Proudly he brought her to his windswept parish. Roxana found herself face-to-face with the reality of being a preacher's wife.

At a time when a sermon was expected to last a good two hours, Lyman preached seven or eight times a week. He also gave lectures in the nearby villages, and conducted services in the Montauk settlement. He was appointed trustee and principal of Clinton Academy, the first academy to be founded in New York State. In his free time he went hunting and fishing—for relaxation, and to fill the Beecher larder.

The gifted Roxana, too shy to take an official role in parish affairs, devoted herself to home and family. Life in East Hampton was as busy as it was Spartan. The mansion of Lyman's new friend John Lyon Gardiner, seventh Lord of the Manor of nearby Gardiner's Island, had fine carved furniture; the sparse furniture in East Hampton cottages was locally made. Floors were kept tidily sprinkled with clean sand. Occasionally there might be a small rag or braided rug, but none of the currently fashionable "floorcloths" and certainly not the silken carpets of the rich.

Roxana longed for a floorcloth. When Lyman received a cash gift from Uncle Lot Benton, he "had an itch" to spend it immediately on a gift for her: a bale of cotton specially imported for her from New York City. She spun it herself; had it woven; laid it and sized it and painted it with pigments she ordered from New York

10

and ground and mixed herself. The preacher's wife's beautiful parlor, her flowery floorcloth, her own framed watercolors, and the miniatures she painted on ivory became the wonder of the village. Her garden foamed with flowers in the summertime. Roxana cheered and comforted her husband, she spun and wove and sewed, she cooked and cleaned with the help of two young "bound girls" (indentured servants), sisters in their very early teens. And, as Lyman had eagerly hoped, she bore him children.

One after another they came, in swift succession: Catharine, William, Edward, Mary, George—little Christian soldiers whom Lyman could raise up to "win souls to Christ" or to be preachers' wives and preachers' mothers. Lyman's salary climbed to $400 a year but was still not enough to meet expenses. Roxana did what most wives of her class and situation did—opened a school in her parlor, and took some of the young girl students in as boarders. Lyman was supposed to help teach, but Lyman loathed teaching. Besides, he was so busy. After three years of his backbreaking routine he had had a breakdown and had been unable to resume full parish duties for a year. Roxana grew frail, but she found time for her art, time to encourage and applaud her husband, time to fill her children's lives with joy and laughter.

In 1804 two Revolutionary War heroes, Aaron Burr and Alexander Hamilton, fought a duel to the death on the cliffs of the New Jersey Palisades. When the pistol smoke died, Hamilton was dead, Burr disgraced, and Lyman Beecher had found a new cause.

"Dueling is a great national sin," he thundered from his pulpit. He repeated the sermon at General Synod, the highest governing body of the Presbyterian Church, urging a resolution for the formation of societies to outlaw dueling.

To his astonishment, he met with strong opposition, for dueling as a means of settling matters of honor was entrenched in the American culture. Lyman Beecher, a thirty-year-old country preacher, found himself opposing—and winning over—the most prominent old doctors of divinity in the Presbyterian Church. "Made [their arguments] ludicrous," he reported jubilantly to

Roxana. "Never made an argument so short, strong, and pointed in my life. . . . Oh, I declare! If I didn't switch 'em an' scorch 'em an' stamp on 'em. . . . It was the center of old fogyism, but I mowed it down. . . ."

The anti-dueling sermon was soon published, and brought Lyman national recognition.

That same year, Roxana's sister Mary fled for refuge to the Beechers after a traumatic, brief marriage to a Jamaican planter. Mary Beecher, born the following year, was named for her, but it was five-year-old Catharine who became Mary Foote Hubbard's favorite and confidante. In 1807 George was born; in 1808 a little girl who did not live. By 1809 Lyman concluded that it would be impossible to continue trying to live on $400 a year. Even with the utmost thrift, even with the income from Roxana's school, they were $500 in debt.

He served notice to the presbytery that he would not be able to remain in East Hampton unless the church increased his salary by $100 and paid off his debts. That said, he left for New York City, where he had been invited to fill the pulpit of Brick Church for a few weeks. Roxana, writing to him there, gave vent to her frustration. Ministers of the Gospel were held in such low esteem that congregations would not pay their pastor in a year what they willingly spent in that same year for luxuries like tobacco!

At that point the celebrated Judge Tapping Reeve of Litchfield, founder of the first law school in the country, wrote a letter to the Rev. Lyman Beecher, inquiring whether he would consider a call to the pulpit of the Litchfield Congregational Church.

Lyman, his spirits kindled, journeyed to Litchfield to preach for a few Sundays. He found himself in what was for him a whole new world.

If Boston was America's New Jerusalem, Litchfield was a New Eden in the Connecticut hills. Its fame had spread, not only to the nation's capital, but to the courts of Europe. Litchfield was located in a place of natural beauty, on the direct North-South transport route that had developed during the Revolutionary War.

The "new" church, built in 1762 to replace the original of 1723, rose proud and serene on the town green. From there the principal streets ran out like the arms of a cross—East Street and West Street, South Street and North. Here lived the gentry of Litchfield in their white wood houses, Georgian or Federal style, with widow's walks, Palladian windows, and imposing porticos: Judge Tapping Reeve; Colonel Benjamin Tallmadge; Oliver Wolcott III, U.S. Secretary of the Treasury; the Seymours and the Sheldons, the Tracys and the Daggetts, the Demings and the Buells. On the side streets stood the neat houses of the less well-to-do.

Judge Reeve proved to be a dignified Federal aristocrat in dark broadcloth breeches and cutaway coat, black hose and boots and fine white linen stock—styles Lyman himself copied, but quality of which he could so far only dream. Now in his sixties, the judge had created the case-study method of teaching law, and young men came from all over America to learn from him. His wife, Sally, whose graciousness was equaled only by her size, was a granddaughter of the famous Jonathan Edwards, daughter of a president of Princeton College, and sister of the Aaron Burr whom Lyman had vilified in his anti-dueling sermons. Despite this, the motherly Mrs. Reeve was prepared to take the Beecher family under her wing.

Before Lyman's visit was over, the congregation voted unanimously to call him as their pastor. The salary paid would be $800 a year, plus the all-important firewood.

Back in East Hampton, Lyman sold the cottage for a profit of $1,000, and preached one final sermon on damnation. Then he set off for Connecticut to find a new home for his growing family. He found the people of Litchfield "impatient for my arrival."

With the aid of Judge Reeve, Lyman Beecher purchased a house on a one-acre corner lot on prestigious North Street, not far from the Tapping Reeve home and law school and Miss Sarah Pierce's Female Academy. When Roxana arrived, bringing the children, she was greeted by a cultural paradise in the full glory of New England spring and a house that did not live up to its surroundings. Square and two-storied, the old white building had four rooms upstairs and four down, a windowless attic under the pyramid roof, and an L on the ground floor that accommodated kitchen, well room, woodshed, and carriage house. This sounded large, but was hardly adequate for the Beechers' extended family.

Then there were the animals—the horse and cow, the chickens, the cats and dogs. And the rats! The house was infested with generations of them, just as the church was infested with families of mice. Rats in the storeroom and cellar, rats in the kitchen, rats in the attic and the walls and (sometimes) rats in the bedrooms. They outnumbered, and tormented, the household cats. The younger children played with them. Catharine, who at ten was already quite a poet, wrote funny poems about them.

A year and a month after the move to Litchfield, Roxana set aside housework and art and took to her bed to deliver her sixth living child, the one that should have been a boy. There was a perfectly good, scarcely used name waiting for her, left by the sister who had borne it briefly. The parents added a middle name, and the baby was christened Harriet Elizabeth. She was a true Beecher, with the family's heavy-lidded blue-gray eyes. From infancy she seemed to retreat away behind those eyelids, lost in some mystical inner world of her own.

Lyman adored his new daughter; he adored all his children. To the young Beechers, Mama was a source of peace, serenity, and comfort, but Papa was *fun*. Papa could skate and sleighride with the best of them. Papa made life one long adventure. He demanded immediate obedience and believed in strict discipline, but he rarely had to exercise it. His moods seesawed from exhilaration to despair and back again, and his children's did as well. His temper, as he had warned Roxana on their honeymoon, was "quick, and quick over." Even with the rats, life for the Beecher children was rollicking. Church services were long, and the box pews hard, but that was *Papa* up there in the pulpit with its great canopy, his grand voice rolling out like organ music. For Harriet especially, Papa in the pulpit was a wondrous thing.

So were the church mice that lived in the pulpit's base. Churchgoing in the early nineteenth century was an all-day affair, and families who came from a distance brought hampers of "cold lunch" to eat on the lawn between the first sermon and the second. When the weather was wet, or cold, this refreshment was usually taken in the pews. The mice had learned this promised a future feast. Harriet would see their bright eyes shining through the mouseholes in the pulpit base. If Lyman began to speak quietly, the mice would venture out for crumbs of bread and cheese, only to scamper back again when the great voice thundered awful words like depravation and damnation.

The Beecher household continued to enlarge with servants, relatives, and boarders. By 1812 there were six children, Lyman and Roxana, Lyman's orphaned ward, Roxana's sister Mary, two schoolgirl boarders, and two young indentured servants, all living under the parsonage roof along with the cats, the dogs, and of course, the rats. Fortunately the house expanded also after Roxana received a small inheritance. An imposing new wing was added, its whole ground floor devoted to a proper parlor large enough to accommodate both "ministers' meetings" (vigorous debate amid clouds of tobacco smoke) and "musical soirees" (piano, song, and flute). The second floor contained more bedrooms, and the arched attic became Lyman's study.

Not long after Harriet's birth Lyman's father died, and his unmarried half-sister Esther and her mother moved from New Haven into half of a house just round the corner from the Beecher parsonage. Aunt Esther bristled easily, but she was an avid reader, a great storyteller, and an ardent naturalist who could fascinate the children with her animal lore. Aunt Mary had tales to tell also, but they were darker stories, not for children's ears. If she shared details of her tragedy with any of them, it was with Catharine. Now close to entering her teens, Catharine often sat beside the hammock in the kitchen where Aunt Mary habitually lay, coughing her life away into bloodstained handkerchiefs.

Then, suddenly, Aunt Mary was gone, leaving Catharine devas-

Harriet Beecher Stowe's birthplace, Litchfield, Connecticut

tated and two-year-old Harriet with a lasting memory of a beautiful doomed woman and of adult whispers that had passed over her head like some terrible, mysterious shadow. *Slavery.* Slavery had in some way snuffed the life out of Aunt Mary. For Harriet, her aunt's tragedy became dark thread in the tapestry of family legends: Something had happened to her in the islands that had destroyed her marriage and sent her fleeing home to die. And that something had to do with slavery.

Aunt Mary was gone, but Grandma Beecher and Aunt Esther had come. So did "young lady boarders"—money was scarce again, so Roxana took in some students from Miss Pierce's Female Academy. But from Harriet's point of view the most important new arrival came ten days after her second birthday. He was a plump boy baby whom his overjoyed father christened Henry Ward.

Harriet and Henry Ward bonded immediately and for life. They were in many ways an odd combination. From infancy Henry was always plump, Harriet small and slender. Harriet darted like a butterfly; Henry was clumsy. Harriet's mind was quick, Henry's was not. Harriet had a gift for words; Henry's, as an aunt remarked, often came out sounding as though he were speaking Choctaw. Henry was an extrovert, Harriet lived inside her head. But both were actually deeply shy, really opening up only to those they knew and trusted. Both had the "Beecher face" with its heavy-lidded blue-gray eyes. Both had the same, as-yet-unchanneled fires within them. Above all, there was between them absolute empathy, absolute faith, and absolute trust.

One of their earliest bits of mischief came when Harriet, rummaging unseen in cupboards as small children do, discovered what she took to be a bag of onions. Grown-ups' food, something not served to children and therefore much to be desired! Harriet at once shared her discovery with Henry and the round brown objects were promptly eaten. To the children's disappointment they tasted odd, rather sweet, not nice at all. Then Mama appeared. Mama did not scold; she never did, but her lovely face grew very sad. The brown things had been not onions but expensive tulip bulbs, a gift from her brother John. Now, she explained to the small culprits, there would be no beautiful red and yellow flowers in the spring.

The incident, and the way Roxana handled it, left an indelible mark on Harriet. It was one of the few memories of Roxana that she would have. In October 1815 Roxana gave birth to another son, named Charles, with her own gentle nature. During the winter and spring, while Roxana was not well, author Maria Edgeworth published a children's story, *Frank*. Novels, regarded as immoral influences, were normally banned from the parsonage. But Miss Edgeworth was different; Miss Edgeworth was *educational*. Roxana read *Frank* aloud to her children, giving Harriet one more lasting memory.

In the middle of that damp, sultry August, Lyman and Roxana stole time to take tea one afternoon with parishioners who lived a few miles out of town. A cold wind sprang up as they started home. Roxana, shivering, huddled against her husband. She had a sudden premonition of heaven, and Lyman found himself unable to laugh away her fears.

Lyman had to leave before breakfast the next morning for a week in New Haven. Back in Litchfield, Roxana developed chills and fever and was forced by her worried family to remain in bed. She had developed "galloping consumption," probably contracted while nursing her sister Mary through the same fatal illness. Lyman returned home to find his beloved wife close to death.

For another week the days dragged by, the house filled with anxious whispers and unnatural hush. Roxana's spinster sister Harriet came from Nutplains to nurse her through her dying. Once a day five-year-old Harriet was allowed to pay a visit to the mother who lay so still, red spots burning on the cheeks of her white face. Whenever any of the children went outside, everyone they met stopped them to ask for news.

The whole of Litchfield was praying for the preacher's wife. On the night of September 24, 1816, Harriet dreamed that her

Lyman Beecher, c. 1815
(Courtesy of the Litchfield Historical Society, Litchfield, Connecticut)

mother was well at last. She awoke, joyful, to find the house full of the sounds of grief. Roxana was dead, and when the children were taken into the bedroom to say good-bye it seemed to Harriet that the still cold figure was a stranger whom she had never known.

The mourning rituals continued. Crepe on the door; black clothing for the children. Lyman's face a rocky mask of grief. Henry and Charlie were considered too young to attend the funeral, but Harriet went. She heard the orations, took the solemn walk to the cemetery, saw the coffin lowered in the ground. A day or so later, sixteen-year-old Catharine looked out the window to see Henry, gold curls flying and little black skirts upended—boy children were put "in petticoats" until they were five or six—digging industriously in the earth. He was trying to "dig his way down to heaven" to find his mother.

Harriet herself was scooped up by her godmother, Aunt Harriet Foote, and taken back to Nutplains for their mutual comfort. There was a long, grief-filled ride, and an after-dark arrival at a lonely farmhouse. Then the bewildered child was in a parlor full of firelight, in the arms of a weeping white-haired woman who was her grandmother.

Mama was gone; Mama had become a shining memory, a legendary bright angel almost too good for this world. Harriet's life had been forever changed.

III

"Hattie Is a genius"

1816-1817

THE NUTPLAINS FARM was a house ruled by women. It was Harriet's first experience of women who were aware of their own importance.

Grandma Foote was a white-haired lady who, despite having a Continental Army general as a father, had married a Tory (a person loyal to the British Crown) and had been a British sympathizer throughout the American Revolution. She was still, in her heart, a monarchist, and regularly read the traditional Prayer for the King and Members of the Royal Family. The Footes were Episcopalians, members of the American version of the Established Church of England. On the great round table in the parlor, Grandma Foote's workbasket kept close company with her books—Bible and prayer book, religious texts, the works of Shakespeare and Dr. Samuel Johnson. Grandma Foote knew her Bible almost by heart, and spoke of the prophets and apostles as though they were personal friends. She was emphatically not a believer in the fire-and-brimstone doctrine of the Puritans. The God she spoke of to Harriet was a God of Love.

While Grandma Foote was the official head of the family, it was really Aunt Harriet who ruled the household. Grandma was gentle and easygoing, as Roxana had been; Aunt Harriet was austere, efficient, and growing very peppery as she neared her forties. She was determined to bring "Niece" up as a proper lady. Harriet, age five and a half, must be addressed by the servants as "Miss Harriet." Harriet must not romp around like a nasty boy, must always be soft-spoken, must keep her dresses spotless and unwrinkled, must have regular lessons in needlework and catechism.

The latter presented a problem. *Which* catechism—the Episcopalian, which Aunt Harriet felt essential for Harriet's soul, or the Congregational, which Lyman considered equally essential? To Harriet's dismay, Aunt decreed that she must learn *both*. The Congregational catechism was the hardest—in all senses. To Harriet's relief, Aunt soon decided that Congregationalism could wait until Harriet returned home. While at Nutplains, she attended the Episcopal Church with her Foote relatives, and was entranced by the color and beauty of its services.

As Harriet learned to read, she became an avid reader like her father. No one told her that Shakespeare was too advanced for her, or the Bible too difficult to understand. She learned the art of reading aloud by reading to her grandmother.

Uncle George Foote, the one man in the household, enthralled her by reciting the thrilling ballads of Sir Walter Scott, and answered her questions by reading aloud from the encyclopedia. Even severe Aunt Harriet unbent to tell stories on family and neighborhood, past and present, in a way that had Harriet doubled up with laughter.

Uncle Samuel Foote, the sea captain, was off on a long voyage, but his presence was felt throughout the Nutplains house. The bed Harriet shared with her aunt was canopied with exotically colored linen from India, patterned with strange plants and birds and Chinese figures. In the parlor were mats and baskets from the East Indies, frankincense from Spain. Other treasures were locked away in drawers, to be displayed and told about one by one for the entertainment of a little girl. Some keepsakes tugged at the heart—embroidery done by the "Foote girls," letters written by

Aunt Mary; needlework and paintings by Roxana. Harriet's mother was still alive for her at Nutplains.

When Harriet returned to the Litchfield parsonage in the summer of 1817, she found great changes. To his own relief and his children's dismay, Lyman had persuaded his half-sister Esther and her mother to give up the immaculate privacy of their own home and move into the parsonage. Esther was a woman who believed in order and method, "a place for everything and everything in its place." She promptly set about making order out of the chaos of Lyman's home. Lyman, diplomatically, had gathered his brood about him in advance and carefully explained that Aunt and Grandma were not coming to take Roxana's place, nor to usurp Catharine's new role as substitute mother to the younger children—they were coming to *help*. The Beecher children loved Aunt Esther, and tried valiantly to adapt. But it wasn't easy.

A year can make enormous changes in children—in themselves, and in the way they see their world. Harriet had had a year of being an only child in a family of three grown-ups, a girl in a house run by women. There had been family history everywhere around her, and soft voices. There had been quietness. There was none of the bustle and clutter of a busy parsonage; none of the almost too exciting give-and-take of dinner-table arguments during which Lyman taught his children to debate. Above all, there had not been the beloved but overpowering figure of Lyman Beecher.

"Hattie is a genius," Papa had often said. She only had to peer, on tiptoe, into a mirror to see that she was a Beecher. At Nutplains, Harriet discovered the other side of her heritage in herself. She discovered she loved serenity, and quietness, and order. She loved—no, she *needed*—beauty. She had Roxana's talents for handwork, and art. She loved music and poetry. She loved stories—family stories, stories told aloud or on paper, stories made of part fact and part imagination. She loved having a chance to be alone. She discovered that her shyness was inherited from her mother.

She came back to a parsonage much more organized and

orderly, but still full of people and noise. Mama was gone, but Aunt Esther presided over Rachel and Zillah in the kitchen. The rats still played games at night, bowling stolen corncobs in the space between bedroom ceilings and attic floor. The cats were still having kittens, and catching mice, and sharpening claws on the furniture. The dogs were still in and out—including at church, for when families attended church their dogs did, too, and the Rev. Mr. Beecher's dog Trip liked to park himself at the base of the pulpit and howl if he did not enjoy the singing. The hilarity and arguments at the dinner table still went on, despite Aunt Esther. There were still the boarders.

Henry Ward was four now, taller if not thinner, looking forward to entering school in the fall. George was ten, and a scholar at Miss Collin's school. Mary, at twelve, was definitely the prettiest of the sisters and fast becoming a proper young lady. Edward, fourteen, was "fitting for college" at South Farms Academy in Litchfield. William, one year older, was the "slowest" of the family, and he knew it. He had been sent away to school for a year and come home a dismal failure. Now he was working in Mr. Collin's store.

Catharine was now "Miss Beecher," a title etiquette reserved for the eldest daughter. Her light brown hair hung in long ringlets beside her face, in the style popularized by the heroines in romantic poems. No one would ever call Catharine romantic-looking, or even pretty, but there was something very appealing about her vivacity and her quick mind. Catharine had almost completed her studies at Miss Pierce's school, where the Beecher girls would receive free tuition in exchange for Lyman's serving as school chaplain. Catharine had discovered a real gift for homemaking, and for organization; she had become her father's secretary and confidante. She was still full of fun and laughter, but there was a new seriousness about her.

Lyman had had an agonizing year. All the things that he had most firmly believed—that life was only a prelude to heaven, that we should rejoice when our near and dear were "gathered to their heavenly home"—had become hollow to him. He could *not* rejoice that Roxana was gone. Eventually he regained his equilibrium, but his sermons never again contained those particular platitudes. The rock-hard foundation of his theology had begun to crack.

Great winds of change had been sweeping through the Western world in the first two decades of the nineteenth century. A bloody revolution in France had driven king and queen from throne to guillotine. Napoléon Bonaparte had gone from peasant to dictator, and almost made the whole of Europe part of his French Empire before he was finally defeated at Waterloo. There had been an outburst of creativity—in art and literature, in music, in education, in scientific thought. An "industrial revolution" was transforming farming and manufacturing from manual labor to work done by machines, taking crafts and trades out of the homes and into factories. In the New World, the world's first democratic nation was trying to find a balance between the rights of the states and the power of the central government, and trying to find its place in the world. As so much changed, people's beliefs were changing also.

Harriet, with Henry Ward scuttling along beside her, went for the first time to a "real school"—the Widow Kilbourne's "dame school" on West Street. It was the kind of early education that gave "dame schools" a bad name. All the Widow Kilbourne excelled at was rote learning and corporal punishment. Henry was no good at the memorizing she demanded, and so was judged to be, like William, "stupid." This was a judgment his indignant family did not accept. Harriet was good at reading, and she had a remarkable memory. But her real learning was taking place in Lyman's study.

High up in the "new garret," the study was Lyman's refuge from family and parishioners. Here were Lyman's writing table and his big chair, its arms wide enough to support his open Concordance and his open Bible. The big window looked out through steel-blue pines to Great Pond, where Lyman and the boys went fishing. But the primary magic of the room, besides the comforting security and silence, was its books. Books of every size and shape and color. Books of every kind, from references, sermons and religious essays, to poetry and Shakespeare and a whole set of huge folios titled *Lightfooti Opera*. The shelves circled the room, rising from floor to the arching eaves. It was a place where a small shy girl could curl up in a corner, and hear the quiet scratching of her father's pen, the occasional rustle of a page turning, and feel safe.

There were barrels of pamphlets and old sermons in the study—everything from *An Appeal on the Unlawfulness of a Man's Marrying His Wife's Sister* to a copy of the *Arabian Nights*. Harriet stumbled onto this one rainy day, and it became her magic carpet. She read it daily. She also discovered a torn copy of Shakespeare's play *The Tempest,* full of shipwrecks and sorcery and a secret, enchanted world. But most exciting of all was the day Lyman brought home a two-volume edition of *Magnalia Christi Americana* by Cotton Mather, the famous Puritan preacher in the days of the terrible Salem witchcraft trials.

The *Magnalia* was a seven-book, supposedly accurate history of the Puritans in New England: the settlements; their judges, governors, and ministers; evidence of "divine providence"; the Puritans' "wars of the Lord" against such powers of darkness as witches, heretics, the Native Americans, and the Quakers. Mather had impeccable Puritan credentials, but his writing was what was called "fantastical"—full of literary allusions and quotes in foreign languages; full of violent images and extremes of passion. Some of the images made Harriet shudder; the new words and the way Mather used them entered into her brain like surges of strange music. The *Magnalia, The Tempest,* and *Arabian Nights*—and the Bible—were being filed away in Harriet's memory. She was discovering the power of words—*on paper,* as well as from the pulpit—to evoke images, induce powerful emotion, and alter people's ways of thinking. It was a lesson she learned well.

The hours in Lyman's study—with and without her father—made up in part for all the times she was left out of the adventures her brothers had with Lyman. Such manly excursions they had together—roughhousing, hunting, all-day fishing trips across Great Pond to Pine Island. How empty the house seemed without them, and how exciting their return at twilight with strings of perch and pickerel and bullheads, armfuls of sweet grass and wildflowers. Lyman himself presided over the frying pans, for he thought no woman could cook fish well. He demolished the neatness of Aunt Esther's kitchen. For sister Mary, the lady, such excursions had no appeal; Catharine, to Harriet, seemed often more a grown-up than their father. It was Harriet who felt the injustice of being left out because she was a girl.

Toward the end of 1817 Lyman again left his children in the care of their Aunt Esther and went off on a journey. His return came late one evening. Harriet, Henry, and little Charlie were sound asleep in the nursery when an excited bustle from below awoke them. Lyman's great voice shouted up to them, "Here's Pa!" From behind him, as he entered the children's room, came a woman's voice calling out gaily, *"And here's Ma!"*

Harriet sat up, still half asleep, to see a smiling young woman with bright blue eyes and auburn hair bending over them. She kissed the children and told them that she was now their mother.

IV

"It Is a Slander on My Heavenly Father!"

1817–1822

UNBEKNOWNST TO HIS CHILDREN, Reverend Lyman Beecher had had a private mission in mind when he paid that first visit to Boston. He was lonely. His children needed a mother; he still hoped to have more sons. In addition, churches expected to benefit from the unpaid labor of their pastor's wife—as official hostess, leader of the church's women's activities, and a one-woman "aid society" to the parish needy. Shy Roxana had done none of these things, but Roxana had been special, and East Hampton and Litchfield had revered her. There could be only one Roxana in Lyman's life, and Lyman knew it.

His first marriage had been for love; this time he looked for a woman who would fill a job description: physically strong, sensible, supportive, an asset to the parish and preferably well-connected. Harriet Porter of Portland, Maine, was all those things. Her father was an eminent doctor. One of her uncles was governor of Maine, another a member of Congress, a third a senator. Lyman met her while she was visiting relatives in Boston; within the week they became engaged. Short months later, the marriage took place in Portland. Her wedding journey was a

series of visits to relatives, winding up with the nighttime introduction into her new home and family.

Harriet Porter stepped into the Litchfield nursery happy and
smiling, a young woman who loved children and was eager to be
their mother. She didn't know she never had a chance. In death,
Roxana had been transformed from much-loved wife and mother
to an immortal angel. She lived on in her children's hearts—and in
her husband's.

Catharine, at least, had known of the engagement and
exchanged correct, formal letters with her future stepmother. The
younger children had had no such warning. Harriet Porter was
cool and precise and silvery-voiced, so elegant and aloof that she
filled the young Beechers with awe. They felt rough and countri-
fied in her presence. She had high standards in manners, deport-
ment, and dress. Order and method were as much a part of her as
they were of Aunt Esther—who was still there, along with the
now-ailing Grandmother Beecher. In no sense did Harriet Porter
have a clear field as mistress of the house.

Lyman soon had a run-in with his new wife, one that must have
stirred up strong memories. It happened when Lyman, who loved
to read aloud, was treating his bride to Jonathan Edwards's famed
sermon on "Sinners in the Hands of an Angry God," a terrifying
exposition of the Calvinist doctrine of predestination. All humans
were sinners and deserved damnation, the doctrine went; even the
most virtuous life could not change that fact. God, all-powerful
and all-good, through His grace (love given though undeserved)
"elected" some sinners to join the angels in heaven anyway. Not
all—for if all were saved, how could the power as well as the love
of God be demonstrated? Being all-knowing, God had known
since the dawn of time who would and who would not be saved.
Surely, if humans truly loved God they would rejoice even in their
own damnation, if that was their fate, since it served to proclaim
God's greatness. Only after a person could reach that point of sub-
mission would a realization of "election" come—if it were to
come. Once the souls of the Elect reached heaven, God permitted

them to look down and behold what they had been spared—the torments of the souls in hell, which Edwards graphically described and Lyman Beecher dramatically orated.

On and on he went, as Harriet Porter's face grew pale with outrage and the red patches on her cheeks grew brighter. At last she had heard all she could stand. She swept out of the room proclaiming, "Mr. Beecher, I will not listen to another word! It is a slander on our Heavenly Father!"

For Lyman, it was as though ice water had been flung into his face. For a second time, a woman had cracked the foundation of his orthodox theology. He was not aware of the crack yet, but it would grow. Small Harriet, curled on the sofa, had been an accidental eavesdropper. The words became burned in her memory, too.

Revival fervor swept the state around this time. To the Old School Presbyterians, the idea of revival services was heretical and absurd. If God predestined each soul, long before birth, to heaven or to hell, what was the use of holding revivals? Everyone's fate was already sealed. Presbyterians of what was coming to be called the New School said, "Yes, *but* . . ." If God was Absolute Good, perhaps He "predestined" *every* soul to heaven, and it was the sinner's "free will," choosing a state of sin rather than surrendering to conversion and a state of grace. . . . If there was even a chance that this was the case, then surely it was almost the duty of the converted to hold revival services?

The crack in Lyman Beecher's orthodoxy was widening. He threw himself feverishly into the revival movement and the winning of souls, and overworked himself into another breakdown. He feared he had consumption, but at last found a Boston doctor who diagnosed dyspepsia. It was a recently coined name for an increasingly common ailment, a combination of indigestion and other stomach troubles, depression, and mental exhaustion.

The treatment called for fresh air, physical activity including useful labor, and a respite from books and intellectual study. Lyman stopped laboring so over his Sunday sermons and began to speak extemporaneously. He was very good at it, he discovered.

He also found that he liked some of the physical labor, especially gardening. Especially when he could draw his children into it. He had already discovered the advantages of that in connection with the annual "wood-spell" at which the congregation delivered the minister's annual supply of fuel.

Wood-spells occurred in February, after farmers had finished their winter cutting. Great preparations had to be made in advance—pies baked by the dozen and stacked to freeze in the outdoor shed, beer brewed by the gallon for the traditional "flip." Even Lyman Beecher could not put a stop to that. On a clear, cold morning the word would go out: *Today was wood-spell day.* The parsonage womenfolk would hastily make cakes and doughnuts and warm up the pies. The small boys would carry in the beer and cider, and heat flip-irons in the kitchen fire to thrust into the brew. Soon the sleds would arrive with their loads of wood.

Somehow Lyman never managed to arrange in advance to have the wood neatly stacked conveniently near the house. "Oh, toss it over there," he would say, pointing vaguely. Somehow "over there" was always exactly on the spot where, in early April, Lyman would find he wanted to plant his cucumbers and melons. The men of the parish, warming up inside with food and flip, thought with amusement that the preacher's mind was counting the logs to make sure the church's contract with him was fulfilled. They were only half right. Lyman *was* counting. He was also scheming to get the better of a New Haven friend with whom he had an annual race to produce the first cucumbers. New Haven had the warmer climate, but Lyman knew about cold frames. The huge pile of logs kept the earth beneath it warm and dry.

Two months later, Lyman would cheerfully announce at breakfast that wood-splitting day had come. Out they trooped into the yard, he and all his boys. The axes would swing, the chips would fly, the jokes and stories poured out one after the other in grand Beecher competition. Then there was a great piling and moving and stacking and sweeping up of chips. Harriet would be "sucked into the vortex of enthusiasm by father's well-pointed declaration that he 'wished Harriet was a boy, she would do more than any of them.'" She would "put on a little black coat which I thought looked more like the boys, casting needle and thread to the wind, and working like one possessed for a day and a half, till in the afternoon the wood was all in and piled, and the chips swept up. Then father tackled the horse into the cart, and proclaimed a grand fishing party down to Little Pond. And how we all floated . . . and every one of us caught a string of fish."

These rare moments of being "one of the boys" were precious to Harriet. And Lyman, erecting his cold frame on the soft earth where the wood had lain, always won the contest for earliest cucumbers.

In 1818 on the Fourth of July Harriet heard old Colonel Tallmadge, in his Revolutionary War blue and gold, read aloud the Declaration of Independence. Lyman entered into the full glory of a Doctor of Divinity degree, conferred on him by a college in Vermont. Henceforth he would be *Doctor* Beecher.

The following year, Grandmother Beecher died. Lyman, motherless from birth, raised by an aunt and uncle, had hardly known his stepmother; between them there had been respect but no real emotion. Perhaps that was why he had thought he could bring a stepmother into his own family in such a cavalier fashion. He never seemed to sense that anything was wrong. There were never any outward signs; all the young Beechers knew their manners. But subtly, steadily, Roxana's children were uniting in a solid rank that Harriet Porter could not join. Her voice grew sharper, her smiles became less frequent.

In October 1819, Harriet Porter's first child, Frederick, was born. Edward, now sixteen, went off to Yale. William was apprenticed to a cabinetmaker in Hartford. The family was relieved that he might at last have found his niche, but worried over the possibility of Henry Ward's having a speech defect. George was still quiet and studious, Mary studying at Miss Pierce's, Charlie amusing everyone with his mischief. There were *five* boarders in the household now—Lyman's salary had not kept pace as his family grew.

Fun-loving Catharine, having managed to get through Miss Pierce's school while doing very little work except piano practice—and a bit of cheating—went off to Boston to study piano and art. She said it was to prepare herself for teaching school, so she could help the family by being self-supporting. That undoubtedly was part of it. But she was also nineteen, everyone's big sister, and for the past three years she had made, by hand, all her brothers' and sisters' clothing in addition to her own. Freedom beckoned.

With Catharine gone, Harriet, who had already graduated from the nursery to the trundle bed that pulled out from under the big bed in the girls' room, moved up into the bed with sister Mary. For Harriet, the high point of the year was that she entered Miss Pierce's school for girls. Miss Pierce had waived the minimum-age requirement especially for her!

Sarah Pierce, a formidable, charming woman, made an indelible mark on all her pupils. Learned, elegant, and accomplished, she also had revolutionary ideas about the proper education for women. Her students were taught all the arts and graces—music and dancing, sewing and embroidery, painting and drawing and how to write "a fine hand." They also studied nearly everything their brothers studied. When Harriet entered the school, the curriculum included history (European and American), geography, literature, grammar, chemistry, astronomy, botany, natural and moral philosophy, and logic. John Pierce Brace, Miss Pierce's nephew, had become her assistant principal. The student body sometimes numbered as many as 130.

Miss Pierce understood young girls well, and saw to it there were strict rules and plenty of amusements. Litchfield life was very social. There were afternoon tea drinkings, and evening sleighrides, and there were dances—schoolroom dances at the Academy; Law Students' Balls in the Phelps Tavern Assembly

Room; private dances and cotillions. Miss Pierce's young ladies had to be back home by 9 P.M., and evening parties were forbidden for those under seventeen. There were also the serenades. They involved one or more law students in good voice, a flute and any other available instrument, and a young lady's window under which to sing.

Harriet was much too young for any of this, but it was exciting to hear her classmates talking about them when a teacher could not hear. She was certainly part of the afternoon promenades when Miss Pierce's young ladies, walking two by two, took their well-chaperoned daily walk beneath the whispering elms of North Street. The young men from Judge Reeve's Law School always managed to be "taking the air" themselves at the same time.

Young men—even future lawyers—no longer copied the dignified style of Tapping Reeve. Gone were knee breeches and shoulder-length plaited hair. Now the fashion was for the long, snug "pantaloons" that had been the street fashion of the French Revolution, and short-cropped, tousled hair (a style originally called *à la guillotine*). For women, the slender, very high-waisted gowns and classical hairstyles of Roxana's day had given way to more "romantic" fashions—waistlines about an inch below the bust, skirts belling out at hemline, hair up in curls with long ringlets falling in the style Catharine Beecher already had invented. This was all part of the Romantic Movement that had begun in Germany, and the "Byron fever" that was sweeping America since the poetry of George Gordon, Lord Byron, crossed the Atlantic.

The Romantic Movement in art, music, and literature had thrown out the symmetry, order, and formality of the classics. Now "Nature" (with a capital *N*), "moods," "passion" were all. Lord Byron was part of the Romantic Movement, but he was also a whole lot more. He was young, he was world-weary, he was as beautiful as it was possible for a man to be. He had the look, in fact, of someone far gone with consumption—a look he induced by a combination of dieting and purging, but his adoring public

Byron
Painted by Alonzo Chappel, likeness after a
painting by Thomas Phillips
(Stowe-Day Foundation, Hartford, Connecticut)

didn't know that. His writing was filled with vivid imagery. Moreover, he was a scandal. The Litchfield ladies whispered over their teacups about his ill-starred marriage, the British noblewomen who pursued him, his possible insanity. Miss Pierce's students, reading his poetry on the sly, hid their blushes and agreed how terrible it was that his wife had deserted him. Their hearts beat faster over the "Byronic hero" that he wrote about—moody, silent, torn by remorse and passion but unrepentant. The Byronic hero was a quite accurate likeness of Lucifer, the Fallen Angel, in Puritan poet John Milton's *Paradise Lost*.

Harriet, young as she was, had read Milton—because Lyman did—and she had read Byron. Aunt Esther's escape from Beecher hurly-burly was her own quiet room and her many books. Harriet was allowed to escape there, too, just as she did to Lyman's study. Aunt Esther owned a set of Byron's works, and Harriet happened upon *The Corsair*. She fell instantly, and passionately, in love with Byron.

Some of his writing, not surprisingly, she found confusing. "Aunt Esther, what does it mean—'One I never love enough to hate'?"

"Oh, child," Aunt Esther replied comfortably, "it's one of Byron's strong expressions."

None of the adult Beechers found anything wrong with Harriet's reading Byron. For one thing, he was a genius—Lyman Beecher had an admirable ability to appreciate the works of a genius while deploring the genius's morality. For another, Byron wrote *poetry*—an exalted, uplifting literary form, not like the new novels that glorified commonplace lives and sinful acts while pretending to preach against them. The older Beechers discussed Byron, the state of his writing and the state of his soul, at the family dinner table.

There was much beyond Byron being talked about there. 1820 was a watershed year. America was growing restless. The Louisiana Purchase in 1803 had opened up a whole new western territory for settlement. Eli Whitney's invention of the cotton gin ten years earlier had made cotton a cheap and profitable crop—so long as it was grown by slave labor.

Slavery, the "peculiar institution" as it was called, cast over America a dark shadow. Now southern farmers were pushing into the Louisiana Territory, and bringing the peculiar institution with them. The North objected, vehemently. When Missouri applied for admission as a slave state, a bitter battle in Congress began. Finally a compromise was struck: Missouri would be admitted, with no mention of slavery; Maine would be admitted at the same time, keeping the balance between the number of slave states and free; in future, slavery would not be permitted in the Louisiana Territory north of 36°x 30'.

The Missouri Compromise was the spark that set off the Abolitionist Movement, and it was among the clergy and elders of the northern churches—and the women of the church ladies' aid societies—that the movement took form.

For the moment, the Beechers were occupied with matters closer to home. The "black canker"—scarlet fever—struck the parsonage in June. Harriet was terribly ill with it, and baby Freddie died. 1821, too, was full of troubles. Charlie had another accident, a fall that resulted in a rusty nail being driven into his knee. His leg became crooked; the wound would not heal. In July Lyman had another breakdown. He took leave from his clerical duties and tried to travel, riding alone as far as Niagara Falls. His voice had failed. He submitted to a tonsillectomy, undergoing the dual agonies of surgery without anesthetic and fears of permanently losing his pulpit voice. He also feared cancer.

He came home no better, and in September took his wife on her first visit back to Maine. With Aunt Esther in poor health, Aunt Harriet Foote came to take charge in the parsonage. Catharine was off teaching art and music in New London. But Edward was home on vacation, and Harriet was there with her nose constantly in books. George and Mary were both there studying—he for Yale, she in the hope of joining Catharine as a teacher. Charlie was able to limp around again, but the family was beginning to fear that Henry Ward had a speech impediment.

Dr. and Mrs. Beecher returned to Litchfield to find Charlie's knee again an open wound.

The wound healed enough for the family to celebrate a Thanksgiving family reunion. Among the Puritans, Thanksgiving was the great annual religious celebration, and this Thanksgiving, after a year of sadnesses, held promise of new life. Harriet Porter was pregnant again. And Catharine was in love.

Her sweetheart was a mathematical genius named Alexander Metcalf Fisher. In his mid-twenties he was already a full professor at Yale, where at eighteen he had graduated first in his class. He knew Latin, Greek, and Hebrew; he had studied theology, astronomy, and architecture; he played piano and wrote music. And he fell in love with Catharine Beecher through her poetry, which was now being published regularly in *The Christian Spectator*.

Their courtship was made up of poetry and music and long, frequent letters. Very soon they were speaking of marriage. At the Beecher Thanksgiving reunion Catharine was radiant. Lyman had given his enthusiastic blessing to her engagement. She resigned her teaching post and began to make ready for a wedding.

It could not take place for at least a year. Yale was sending Professor Fisher to Europe in the spring of 1822 for several months of study and scientific errands. Meanwhile, Catharine could fill her hope chest, and Lyman would have time for serious conversations with his eldest daughter. There was only one flaw in the admirable Professor Fisher. *Had he been "saved"*? If not, could Catharine live with the knowledge that they might be together in this life only?

Most of this theological discussion went on behind Harriet's back or over her head. She was going through an awkward age, "owling about," her eyes on the printed page or half hidden behind their heavy lids. In her family's eyes, she had lost any earlier charm and had turned "peculiar." Her stepmother was in the last months of pregnancy. To Harriet's relief, Grandma Foote invited her to Nutplains. She went in January 1822.

At Nutplains she found not only books, and quiet, and the color and poetry of Episcopal church services. She found her Uncle Sam.

Samuel E. Foote was a sea captain whose mastery of sail was world-famous. He was both an Episcopalian *and* a free-thinker who respected his brother-in-law Lyman Beecher but found much to question in Puritan narrow-mindedness. Above all, as a world-traveler, he understood that tolerance was a great virtue, not a great sin. He had carried on shipboard people of every nationality and persuasion. Race didn't matter; religion didn't matter. Good people were good people, and equals were equals. Again at Nutplains, Harriet was entering a whole new world, this time of ideas. She soaked up her uncle's stories.

The new baby, Isabella, was born in February. On the first of April Professor Fisher sailed for the British Isles on the packet boat *Albion*. Catharine waited eagerly for his first letter. Weeks went by. Harriet came home.

On June 2 Catharine received a letter, not from her professor, but from Lyman, who was in New Haven.

> My dear Child,
> On entering the city last evening, the first intelligence I met filled my heart with pain. It is all but certain that Professor Fisher is no more. . . .

On April 22 the *Albion* had been shipwrecked on the cliffs of Ireland.

Catharine's lover was gone, and she had no way of knowing whether his soul was in heaven or in hell.

V

"Who Wrote That?"
"Your Daughter, Sir!"

1822–1824

THE WRECK OF the packet boat *Albion* sent dark thrills running through a nation drunk on the tragic romanticism of Byron's poems. A small ship, storm-tossed, was dashed upon wild Ireland's cliffs. Of its twenty-three passengers, one alone survived, clinging through the night to jagged rocks until rescued, close to death.

That survivor was *not* Professor Fisher, and there was nothing romantic about the tragedy for the Beechers. Lyman hurried home from New Haven to comfort his oldest daughter. Now she, like he before her, was going through the agony of not knowing whether a beloved one was "saved." But there was one huge difference. Roxana had become a dutiful parishioner of Lyman's churches. Lyman had had seventeen years with her, day and night, in which to become convinced that she was not merely "naturally good" but one of God's own angels. Catharine had no such basis for assumption where Dr. Fisher was concerned. Nor did Lyman.

"I can only say that many did and will indulge the hope that he was pious," was the best he was able to write to his grieving daughter. "May God preserve you, and give me the joy of beholding life spring from death."

Lyman found in Litchfield a household stunned with grief, and a once-laughing girl, eyes swollen with weeping, pacing the floor in torment. He offered her, out of his rock-ribbed beliefs, two comforts: Dr. Fisher might have been one of the Elect, and had just not shared the details of his conversion with her. Or he might have experienced conversion in the last storm-lashed hours of his life.

Catharine scarcely heard—or if she heard, could not accept. In her mind's eye were the too-few hours she had spent with her professor, and all the goodness of him. In her heart were all the words that he had spoken, and everything that they had shared. Why would he not have shared so important a thing as his conversion? Why would God damn anyone as good as he?

Ringing in her ears were all the thundering words of salvation and damnation she had heard her father preach . . . all the vivid images she had heard him read aloud from the Bible and Jonathan Edwards and *Paradise Lost*. By the hour Lyman sat at his desk, trying to have a doctrinal "disputation" with his suffering daughter, the tears often running down his own cheeks. By the hour Catharine moaned and sobbed, paced restlessly or froze in the rigid grip of anger. Henry Ward, now a stocky boy of ten, watched from the hall in a state of vague comprehension. Harriet saw and heard it too, the imagery even more vivid for her than for Catharine, and stored it all away inside her silence.

Eventually a letter of condolence came for Catharine from the surviving passenger. It included a description of his last sight of Dr. Fisher, with face bloodied and bowed in a state of anxious meditation. On salvation? Or on the prospect of eternal death? That was the riddle that ripped at Catharine's soul.

"Oh, Edward, where is he now? Are the noble faculties of such a mind doomed to everlasting woe?" Catharine cried out in a letter to her brother at Yale, recently converted and planning to follow his destiny into the ministry. "Could I but be assured that he was now forever safe, I would not repine."

Edward was a generation further than Lyman removed from their ancestors' merciless Calvinist logic. He was also, at nineteen, wise enough to urge Catharine, "You have talent and influence, and cannot you consecrate them . . . and live to do good? . . . let the tide of benevolence and love once flow in your heart it will increase forever and bury all your sorrows. . . . Mr. Fisher I hope and believe is not lost."

Edward had more influence over Catharine than anyone except Lyman. The letters went back and forth between them until her moans of grief were overcome by a stern calm.

Presently word came to Catharine from her professor's grieving parents. Ever methodical, Dr. Fisher had left instructions that if anything happened to him before he could make a proper will, "my friend Catharine E. Beecher should receive two thousand dollars" out of his estate. She was also to receive his library and papers.

Catharine left for a visit with the Fishers, a visit that lasted for more than a year.

Spring turned to summer and lengthened into autumn. Edward graduated from Yale—first in his class; Phi Beta Kappa. He was appointed headmaster of the Hartford Grammar School. This meant George could study there with free tuition. William was in Boston. Mary, now seventeen, and Harriet were the oldest children still at home. Both were attending Miss Pierce's school. Mary was pretty, popular, and a model student. Harriet was not.

She was living, more than ever, inside her head or inside books. Books were where she found joy, and life, and color, passion, hope. Though she did not fully realize it, Catharine's tragedy, and the sudden comprehension of Calvinist theology that made it worse, had eaten deep into her own soul. Lately Lyman had been pressing his children on the subject of their own salvation. Harriet wasn't sure exactly *what* she believed, or what conversion was— she only knew the absence of it was terrible.

There were two bright spots in the dark night of Harriet's adolescence. One was when the cartons arrived from Catharine, containing Dr. Fisher's books. Like a good father, Lyman immediately confiscated them for inspection. Many books that could be read without harm by a mature—and converted—man could be unsuitable for children's vulnerable minds or the delicate sensibilities of ladies. He was troubled at first to discover novels in the cartons. Then he noticed that some were by an author noted as a poet, whose works were praised by persons he respected. He opened one of these novels, settled himself, and began to read.

Hours later he came plummeting down the stairs from his garret study, his hair all awry and his eyes glowing. "You may read [Sir Walter] Scott's novels," he announced. "I have always disapproved of novels as trash, but in these is real genius and real culture, and you may read them."

Read them the Beechers did. In one summer they went through *Ivanhoe,* with its crusades and tournaments, dark doings in the English court, and the beautiful Rebecca so cruelly persecuted for her Jewish faith, seven times. Harriet could recite many of the scenes from memory.

The other bright spot for Harriet at this time was her first real discovery of a gift for writing. It came about through the influence of Miss Pierce's nephew and assistant, John Pierce Brace. A born teacher, he taught Historical Criticism, Rhetoric, Moral Philosophy, and Taste to the older students. But it was in teaching Composition that he truly excelled. He stimulated his students' minds, led them through fertile fields of thought and imagination. Most of all, he believed implicitly that in order to write well one must first have something one really wanted to say.

The blood of her heroic ancestors ran in Harriet's young veins. Hearing Colonel Tallmadge read the Declaration of Independence had "made me long to do something, I knew not what: to fight for my country, or to make some declaration on my own account." Brace could not show her *what,* but he could show her *how.*

Hour after hour she sat, unnoticed, listening to Mr. Brace's conversations with his older students. And she began to write.

Up in Massachusetts, Catharine was struggling to find firm ground on which to stand. She had read her fiancé's journal, and one agonizing question had been answered. He had never had the terrifying mystical experience of conversion—not unless it had come to him in his final hours. *Could* the absence of that damn him? Catharine began to doubt.

She poured her thought and questions out to her father and her brother Edward. Back their letters came, forming a kind of anvil against which she could hammer out her own beliefs. Catharine was experiencing a new kind of conversion—from fear of God to absolute faith in God's grace and love. In the process she changed from a laughing girl into a basilisk of a woman, firm in principles and beliefs.

Catharine was twenty-four, and in the eyes of her generation already an old maid. Her love, and her dream of a home and children of her own, were gone. But she had Dr. Fisher's $2,000, and she had his books. She meant to earn her living. The best path open to her was to start a school.

Now she regretted the hours she had wasted in Miss Pierce's school! The only things she was equipped to teach were art and music. Actually Catharine didn't like teaching any better than Lyman did. What she really wanted was to be headmistress, and hire others to do the actual teaching.

Lyman, who did a great deal of traveling on church business, reported that Hartford could use a good "female school." Edward was there, which would be helpful. Catharine would have no difficulty getting students.

In the spring of 1824 Catharine opened her Hartford Female Academy with fifteen pupils, and sister Mary—now eighteen and one of Miss Pierce's finest graduates—as principal teacher.

Harriet was now the oldest Beecher child still in the nest. That school year of 1823–1824 would be her last, and best, at the Litchfield Female Academy. At last she was twelve, the entry age for other pupils. For the first time she was commended for excellence—in music and in English. And she was writing. She wrote an essay so good that Mr. Brace chose it as one of three to be read aloud at the great Exhibition of Work that annually closed the school's spring term.

Not for nothing had Harriet been listening to all her father's sermons, all the family legends, all of Catharine's struggles of the soul. Her essay's title was "Can the Immortality of the Soul Be Proved by the Light of Nature?"

Not for nothing either had she read her father's books. Among them were not only *Pilgrim's Progress* and *Paradise Lost* but also the work of Alexander Pope, the great rationalist poet of seventeenth-century enlightenment and secular skepticism. His *Essay on Man* had declared outright:

> *Know thyself, presume not God to scan;*
> *The proper study of Mankind is Man. . . .*
> *A Being darkly wise, and rudely great:*
> *With too much knowledge for the Skeptic side,*
> *With too much weakness for the Stoic's pride,*
> *He hangs between; in doubt to act, or rest;*
> *In doubt to deem himself a God, or Beast . . .*
> *Sole judge of Truth, in endless Error hurled:*
> *The glory, jest, and riddle of the world!*

Never mind that Pope's long poem ended up, "Though Man's a fool, yet GOD is wise." This was strong stuff. It reeked, in fact, of heresy, as well as psychological insight. And Harriet at almost thirteen understood it well enough to relate it to her topic, and to all those Beecher dinner-table disputations and Beecher legends—and to the Calvinist catechism that she had, after all, learned. "What is the chief end of man?" was its first question, and the answer focused firmly on God, not on mankind.

"It has been justly concluded by the philosophers of every age," twelve-year-old Harriet wrote, "that 'The proper study of mankind is man,' and his nature and composition, both physical and mental, have been subjects of the most critical examination. In the course of these researches many have been at a loss to account for the change that takes place in the body at the time of death. By some it has been attributed to the flight of its tenant; and by others to its final annihilation."

She was confronting the Calvinist struggle of the soul—and sister Catharine's struggle of belief—head-on.

Mr. Brace had "set the topic" for these essays. Several of Harriet's classmates, all older than she, had "written strongly in the affirmative." Harriet "chose to adopt the negative." When her essay was chosen to be read aloud, she was overwhelmed at the "proud distinction."

She did not have to read it herself. That would have been not only a terrifying ordeal, but most improper. Having to speak out in public, from a platform, would have been an assault on any lady's modesty.

All of Litchfield's intelligentsia turned out for the Academy's closing exercises. The young ladies of the Academy clustered together, in their pretty, pale high-waisted gowns, with downcast eyes and many sidelong glances toward their admiring Law School beaux. Their elders watched benevolently. Up on the platform with the great men of Litchfield sat Dr. Beecher, pastor and school chaplain. The program moved steadily on toward essay time. Harriet's heart was pounding.

She had always been too shy to take part with Catharine and her brothers in the dinner-table disputations, but she had learned from them. Lyman loved to do just as Mr. Brace had done—throw out a controversial topic and watch his children pounce on it like little foxes. He insisted upon arguments built on strong logic and backed up with references to the "Elders of Zion," scriptural or otherwise. He almost always won the debates, but then generously complimented his children on what they had argued well, and showed them how they could have built up stronger cases. Harriet had tried to do so in her essay, but the conclusion her logic—and heart—led her to was not the Puritan God of wrath and vengeance.

"The sun of the Gospel has dispelled the darkness that has rested on objects beyond the tomb. In the Gospel man learned that when the dust returned to dust the spirit fled to the God who gave it. He there found that though man has lost the image of his divine creator, he is still destined, after the earthly house of his tabernacle is dissolved, to an inheritance incorruptible, undefiled, and that fadeth not away, to a house not made with hands, eternal in the heavens." Harriet knew her Scriptures well, and they had led her at last past the terrors of hellfire to a trust in the God of Love.

Up on the platform, his features stern but kindly, the celebrated Dr. Beecher was prepared to be gracious about the literary effort of Miss Pierce's young lady scholars. But as the formal phrases of one composition rolled out, his ears pricked up. Then his face brightened. At the composition's close he leaned over and inquired of Mr. Brace, "Who wrote that composition?"

Back came the proclamation, with the satisfaction only a gifted teacher of an underestimated pupil could know.

"YOUR DAUGHTER, SIR!"

Lyman Beecher's face became one great proud beam.

Harriet's blue-gray eyes glowed; her face lit up. For once she looked actually pretty. It was the proudest moment of her life.

VI

"Then Has a New Flower Blossomed in the Kingdom . . ."

1824–1825

WHAT HAPPENED "when the dust returned to dust" weighed on Harriet's heart as the sweetness of June turned into the heat of summer. She trusted in the "house not made by hands" and a God of Love, but all her Puritan blood, all her father's sermons, cried out that that answer was too easy. It was not just Catharine's tragedy; it was not just Lyman's nudging his children toward the terrifying ordeal of conversion. Byron was dead.

George Gordon, Lord Byron, in his thirties a dissolute but still luminous fallen angel, had died of the fever while in Greece, where he had gone to help the Greeks revolt against their Turkish masters. He died in April; it took two months for the news to reach Litchfield. Lyman heard it, and went home to announce sorrowfully, "Byron is dead—*gone*." To Harriet, his voice was like a tolling bell. After a silence he went on. "Oh, I'm sorry that Byron is dead. I did hope he would live to do something for Christ. What a harp he might have swept!"

That afternoon Harriet took her basket and climbed Chestnut Hill to gather strawberries. Instead, she "lay down among the daisies, and looked up into the blue sky, and thought of that great eternity into which Byron had entered, and wondered how it might be with his soul."

The devout on at least two continents were wondering the same thing. Byron had been raised by his Scottish mother in a stern Presbyterian Calvinism, but he had run away from it into a feverish search for pleasure. To Lyman, the thought of all that talent, all that potential, lost so young and lost forever, was true tragedy. The thought that he, Lyman Beecher, might have been able to bring Byron to a state of grace weighed heavily upon him.

On Sunday he mounted the steps to his Litchfield pulpit and gazed solemnly down at his waiting congregation. Beyond the tiers of windows, heat hung heavily in the air over the rolling hills. Inside the church the great and small of Litchfield, the law students and Miss Pierce's young ladies sat languidly in their accustomed places. Suddenly Lyman pushed his spectacles up onto his rampant hair and took off on one of the mesmerizing, spontaneous flights of eloquence that made his listeners bolt upright in their pews.

His voice rolled out like great chords on an organ, and his words were all on Byron. No amount of genius or of brilliance could save vice from perishing in its own fires, he thundered. Goodness only was immortal. And to throw away one's life, to misuse one's gifts and powers as Byron had done, was a terrible waste and a sin against God. His words etched themselves deeply into Harriet's mind.

Byron's death had brought her face-to-face with what she had been trying to ignore all through the time of Catharine's troubles—the subject of "conversion." Her *own* conversion—or rather, the absence of it. Harriet believed in God. She tried to be good, and to bend herself to God's and Papa's will. She shivered over thoughts of hellfire and damnation. Yet she couldn't, she simply couldn't bring herself to a state of agony over her state of depravity, and a sense of deserving—even being willing—to be damned.

That summer Catharine and Mary came home from Hartford, full of news about Catharine's school. It occupied rooms above a harness store on Main Street—an excellent spot, at the sign of the White Horse. Hartford was a bustling city, population around five or six thousand. Its Main Street was paved with cobblestones, there were fascinating shops, and three times a week stagecoaches stopped at Ripley's Coffee House to pick up passengers for faraway Boston or for New Haven, five hours' ride away. Lyman's friend Dr. Hawes was pastor of the Congregational Church. There was a Hartford Museum of Curiosities and Paintings, and the Jubal Society gave concerts at the Episcopal Church.

Best of all, Catharine's school was a success. It had had fifteen students in its first session, more in the second, and even more promised for fall of 1824. Catharine had based her curriculum on the progressive example set by Sarah Pierce: Natural and Moral Philosophy, Chemistry, History, Rhetoric, Logic, Latin, Algebra, and Drawing, with Botany planned as a future addition. Catharine kept school in the mornings, hearing recitations in the first six subjects and teaching an algebra class. She was actually teaching Latin, too, having made her first acquaintance with it in a cram course under brother Edward during the two weeks before her school opened. Now she was managing, with Edward's help, to keep a lesson or two ahead of her students. Mary presided over the afternoon sessions, teaching drawing and other genteel subjects and hearing recitations.

Lyman Beecher could feel pleased. Catharine—whether she liked it or not—had found her calling, Mary a safe niche for the present. Edward was making a fine name for himself. Mrs. Beecher was expecting another baby. There remained the question of Harriet. She was indeed a genius; the Exhibition Day essay had established that fact firmly in her father's mind. She was also small, and plain, and "peculiar" in the way she kept so much to herself and was given (like her father, though he would not acknowledge that) to fits of moodiness and melancholy alternating with an odd kind of inner exaltation. Where was the best place for a thirteen-year-old female genius to flourish? At Miss Pierce's Academy for another year or so? With her father, wherever he was? Lyman was away from Litchfield a great deal these days and growing restless.

If he left the Litchfield church, and the Academy chaplaincy, his daughters would no longer receive free tuition there.

Catharine, with one eye on her school's growing enrollment and the other on how much she hated teaching, knew exactly what should be done with Harriet. Within the next year, Catharine's school would need another teacher, and who could be trusted more—and be paid less—than her little sister? Catharine had already arranged where Harriet would live in Hartford. Mr. Isaac Bull, who had a wholesale pharmaceuticals business in Hartford and several children, wanted to send one daughter to Miss Pierce's school. If she could board in Litchfield with the Beechers, the Bulls would take Harriet in. This sort of exchange of children between families of like minds was very common.

Before Harriet knew what was happening, her trunk was packed, and she was on the stagecoach with her sisters, headed for the great city thirty miles away.

Catharine, kindly as well as efficient, had arranged for her two best students to write to Harriet, welcoming her in advance. They became the first friends Harriet had ever had.

Both were older than she. Catherine Ledyard Cogswell was the daughter of Hartford's most prominent doctor; the prettiest, most popular girl in school. Harriet, always deeply moved by beauty, promptly became one of her admirers. Georgiana May, daughter of a wealthy Hartford widow, was, like Harriet, plain and quiet. Catherine Cogswell was for Harriet like a bright dancing light; Georgiana like a sister or a mother. Harriet admired Catherine; Georgiana admired *her*. The bond that developed between Harriet and Georgiana would endure for life.

The greatest thrill for Harriet was that she had a room of her own. It was only a small hall-bedroom (as such "extra" rooms were called)—scarcely big enough to hold the customary narrow bed, the straight chair and table, the hooks for dresses. But it looked out on the Connecticut River, and it was *all her own*. Only a shy child from a large and boisterous family could fully appreciate what that meant.

Life in the Bull home was full of novelty. One of Mr. Bull's sons kept a retail drugstore at the sign of the Good Samaritan. The other two were clerks in their father's wholesale house on Front Street. They were all musical. Morning and evening family worship in the Bull home was enlivened by rousing hymns, enhanced by flute accompaniment and the rich soprano embellishments of Miss Mary Anne Bull. Miss Bull was one of Hartford's reigning beauties, and a soloist in the church choir. Her favorite suitor, Samuel Collins, would sit in speechless wonder in the parlor, gazing on his beloved's long dark curls, cascading from a comb high on her head, while Harriet observed them both with interest.

School, in spite of new friends, was a less comfortable place. Harriet had no illusions about the fact that, as a Beecher, much was expected of her. Catharine, her eye on the future, threw Harriet into Latin class. No one else was beginning Latin that session, so Harriet received the awful honor of her sister's individual attention. Soon Catharine had Harriet wrestling with the odes of Ovid, and found a private tutor to teach her Italian and French.

In after-school hours, Harriet and Georgiana walked along the banks of the Park River, at the west end of Hartford. There, under the whispering trees, Harriet talked and talked, thoughts and dreams gushing out that had been dammed up all her life. Georgiana was the listener Harriet had always needed—comforting, reassuring, admiring, and absolutely loyal. To her, Harriet poured out everything—her passion for Byron and her grief for his lost soul; her dreams and fears; the story of her life. Georgiana listened, and sympathized, and encouraged. They talked of how someday, far in the future, they would both build their dream homes here beside the river. The quiet, sun-dappled riverbank was a sanctuary for Harriet.

But her real sanctuary was her room. Here Mrs. Bull took care of her when she fell ill. Here she studied the textbooks Catharine assigned to her, and read the books she craved. Here she became a writer.

Her triumph at Miss Pierce's had kindled a fire in her that could not be quenched. *Now* she knew why moods and daydreams came to her, so vivid at times that they were truly visions. *Now* she knew why she took to reading as to a drug; why she felt everything so deeply, so intensely. All her life Harriet had heard about the Calvinist doctrine of "the calling"—being called to a ministry in whatever work one did, whatever one's gifts and talents. She knew, quite suddenly and clearly, that her gift and calling was to be a writer. It was an ambition she confided only to Georgiana.

Catharine kept her busy with school assignments but secretly, slowly, Harriet began to write. In typical Beecher fashion of doing things on a grand scale, she chose to write a drama on the ancient Latin lines, but with a dash of Shakespeare thrown in—she was writing in iambic pentameter.

She set her verse drama in ancient Rome, in the days of Nero and the Christian persecutions. Her hero was Cleon—young, rich, an Olympic champion from Greece, and as handsome as a god. In other words, Lord Byron. But a Byron who, although throwing his life away in wasteful living, was not yet totally beyond redemption. Because this was going to be a *Christian* epic, and she, Harriet, was going to do in it what she hardly dared realize she had longed to do in life—save the fallen angel's soul.

Harriet began her play in Shakespearean fashion, with two young nobles talking on a street in Rome.

Lentulus: And so you missed the banquet—'tis a pity!
. . . . why, this same Cleon,
He is a perfect prince in entertainments. . . .
Such show of plates and cups both gold and silver,
Such flaming rainbows of all colored stones. . . .
Lucullus: And so the emperor himself was there. . . .
He takes to this young lord with special favor. . . .
Cleon seeks pleasure with a ravening thirst.

Then, in "An apartment splendidly furnished," Cleon, "reclining on a couch," was visited by a figure from his youth, an "aged philosopher" whose attitude and rousing lecture bore strong overtones of Lyman Beecher:

Diagoras:	I hear thou art the common talk for waste,
	And that in riot and loose luxury
	Thou dost outstrip even these degenerate days. . . .
	And thou companion of the very scum,
	The very dross and dregs of all mankind; . . .
	Is this the Athenian Cleon? Is this he
	Who drank philosophy and worshipped virtue?
	This he who triumphed in the Olympic race
	Followed by wondering eyes. . . .
	Rememberest thou the glory of those days?
	. . . canst thou tamely sink into a brute?

Of course Harriet's Cleon could not; would not. He would experience conversion, undergo the most terrible of tortures in pagan Rome, and not recant his newfound faith. He would become a "soldier of the Lord."

All this would take time. Harriet was becoming drunk on her own creation. She "filled blank book after blank book with this drama. It filled my thoughts sleeping and waking."

Then Fate swept down in the person of Catharine Beecher. In spite of—or perhaps *because* of—her own position as Beecher family poet, Catharine had no tolerance for Harriet's literary extravaganza. If Hattie had so much free time, she could put it to better use in study and written analysis of Joseph Butler's *The Analogy of Religion, Natural and Revealed, to the Constitution and Course of Nature.*

There it was again for Harriet—the question of Religion and Nature. She had been trained to do as she was told, and she did so now, dutifully, grieving only in private over her unfinished masterpiece. But analyzing the dry chapters of Butler's *Analogy* taught her literary structure—and more importantly, how *not* to be boring.

Spring came; then summer. Harriet produced a translation of Ovid that justified Catharine's faith in her, and was good enough to be read at Exercise Day in June. Then the Beecher sisters went back to Litchfield for the summer.

There was a new baby in the parsonage, named Thomas. Harriet's fourteenth birthday was celebrated. She was old enough now to participate in some of the Litchfield social life along with Mary. There were rides to the lakes, and boat rides, and picnics with ham and chicken and a vast variety of cakes. On the outskirts of town Bantam Lake sparkled in the sunlight. On North Street the young men from the Law School still tipped their hats to those tantalizingly demure young ladies from Miss Pierce's school. Lyman still dazzled his parishioners from the canopied pulpit of the church. But it was no longer certain how long he would remain there. Old-style fire-and-brimstone Calvinism was losing its appeal; even Lyman at times was vaguely straying. The competition of Unitarianism loomed ever larger. Worst of all, and most to the point of Lyman's thinking, the salary he received could no longer support his family. Lyman, quietly, cautiously, was planning to move on.

But he still preached the Gospel of Christ and of Calvinism, and he still held his audiences. Communion Sunday approached. The Congregationalists "took the sacrament" once a month, and it was the only time that the converted and the unconverted were visibly separate in the congregation. Only those "under conviction" could come forward to the Communion table with its snowy cloth, could eat the bread and drink the wine held out to them.

The Sunday dawned, dewy and fresh, with the scents of hay and roses. Harriet was painfully conscious of her lack of conversion. For months she had been trying to screw herself into a state of agony over her sins, but it hadn't worked. The Communion service, starkly beautiful in the Calvinist tradition, moved her deeply, but she was an outsider at the feast. Then her father began to speak.

Frequently Lyman's sermons were, as Harriet privately admitted, "as unintelligible to me as if he had spoken in Choctaw." But today he was preaching what he called a "frame sermon," speaking from deep feeling and inspiration rather than from the written word. He took as his text the words from the Gospel of John: "Behold, I call you no longer servants, but friends."

He spoke of Jesus as the friend everyone longed for—unconditionally loving, patient, compassionate. Oh, how much I need such a friend, Harriet thought. But if she never came to a conviction of her own sins, she would never find one.

"Come, then, and trust your soul to this faithful friend," Lyman urged his parishioners. The words ran through Harriet like a flash of lightning. If Jesus could be trusted, if as the Scriptures promised, He could supply one's every need—why, then He could supply the sense of sin and conversion that she was lacking! She *would* trust Him!

Harriet felt as if her "whole soul was illumined with joy," and "as if nature herself were hushing her breath to hear the music of heaven."

After church Harriet slipped up to her father's study. Lyman was in his desk chair near the window. She found herself falling to her knees beside him. "Father, I have given myself to Jesus and He has taken me," she whispered.

"Is it so?" Lyman gathered her into his arms, his face like sunlight and tears rolling down his cheeks. "Then has a new flower blossomed in the kingdom this day."

He *accepted* her statement. Lyman, who gloried in testing his children, never doubted her conversion for an instant. It was the greatest gift he ever gave her.

Catharine, remembering her own struggles of the soul, wondered audibly how a lost lamb could be brought into the fold so easily, "without being first chased all over the lot by the shepherd." Catharine had come at last to her own difficult peace, but at what a price—she was skeptical of everything, and her tongue was becoming whip-sharp.

In September the Beecher sisters returned to Hartford. Harriet was eager to see Georgiana, and Catherine Cogswell. She tried not to think about the alarming fact that she would be teacher as well as student this session. Catharine had decreed that Harriet would teach students no younger than herself the *Analogy of Religion,* which she had analyzed the previous spring. Later, she would teach Ovid, and other subjects. It was no use protesting that she didn't know enough. Catharine brushed such argument aside. Wasn't *she* teaching Latin via a two-week cram course and daily study? Well then! Sister Harriet could go and do likewise!

There was one more thing Harriet had to do. Her home was in Hartford now, and Lyman had advised her that she should unite with a Hartford church. Supported by Georgiana and Catherine Cogswell, Harriet fearfully went to present herself to Dr. Hawes as a candidate for church membership.

Dr. Hawes knew his duty to her soul and to her father. He listened to her halting account of her conversion, and then looked at her with awful calm. "Harriet! Do you feel that if the universe should be destroyed"—long pause—"you could be happy with God alone?"

"Yes, sir," Harriet stammered.

"You realize, I trust, in some measure, at least, the deceitfulness of your own heart, and that in punishment for your sins God might justly leave you to make yourself as miserable as you have made yourself sinful," Dr. Hawes told her solemnly. That said, he welcomed her into the church.

Harriet went back outside, and the sun had left the sky. The whole world seemed chill. She could not answer Georgiana's anxious queries about how the interview had gone. *Deceitfulness of heart . . . punishment for your sins . . .*

Sister Catharine's skepticism over the ease of her conversion, and Harriet's own guilt about it, reverberated in Harriet's brain in awful counterpoint to Dr. Hawes's words.

Her terrible years had begun.

VII

"I Could Wish to Die Young"

1825–1829

WHEN JOHN QUINCY ADAMS became president of the United States in 1825 he was only the sixth president of what was still a very young country. He was the son of John Adams, the second president, and came from the old Puritan aristocracy. His father's generation had created for this new republic a government that worked, like a great clock, on a system of "checks and balances."

There were many areas in which this delicate balance had not yet been achieved. The Founding Fathers had written a Constitution that left some issues deliberately vague, because otherwise the Constitution would never have been adopted. One was states' rights versus central government. Another was slavery. Those issues had sprouted like two acorns fallen side by side from the Liberty tree, and had grown until by now their trunks were intertwined. They were merging into one mass, inseparable except by violence.

Political issues have personal fallouts. America had been founded by dissidents with strong beliefs. Their descendants found it impossible to separate religion and politics, no matter what the Constitution said. Both were argued constantly and passionately. It was an age of intense mind-searching, intense soul-searching, and intense emotion. All these things came together, like the spiral of a tornado, to strike down on the person of one small girl.

Harriet had crashed from conversion ecstasy into what theologians call "the dark night of the soul." She questioned her worth, her calling, her relationship with God, and her beliefs. Obediently she trotted through her daily duties, seesawing dizzily all the while from highs to lows. Her soul, her health, her very mind were battered.

It might have been because she was away from home. It might have been because of the bewilderments of her new life. It might have been that she had inherited the Beecher tendency to dyspepsia, or that she was so weary—her day started at dawn, ended long hours later, and she couldn't sleep. It might have been because she was fifteen.

All Harriet's intensity was focused on herself. Her heart pounded in her chest; her pulses pounded in her ears. She was overcome by dizziness, and weakness, and consciousness of her own shortcomings.

Back in Litchfield, Lyman Beecher had reached a milestone. Now fifty, he was the most famous preacher in America. Once more he appealed to an adoring congregation for a raise in salary. Once more it was denied.

Lyman informed his church board that he could not afford to stay in Litchfield. Within twenty-four hours he received a call from the new Hanover Street Church in Boston. To Lyman, this was another sign of God's hand on his shoulder, a miracle no less real for the fact that he'd heard rumors in advance about the Boston call.

Boston! That hotbed of Unitarian heresy! Lyman was young again, a racehorse champing at the bit. His joy was increased because Edward, completing studies at Andover Seminary, was called to the pulpit of Boston's famous Park Street Church. *Two* Beechers to combat Unitarianism in Massachusetts!

In the summer of 1826 Harriet joined her father and step-mother in their new home on Sheaf Street in Boston. Lyman, re-energized, was tearing hither and yon, his great voice rolling out against the Unitarians from the pulpit and his great personality rolling, like one of the new steam engines, over everything in its path. His heart was large, but he no more noticed the spiritual misery of one teenage daughter than he noticed the insects in the grass of Boston Common.

Edward was in Boston, and Edward did understand what Harriet was going through. But he was only twenty-three, newly ordained, and grappling with the enormously difficult task of pastoring a large and famous church. Nonetheless, he made time to talk gently with his little sister, trying to help her find her way. With Edward, Harriet found a mousehole-sized place of peace. Then she would return to Sheaf Street, and her peace grew cold.

It was no one's fault; it was everyone's fault; it was simply the Beechers being Beechers. It was difficult for Lyman to be aware of anything that wasn't larger than life. It was difficult for Harriet to assert herself. The domestic side of Sheaf Street life focused on the young children, her half brothers and sisters. The relationship between stepmother and stepchildren was no relationship at all.

The family, in a kind, disinterested way, was vaguely aware of Harriet's misery. Or perhaps Catharine and Edward, who were well aware, made the rest of the Beechers address the problem. Had Harriet been working too hard? Studying too hard? Maybe she should take a break from teaching and remain in Boston for the fall. So she did, moping her way about until her moods grated on her father's nerves.

Lyman was facing frustrations of his own. He, who had believed so fervently in the old Connecticut theocracy, was faced now with a bitter irony. In Massachusetts, not really a theocracy, all power was concentrated in Unitarian hands. The elected officials were Unitarians, the judges were Unitarians, the professors and trustees of Harvard College were Unitarians. The rich and fashionable, the literary and intellectual elite were Unitarians.

Even a fund established specifically to sponsor a yearly lecture on the Trinity was now being used for an annual lecture against that doctrine.

Lyman relieved his feelings with outbursts of emotion during family prayers, and with vigorous assaults on the parsonage woodpile. He kept a load of sand in the cellar for the express purpose of shoveling it from one side to the other. He installed climbing ropes and parallel bars in his backyard, and astonished visitors with his gymnastic feats. Harriet had no such outlets; a lady didn't *do* such things. She wasn't writing anymore, except for desperate letters.

Presently Catharine was writing to her father in alarm.

> I have received some letters from Harriet to-day which make me feel uneasy. She says, 'I don't know as I am fit for anything. . . . I could wish to die young, and let the remembrance of me and my faults perish in the grave, rather than live, as I fear I do, a trouble to everyone. You don't know how perfectly wretched I often feel: so useless, so weak, so destitute of all energy. . . . Sometimes I could not sleep, and have groaned and cried till midnight, while in the daytime I tried to appear cheerful, and succeeded so well that papa reproved me for laughing so much. . . . I make strange mistakes, and then they all laugh at me, and I laughed, too, though I felt as though I should go distracted.'

Catharine was galvanized by that hint of suicide. "If she could come here [Hartford] it might be the best thing for her, for she can talk freely to me," Catharine wrote to Edward. "I can get her books . . . her friends here could do more for her than any one in Boston, for they love her, and she loves them very much."

It was quite true, but books and love and what Catharine called "cheerful and amusing friends" were not enough to cure acute depression. Nevertheless, Harriet went back to Hartford, and muddled through one day after another.

Catharine's school was so successful that she incorporated it as the Hartford Female Seminary, and "took up a subscription"—sold shares of stock—so that the school should acquire a building of its own. By mid-February 1827 all stock had been subscribed. In the midst of this excitement, Catharine was making further plans for Harriet. Since Harriet had a real gift for art, Catharine decided Harriet must have art lessons and become the art teacher of her sister's expanded school.

During spring vacation Catharine sent Harriet off to Nutplains, in the company of Georgiana May. Nutplains and Grandma Foote could work their healing magic. So, possibly, could the Episcopal Church, though if Catharine was aware of that she did not say so. Nutplains made Harriet feel close to the lost mother whom she missed more and more.

Nutplains that spring was touched with romance. Uncle Sam the sailor had come home from the sea and married! Elizabeth Elliot, who was now Aunt Elizabeth, had not accepted the proposal until the captain had agreed to turn landlubber. Their wedding journey west was a search for a new place to live. The bride and groom returned to Nutplains with their minds settled on Cincinnati, the "Queen City of the West," where Uncle John P. Foote was in business.

Romance also blossomed closer to home that summer of 1827. Pretty, gentle Mary Beecher was in love with the wealthy young Hartford attorney Thomas Clapp Perkins. The Clapp family had, like the Beechers, come over in Governor Winthrop's Great Migration of the 1630s, so this was a marriage between two Puritan dynasties.

The wedding took place on November 7, 1827. Catharine's new school building, which had cost $5,000, was dedicated two weeks later. More than one hundred pupils were enrolled.

Harriet was teaching a course on Virgil. She was studying advanced French. But most of her time was devoted to her art. She was becoming an accomplished painter.

She wrote to Grandmother Foote in January, 1828:

I have been constantly employed from nine in the morning until after dark at night, in taking lessons of a painting and drawing master, with only an intermission long enough to swallow a little dinner which was sent to me in the school-room. You may easily believe that after spending the day in this manner, I did not feel in a very epistolary humor in the evening. . . . The seminary is finished, and the school is going nicely. Miss Clarissa Brown is assisting Catharine in the school. Besides her, Catharine, and myself, there are two other teachers who both board in the family with us: one is Miss Degan, an Italian lady who teaches French and Italian; she rooms with me, and is very interesting and agreeable. Miss Hawks is rooming with Catharine. In some respects she reminds me very much of my mother. She is gentle, affectionate, modest, and retiring, and much beloved by all the scholars. . . . I propose, my dear grand-mamma, to send you by the first opportunity a dish of fruit of my own painting. . . . I wish to improve [a taste for painting]; it was what my dear mother admired and loved. . . . had she lived, I might have been both better and happier than I now am.

Little by little, Harriet was finding her way back to the loving God she had felt so close to that unforgettable summer Sunday when she was fourteen. She was beginning to find a kind of inner peace. This came not *through* the "cheerful" company Catharine had prescribed, but as a reaction *to* it. Harriet was discovering her own way of life.

"All through the day . . . everything has a tendency to destroy the calmness of mind gained by communion with [God]," she wrote Edward in the spring of 1828. "One flatters me, another is angry with me, another is unjust to me. . . . It matters little what service [God] has for me. . . . I do not mean to live in vain. He has given me talents, and I will lay them at His feet, well satisfied if He will accept them. All my powers He can enlarge. He made my mind, and He can teach me to cultivate and exert its faculties."

Harriet's months in the chrysalis of adolescence were going by. In February 1829 she was writing cheerfully to Edward, disputing his interpretation of the Book of Job, and reporting that she now shared her room with three other teachers, including a "Miss Mary Dutton . . . [who] is about twenty, has a fine mathematical mind, and . . . I am told, quite learned in the languages. . . ." The Hartford Female Seminary faculty was growing.

In July, Harriet wrote to Edward, "I have never been so happy as this summer." She was eighteen, and in the eyes of the world she was a woman.

VIII

"Count Only the Happy Hours"

1829–1832

HARRIET LONGED TO BE LOVED. She was capable of intense emotions, intense passions, and she knew it. She still dreamed of Byron, but she had no beaux.

The men who dominated Harriet's world were her father and her brothers. Like them, she had the eagle-like Beecher nose, the blunt Beecher chin. She had the large Beecher head, in more ways than one a heavy burden for her small, frail body. She wore her brown hair in long curls, drooping elegantly on each side of her face from a center part. When she was interested or excited by things around her, Harriet's eyes turned violet, and her mouth could curve generously in a smile. When she "owled" inside herself, her eyelids drooped, and all the light went out.

Boston, during school vacations, provided plenty of interest and excitement. An underground movement against the control of the Unitarians was beginning to boil and bubble, and Lyman Beecher was the yeast that made it happen. Around him he was gathering a group of young men, mostly graduates of Andover College or Andover Theological Seminary, who were aching to fight in the army of their Triune God. They formed the Hanover

Street Church Young Men's Association, and promptly took on Massachusetts politics.

Lyman had discovered that Unitarian politicians were controlling the primary elections. Here was a challenge much to the taste of young men newly of voting age! The Hanover Street Church Young Men's Association—in coalition with similar organizations that soon formed in other Calvinist churches—lobbied successfully for laws against selling lottery tickets and strong drink on Boston Common. They put a stop to Sunday steamboat excursions to Nahant, a North Shore beach resort, on the grounds that excursions violated the Sabbath laws. Committees from the Young Men's Association met and welcomed newcomers to the city— young men seeking to make their fortunes, ripe targets for the merchants of sin. A vibrant youth movement was swelling in a city where the first generation of Unitarian leaders was beginning to grow old.

Lyman started a newspaper called *The Spirit of the Pilgrims*. It gave him a pulpit of paper in addition to the one of stone and wood. He charged around Boston, visiting landmarks made famous by seventeenth-century pulpit-pounders Increase and Cotton Mather, glorying in his Puritan heritage. All this new piety was not dry and dull—it couldn't be, with Lyman Beecher and his eager young men involved. To replace the gambling and drinking, they instituted a series of lecture programs called lyceums. In a time when long church services made everyone a connoisseur of oratory, lectures were popular—and respectable—entertainment. These lectures were particularly inspiring—ladies were not only welcomed but encouraged to attend.

Harriet's vacation visits gave her a chance to see her father in action and with more perspective. They also gave her a chance to re-establish the bond between herself and Henry Ward. Henry, now in his middle teens, had been converted—not to the church, but to the sea, under the fascinating influence of Uncle Sam Foote. Wisely, Lyman had not objected, only pointed out that a sailing man needed to know astronomy and mathematics. He shipped Henry off to Mt. Pleasant Preparatory School. Mt. Pleasant just happened to have as its primary mission the preparation of young men for Andover College and Seminary. Lyman was still hoping.

All this Beecher activity was bound to have a backlash. Catharine was an education pioneer, and some of her ideas smacked of heresy. Years at the Beecher dinner table had taught her that the saving of souls was the chief end of man. Why not of woman? If God gave us minds, surely souls could be saved through education as well as through revival services! *Formation of character,* Catharine told her teaching staff, was the first goal of education. *Imparting information* came second. "It should not be so much the object of the teacher . . . to find out how much has been learned as to communicate knowledge by explanation and illustration." It was the way Miss Pierce and her nephew Mr. Brace had taught, only they hadn't talked about it. Catharine did.

Soon the elders of Calvinist orthodoxy were gnashing their teeth. It wasn't just that noisy Dr. Beecher's noisy daughter was proclaiming heresy (*character* was ordained by God; how could it be trained?). She was a *woman.* Women ought to keep silent in the churches—and in schools, on lecture platforms, and in print.

Mary Dutton, who had become Harriet's friend, left the faculty as the whispers of scandal grew. But for the time, enrollment was still growing. Catharine and Harriet still went riding every morning before breakfast, Catharine on a spirited black horse and Harriet on a white one that at times took off as if he were possessed. Harriet wrote very funny letters to Mary Dutton, relating school and extracurricular activities, and Catharine added as postscript that Harriet was as contrary as a mule. Harriet was developing a sharp edge of mockery in her writing, and a real ability to read people's hidden characters.

In February 1830, Lyman's Norman castle of a church on Hanover Street, Boston, burned down.

There were all sorts of ironies involved. The straight-laced church board had rented storage space in the church basement to a merchant of hard liquor. Lyman, the thunderer against alcoholic drink, had been unconcerned. Somehow, the kegs of liquor caught fire. Blue blazed the rum, the flames licking through the basement windows like the fires of hell.

For some time the Boston newspapers had been having great fun at Lyman's expense, ridiculing him as an arch-Puritan out to legislate morality. People's incomes, as well as their indulgences, were hampered by the influence of the Young Men's Associations. When the fire roared at Hanover Street Church, the firemen simply stood around and watched.

An explosion shook the walls of stone. From an upstairs room, rented out to a tract (religious pamphlet) society, a snowfall of white paper booklets began to fall onto the flames. The firemen, the loiterers, the enemies of Dr. Beecher who had gathered quickly to observe his downfall, were enthralled.

Soon a regular "hymn sing" had broken out.

"While Beecher's church holds out to burn,
The vilest sinner may return . . .
Satan's kingdom's tumbling down,
Glory, halleluia!"

Many jokes were made about Beecher's "oil jug" being broken. The hilarity was observed, and recorded, by one of Lyman's young men—a twenty-six-year-old graduate of Maine's Bowdoin College and Andover Theological Seminary named Calvin Ellis Stowe. He also recorded Lyman's reaction to the fire. In the harsh light of morning, the church board assembled to confront the tragedy. The church's stone steeple had been split in two. Lyman arrived jauntily, surveyed the damage, and boomed out, "Well, my jug's broke, all right!"

Once again the Beecher spirit had been fired up by adversity.

The church congregation rose to meet it, contracting for a new location and new church building on Bowdoin Street. Lyman, having succeeded in thoroughly annoying the Unitarians, launched into a series of six sermons against Roman Catholicism and its "secret plot to overthrow American religious freedom." He still saw no contradiction between belief in the Bill of Rights and belief that Calvinism was and should be America's religion.

In May 1830 Lyman set off for the Presbyterian Church's annual General Assembly in Philadelphia. He came back to Boston with a whole new cause.

In Cincinnati, Ohio, where Uncle Sam Foote and his bride now lived, a new Calvinist seminary was being formed. It had a name: Lane Theological Seminary. It had a charter, a $5,000 endowment and sixty acres of donated land, a board of trustees, and three students. It *had* had a fund-raising campaign, which had failed, and one professor, who had therefore resigned. Nonetheless, the trustees hoped to build a seminary greater than Andover, greater than Harvard, greater than Yale. The chairman of the board was the Rev. Dr. Joshua Lacy Wilson, a Calvinist of the Calvinists.

The seminary needed a president—a dedicated Calvinist whose very presence would attract eastern money. The famous Dr. Beecher's name came up. On the strength of the idea, a rich New York merchant was persuaded to pledge $20,000 to endow a professorship of theology at Lane Seminary for Dr. Lyman Beecher.

It all happened much too quickly. Lyman could not leave his Boston congregation until its new church was built and dedicated, but the Lane trustees elected him president of the seminary all the same. Lyman signed a contract with them. The American West beckoned to the Beechers the way the colonies had beckoned to their ancestors—as a wilderness Eden in which they could raise up a New Jerusalem.

Edward Beecher left the Park Street Church in Boston to become the very young president of Illinois College in Jacksonville, Illinois. Catharine was fed up with the acrimony that was developing around her goals and methods for the Hartford Female Seminary. In the spring of 1832 she and Lyman paid an exploratory visit to Cincinnati. The hard journey took weeks, but the travelers were filled with enthusiasm by what they found at journey's end.

Catharine wrote home to Harriet that from Uncle Sam's home,

in the upper part of the city, she could look across the lower town, across the Ohio River, and see Kentucky. Walnut Hills, where the theological seminary would be built, was two miles out of town, in a cool forest grove. Cincinnati was a paradise, only waiting for the "improvements of taste" the Beechers could bring, and the sort of school that she, Catharine, could found there. She was already thinking of turning the Hartford Seminary over to someone she could trust. An added attraction for Lyman was that he had been offered the pulpit of Cincinnati's Second Presbyterian Church.

Lyman and Catharine were back east in time for Harriet's twenty-first birthday on June 14. Harriet was in limbo. Hartford Seminary would not feel like home if Catharine wasn't there. She was not sure whether her father's house could ever be home for her again. Mary was married. Henry was at Andover. Where did she belong? She was painfully conscious that she had no prospects. Prospects, for a young woman in 1832, meant marriage.

She went back to Nutplains for the summer, needing time to think. She was trying to settle not just her physical future, but her spiritual one, too, and on a logical basis. She knew clearly now that she had fled from the old concept of a wrathful God to a personal belief in a God of Love. Was personal belief enough?

Uncle Sam couldn't help with the questions of theology, but he was wise in the ways of human nature. Years of buffeting around the world had left him with a rare tolerance and understanding. To him, Harriet could confess her tendency to expect too much of people, and the bitter disappointments that resulted; her fear of what other people thought of her; her habit of bristling like a hedgehog; her sarcasm at others' expense.

Soon she was writing to Georgiana May, "[A]s this inner world of mine has become worn out and untenable, I have at last concluded to come out of it . . . give up the pernicious habit of meditation and try to mix in society somewhat as another person would. . . . I am trying to cultivate a general spirit of kindliness towards everyone. Instead of shrinking into a corner to notice how other people behave, I am holding out my hand to the right and to the left. . . ."

Uncle Sam, who sat beside her, had just quoted to her an inscription he had found on a sundial in Venice. *Horas non numero nisi serenas.* "Number no hours that are not serene"—or, translated more colloquially, *Count only the happy hours.*

She resolved to take that as her motto, and to move with her family into the new world of the West.

IX

The Great Westward Migration

1832–1833

THE GREAT WESTWARD MIGRATION of the Beecher family consumed nearly as much time as that first immigrant Hannah Beecher's journey over unknown seas. It was in its own way an equally perilous undertaking.

There were loose ends in the East to be tied up first. Catharine's seminary was now one of America's three most famous schools for girls, but she herself was close to breakdown. As principal she supervised the faculty and taught some classes; chose—in some cases wrote—the textbooks; planned curriculum and lesson units. She conferred with students and with parents. She held social events for the students once a week. She took care of all school business matters. She was also involved in politics.

The State of Georgia was trying to evict the fifteen thousand remaining members of the Cherokee Nation from fertile north Georgia reservation lands coveted by the whites. All the Beechers considered this cruel and unjust, but it was Catharine who wrote a petition to the "Benevolent Women of the United States," had it published anonymously, and organized public meetings to instigate petitions being sent to Congress. Catharine's petition was regarded as a masterpiece of political writing, but it failed in its mission. While anguishing over all this, Catharine had to find a new principal and reorganize the school so it would function successfully without her. She "arranged with [her] teachers that . . . the school should be resolved into a sort of republic and attempt self-government at least for a short experiment." And she persuaded John Pierce Brace himself to take over the management of the school.

In Boston, Lyman Beecher preached his farewell sermon, proclaiming his intent to make Lane Seminary the equal of Andover. "[T]he question whether the first and leading seminary in the West shall be one which inculcates orthodoxy with or without revivals is a question . . . of as great importance as was ever permitted a single human mind to decide." He took for granted both Lane's importance and the importance of his decision that Lane *should* promote revivals.

The last good-byes were said, the trunks and housewares packed, and the caravan was under way. There were so many in the party! Lyman, at almost fifty-seven getting his second (or was it third, fourth, or even fifth?) wind; Harriet Porter, some twenty years younger, no longer well or laughing; her stepchildren Catharine, now thirty-two and a nationally known educator; brilliant George, in his midtwenties, who had withdrawn from Yale Divinity School to travel with the Beecher mass migration; and plain, moody little Hattie. Then Lyman's "second family," Harriet Porter's own brood: ten-year-old Bella; Thomas, two years younger; little James, now four. Five adults, three children, plus Aunt Esther Beecher, once again uprooted. They left New England in the golden days of autumn, heading south and west.

The journey would be made in stages: New York; Philadelphia; across Pennsylvania to Wheeling, West Virginia, where they would board a steamboat for Cincinnati. It was a formidable—and expensive—undertaking. Fortunately the Beechers were experienced in two virtues common to clergy families everywhere—thrift and hospitality. They took for granted that they would stay, as much as possible, in the homes of friends and fellow ministers.

They stayed in New York for several days. New York philanthropist Arthur Tappan's endowment of the Lyman Beecher professorship had been a "matching grant," contingent on Lane Seminary's raising $40,000 to fund two more professorships. More than half of this money had been raised. Lyman discovered that as the seminary's new celebrity drawing card he was expected to hustle for the other half. He proved to be enormously successful.

He met briefly with one of the Van Rensselaers, of the old New Amsterdam aristocracy, and walked away with $1,000. His next day's fishing expedition landed twice that sum. Lyman was in his element. He celebrated his fifty-seventh birthday, and felt like half that age. Four days later Harriet was writing, "Father is to perform to-night in the Chatham Theatre! 'positively for the *last* time this season!' . . . [He] is begging money for the Biblical Literature professorship; the incumbent is to be C. Stowe . . . now the good people . . . are talking of sending us off and keeping him here."

Aunt Esther and Harriet Porter were " 'in the lowest depths, *another* deep'!" Harriet herself was beginning to wonder whether they'd ever get to Pittsburgh, let alone Cincinnati. Her head was spinning in the "agreeable delirium" of New York social life. "There's only one thing about it," she wrote, "it is too *scattering*. I begin to be athirst for the waters of quietness."

They arrived in Philadelphia in the drizzling rain of a Saturday evening after a boat journey that was a comedy of errors. Their baggage was delivered to the wrong New York wharf, so the Beechers arrived in the City of Brotherly Love bedraggled—"poor Aunt Esther in dismay,—not a clean cap to put on,—mother in like state; all of us destitute"—to stay with two "rich, hospitable" Philadelphia families. Fortunately, the trunks arrived a few days later. Lyman was lionized, but he raised very little money.

Their next stop was in Downingtown, a thirty-mile journey away. "Here we all are,—Noah and his wife and his sons and his daughters, with the cattle and creeping things, all dropped down in the front parlor of this tavern," Harriet wrote to Georgiana May. "If to-day is a fair specimen of our journey, we shall find a very pleasant, obliging driver, good roads, good spirits, good dinner, fine scenery, and now and then some 'psalms and hymns and spiritual songs;' for with George on board you may be sure of music." By Sunday they were in Harrisburg, and Lyman was preaching at evening service. Three more days, and they reached Wheeling.

Bad news greeted them. Cholera, a virulent infectious disease of the digestive tract, spread by poor hygiene and polluted water, was raging in Cincinnati. The alarmed Beechers decided to remain in Wheeling for eight days and then complete their journey by land. They were able to hire a "private stage" to transport them all.

At last, after several stopovers and days of jolting over Ohio's "corduroy" (log-paved) roads, the Beechers reached Cincinnati. The ghost of the cholera epidemic remained in the polluted air, in buildings blackened by smoke from endless street fires burned to "fumigate" the city. There were hundreds of new graves in the cemeteries. An orphanage was hurriedly being built to house the small survivors.

Cincinnati was a boomtown that had sprung up after the Revolution on the north bank of the Ohio River, directly opposite the mouth of the Licking River that led into Kentucky's "dark and bloody ground." The name came from the Order of Cincinnati, a fraternal group formed by Washington's generals. The shoreline, or "river bottoms," devoted to trade, was where the original settlement had stood. Two residential terraces rose above it, each some sixty feet higher than the land below. Behind it all stretched virgin forest, thick and dark. On the forest's edge, in the area known as Walnut Hills, Lane Theological Seminary was beginning to rise.

The Beecher house was brick, two stories high, with a long *L* running back into the forest. During the fierce gales of fall and winter they could watch the storm-tossed treetops and hear the roaring of the wind. Both Harriet Porter and Aunt Esther found it most unpleasant. But with Lyman there, surrounded by his Beecher troops, it was charged with what Harriet described as "moral oxygen . . . intellectual electricity."

Lyman threw himself into his new responsibilities. He had walked into a firestorm without knowing it. Dr. Joshua Lacy Wilson, until now the "leading clergyman of the West," pastor of Cincinnati's First Presbyterian Church and chairman of Lane's board of trustees, was an old-fashioned Calvinist. He had suddenly come to the horrible realization that in signing up Lyman Beecher he had hired a "heretic." War was inevitable; the only question was when it would break out.

Catharine marshaled all her executive skills to found her new school. She was as good a fund-raiser as her father; in a short time she had persuaded local businessmen to loan the money, and was luring Mary Dutton to come west to be principal and teacher. This time Catharine was determined not to be involved in day-to-day school operations.

She wrote in a series of letters to Mary Dutton:

> [W]e *must have a school here* such as we would establish if we had health. . . . There never was a better opening or a greater demand. . . . Harriet and I would both help in various ways. I should love to come and preach and sometimes to teach, and Harriet would like the same. . . . The plan is to start a school of the first rate order which shall serve as a model to the West. . . . In three years we could train *principals* and *teachers* to go forth and establish similar institutions all over our country. I see no other way in which our country can so surely be saved from the inroads of vice, infidelity and error. Let the leading females of this country become refined, well educated and active, and the salt is scattered through the land. . . .

In other words, Catharine Beecher was about to start a women's college. Forty young ladies were already enrolled for the spring 1833 semester of the as-yet-nonexistent school. Such was the lure of the rumor, floating through Cincinnati parlors, that the Misses Catharine and Harriet Beecher would own and operate the Western Female Institute.

Harriet was delighted when Mary Dutton succumbed to Catharine's artfully worded appeals. Even with the Foote relations near, even in the intoxicating atmosphere of Lyman's presence, Harriet was a ship without moorings in Cincinnati. All the Beecher women were.

Harriet rhapsodized about the picturesqueness of Walnut Hills in letters to Georgiana May. Her writing skills were steadily improving; her gift for vivid imagery needed no improvement. She had a fine eye for the comic, even when it was focused on her-self—the ability to laugh at herself was her saving grace—but her humor had lost its earlier edge.

Before Mary Dutton arrived in May, a momentous event occurred for Harriet—her first book was published. The previous summer she had begun writing an elementary geography for children. Corey, Fairbank & Webster of Cincinnati wanted to publish it, on condition that Catharine's name appear on it as co-author. Harriet had capitulated. Alas, poor Harriet! On March 8, she beheld in the Cincinnati papers an ad for A NEW GEOGRAPHY FOR CHILDREN BY CATHARINE E. BEECHER. At least when the book itself appeared, it bore the credit line "by C. and H. Beecher."

Somehow the real identity of the author got around in Cincinnati, and had an unexpected side effect. Bishop Purcell, of the Cincinnati Archdiocese, paid a visit and "spoke of my poor lit-tle geography and thanked me for the unprejudiced manner in which I had handled the Catholic question in it." He also expressed great pleasure at the opening of the Western Female Institute; probably in part because Catharine—to her own politi-cal and financial detriment—insisted that no school of hers would ever be affiliated with any particular religious group. Harriet and the bishop became good friends. All this was especially noteworthy, considering that one of Lyman's reasons for coming to Cincinnati was to oppose the influence of the Roman Catholic Church, and he was vigorously pursuing that end.

Something else happened in Cincinnati that March. The steamboat *Emigrant* docked briefly on its way south with a cargo of 150 slaves, "of all ages and sexes," en route to the slave markets of Vicksburg, Mississippi, "under the care of two beings in human shape." The young clergyman editor of the *Cincinnati Journal,* who saw this tragic cargo, wrote a scathing editorial under the headline UNRIGHTEOUS TRAFFIC. Vividly he described the torment of families being torn apart, the degradation of being chained two by two, the horrors of being "sold down the river." He saved his harshest condemnation for the slave breeding farms, where humans were forcibly mated like animals in order to produce more human livestock. Mr. Brainerd worded it more delicately than that; he was writing for a family newspaper, but his meaning was clear.

The *Journal* was the leading Presbyterian paper in the West, and Mr. Brainerd was an admirer of Lyman Beecher. Harriet read that editorial.

The Western Female Institute opened on the first of May. Mary Dutton had arrived, so Harriet was no longer quite so lonely. But she had no other friends, and little time in which to make them. In spite of Catharine's promises, Harriet was tied up teaching at the school all day. She was becoming too introspective again, and she knew it.

That July another outburst of cholera occurred—this time at Lane Theological Seminary. Instead of staying away, Lyman moved into the school dormitory, suspended classes, and turned the institution into a hospital for the duration. In two weeks he had the epidemic halted, without becoming ill himself, but four of his students had died.

By July Harriet's geography had gone into its third printing and again sold out. She received no royalties, because the manuscript had been sold outright to the publishers. But its success was still very satisfying. Unlike most textbooks, Harriet's was no dry recitation of names and facts. She had written it the way she wrote letters, as a continuous narration. She discovered she had a real gift for communicating with children.

Oddly, this was only true in her writing. In person, Harriet was too shy, too afraid (despite her resolutions) of what people would think of her, too remote—even with her students. They never clustered around her as students often do with popular teachers. Harriet's students respected her; they didn't know her.

Unlike Harriet, Mary Dutton was lively and charming and always had a group of student admirers. The parents of one of these had invited Miss Dutton to visit them on their estate in Kentucky. No lady, especially not a young one, traveled alone, and Harriet was the companion Mary Dutton chose to take along. They traveled downriver by steamboat to Maysville, Kentucky, and from there on by stagecoach. It was the first experience for both of them of slave country. Harriet spent most of the visit withdrawn in herself and apparently observing nothing, not even when some slaves were called out and commanded to "cut up capers" for the entertainment of the white audience.

Harriet and Mary Dutton returned to Cincinnati at the end of summer to find that Professor Calvin Stowe had arrived to take up his duties at Lane Seminary. He had brought with him a bride, "a delicate, pretty little woman, with hazel eyes, auburn hair, fair complexion, a pretty little mouth . . . a most interesting timidity and simplicity of manner." Perhaps because of her beauty, because of her timidity, Harriet took Eliza Stowe to her heart at once. They became soul sisters, just as Harriet and Georgiana May had done.

X

The Semi-Colon Club

1833-1834

LIFE IN CINCINNATI became better for Harriet after her friendship with the Stowes began.

Calvin Ellis Stowe had been one of Lyman Beecher's "young men" in Boston. While still an undergraduate at Maine's Bowdoin College he had published his own scholarly translation of Jahn's *History of the Hebrew Commonwealth,* complete with copious notes. He had studied for the ministry at Andover Seminary and gone back to Bowdoin as an assistant professor. He was a little giant, short and stocky, with a large head (like the Beechers), a receding hairline, and soft brown hair that curled at sideburns and at temples. His mouth was wide, firm, and humorous, his eyes dark and magnetic beneath bushy brows. Like the Beechers, he had learned to read young and read voraciously—the Bible (especially fascinating bits from the Old and New Testament prophets), *Magnalia,* Shakespeare and Milton and above all Bunyan's *Pilgrim's Progress.* He had great charm, an unconscious flair for the dramatic, and was considered an expert in what was called "Orientalia." He came from a dirt-poor Massachusetts family, and had just wooed and won the daughter of Dartmouth President— and conservative Presbyterian leader—Dr. Bennett Tyler.

Eliza Tyler Stowe was everything Harriet herself longed to be but wasn't—exquisite, gracious, with a natural charm that was enhanced rather than stifled by her shyness. In other words, she was much like Roxana, Harriet's "angel mother." There was instant intuitive empathy and understanding between the two young women, both lonely, both plunged abruptly into this alien western world.

The city they lived in had a dual personality. It was a river port; a northern city only a river's-width distant from the South. Hundreds of steamboats plied the Ohio River. German Catholic settlers operated slaughterhouses and meat-packing businesses in the bottoms, along with breweries and distilleries. Hogs ran loose in the streets. There were sawmills, paper mills, flour mills, cotton mills. Up on the bluffs, where Harriet's two Foote uncles lived, were handsome brick houses and wide, well-paved streets. Samuel and John P. Foote owned the city's water company. John P. was a trustee of the city's first free high school. Books, magazines, daily and weekly newspapers were being published in Cincinnati. The city had ten hotels, forty churches, and a medical school; a Lyceum (with young lawyer Salmon P. Chase as its guiding force) and a rival Atheneum (founded by Bishop Purcell for his Catholic parishioners). There were museums and theaters. For a while there had been a bazaar, founded by the English widow Mrs. Trollope, who had become a famous author by writing about Cincinnati and the *Domestic Manners of the Americans*. She hadn't thought much of either, to Cincinnati's outrage.

This was the city—both cultural center and rowdy frontier port—in which Harriet found herself, a place different from any she had ever known. It was a ripe time, a ripe place, to begin a whole new life—if she had the courage.

Not many months earlier she had written Georgiana May, "Thought, intense, emotional thought, has been my disease. . . . All that is enthusiastic, all that is impassioned in admiration of nature, of writing, of character . . . in emotions of affection, I have felt with vehement and absorbing intensity,—felt till my mind is exhausted and seems to be sinking into deadness. . . .

81

thought is pain and emotion is pain." Now all that enthusiasm, all that admiration and intensity, began to focus on Eliza Stowe (who seemed more like a sister than her own sisters did)—and on her writing.

It was Harriet who sat by Eliza, lending moral support, when Calvin Stowe came up before the Cincinnati Presbytery to be examined and admitted into membership. The support must have been mutual. Harriet's brother George was also up for examination—in his case for a "license to preach," since he had just completed studies at Lane Seminary.

George's application provided Dr. Joshua Lacy Wilson and his Old-School followers with their first chance to attack "Taylorite heresy" among the Beechers. If son George could be dismissed as a heretic, father Lyman's position would be weakened. The Presbytery turned George upside down and inside out, laying doctrinal traps for him in every question. They had not reckoned on George's intelligence nor his skill at disputation, honed at all those Beecher family dinners. George defeated all challenges, preached his first sermon the following Sunday, and was ordained. He was assigned as a "probationer" at a church in nearby Batavia.

Harriet and Catharine were boarding "in town" that autumn of 1833, in order to be close to their school. The Stowes lived in Walnut Hills, close to the seminary. Almost daily the Beecher "carryall" made the two-mile trip between Walnut Hills and Cincinnati and back—taking Lyman to preaching, meetings, or marketing; taking Eliza to Hattie, or Hattie to visit Eliza or her family.

Excitement sparkled in the air as the trees of Walnut Hills flamed with autumn. Nearly a hundred students were enrolled in the seminary, to Lyman's great delight. Among them was a handsome, tall young evangelist named Theodore Dwight Weld. At thirty he was already well-known in church circles as a modern-day John the Baptist who had wandered through the South preaching evangelical Protestantism, the virtues of manual labor, and the abolition of slavery. Like Calvin Stowe, he had been one of Lyman's "young men" in Boston. Like Calvin, he had charm—plus enormous charisma, magnificent looks, and ability to sway crowds by his oratory. Lyman, who had taken his measure and had great confidence in his own similar gifts, was not worried about Weld's influence over other students. If Weld acted as if he "owned the seminary"—so much so that strangers assumed he was faculty rather than a student—what did it matter? Dr. Lyman Beecher could keep him in line.

Up on the heights and down in town, intellectual and social activities beckoned. On September 11, Calvin Stowe addressed the College of Professional Teachers at its annual Cincinnati convention. This college was not a school, but an association of teachers with members from all the western states. Its meetings were open, and the public flocked into Cincinnati's large churches and meeting halls to hear the lectures and debates. Edward Beecher was one of the lecturers that year, appearing without warning to surprise his family. Harriet was overjoyed to see him. She took great pride in showing him the advertisements for her geography, now in its fifth edition.

In October Harriet received even greater literary recognition. She, along with Catharine, was invited to become a charter member of the Semi-Colon Club.

The club was designed to be a literary and artistic salon of the sort that flourished back in Boston. It was probably the brainchild of Uncle Sam Foote, and it frequently met at his fine house on the heights. Besides Sam and Elizabeth Foote and Elizabeth's sister Sarah Elliot, the members included attorney Salmon P. Chase; Judge James Hall, editor of *Western Monthly Magazine;* novelist Caroline Lee Hentz and her husband; Dr. Daniel Drake, the distinguished Cincinnati physician and public servant; E. D. Mansfield, who as a Litchfield law student had heard Harriet's schoolgirl essay read aloud. And the Misses Catharine and Harriet Beecher. And Professor and Mrs. Calvin Ellis Stowe.

For Harriet, having Eliza and her husband also at club meetings was the icing on the cake.

The Semi-Colon Club's name was a double pun. *Colon* was Spanish for "Columbus," who had discovered a great continent, whereas the club members, who were discovering great (though smaller) pleasure in literature, were semi-colons. A semi-colon was also, of course, a grammatical flourish very popular in literary efforts. The club met at members' homes on Monday evenings at 7:30 P.M. Members provided literary contributions—signed or anonymous—to be read aloud by the chosen "reader of the evening" and then discussed. Following the discussion came refreshments, and then a spirited Virginia reel led by the reader of the evening, who by then must have needed some physical relaxation.

Many, if not most, of the members were a generation older than Harriet, or close to it. She rarely spoke at meetings, but she did screw her courage up to turn in compositions to be read aloud. Most of them were satires—behind the veil of anonymity Harriet could indulge her comic gifts although, as she reported to Georgiana May, "I try not to be personal, and to be courteous."

Her first effort was a letter supposedly from a Bishop Butler, "written in his outrageous style of parenthesis and fogification. My second, a satirical essay on the modern uses of languages. This I shall send to you as some of the gentlemen, it seems, took a fancy to it, and requested leave to put it in the *Western Magazine*. It is ascribed to Catharine, or I don't know that I should let it go." That was Harriet's lack of confidence again.

Her next piece was a put-down of "certain members who were getting very much into the way of joking on the worn-out subjects of matrimony and old maid and old bachelorism." Next Harriet was inspired to concoct an elaborate spoof that gave her, by intention or accident, an opportunity to write in her natural letter-writing style. Her creation pretended to be a series of letters between "a gentleman and lady, Mr. and Mrs. Howard . . . pious, literary, and agreeable." She threw in "a number of little particulars and incidental allusions to give it the air of having been really a letter . . . to give myself an opportunity for the introduction of different subjects . . . different characters in future letters."

When she had finished her masterpiece, Harriet "smoked it to make it look yellow, tore it to make it look old, directed it and scratched out the direction, postmarked it with red ink, sealed it and broke the seal, all this to give credibility to the fact of it being a real letter. Then I inclosed it in an envelope, stating that it was a part of a set that had fallen into my hands. This envelope was written in a scrawny, scrawly gentleman's hand." That done, she sent it on its way to "Mrs. Samuel E. Foote," who was apparently the only person in on the joke. The whole stunt was a great success, and provided Harriet with an opportunity to practice a realistic, conversational kind of writing.

Suddenly, she had a serious use for this skill.

Back in August, Judge Hall's *Western Monthly Magazine* had announced a contest for the best story submitted by November 10, and for the best essay on a literary or scientific subject. The prize for each would be fifty dollars. At the time Harriet had been wrapped up in preparing for her Kentucky trip, and in any event would have been too timid. Now, her anonymous efforts had been praised by people of taste and culture. The contest deadline had come and gone, but in December Judge Hall announced that because the quality of entries had been poor, he was extending the deadline to February 1, 1834, in the hope that competent writers would be encouraged to enter the competition.

Harriet had started writing a character sketch to be read anonymously at a Semi-Colon Club meeting. It was a piece about Uncle Lot Benton, who had been Lyman's foster father. As she wrote about the kind, cranky, down-to-earth old man, all the family stories, all her homesickness for New England came flooding back. Uncle Lot became "Uncle Tim Griswold," and he had a pretty daughter, Grace. Grace had a suitor named James Benton, a young man who "had an uncommonly comfortable opinion of himself, a full faith that there was nothing in creation that he could not learn and could not do; and this faith was maintained with an abounding and triumphant joyfulness that fairly carried your sympathies along with him." He had "a knowing roguery of eye, a joviality and prankishness of demeanor that was wonderfully captivating, especially to the ladies."

Harriet was writing about her father, without illusions but with love.

The characters lived and breathed and talked, and would not be denied. Suddenly a plot was unreeling from her pen. Suddenly she had a short story that kept growing longer.

She quailed from submitting it to being read aloud, even with no name attached. She could not, she admitted, bear criticism. At last, in a state of dread, she turned the story in. Meeting time came; the reader began to read. And suddenly, in that cultured Cincinnati parlor, there they were—Uncle Lot, "James Benton" and his sweetheart, invisible but real, the everyday voices of everyday New Englanders ringing true and clear.

This was genuine art, written out of a real gift. It cast a circle of magic around the spellbound listeners in the quiet room, and even shy, self-doubting Harriet knew it.

XI

City under Siege

1834

JUDGE HALL SOON ferreted out the identity of the author whose story had so captivated the Semi-Colon Club. Sam Foote's quiet little niece had captured on paper a slice of Americana as yet unknown in literary circles, and the judge was astute enough to recognize it. He pressed Harriet to submit her story in the *Western Monthly Magazine* competition.

Harriet's story carried off the fifty-dollar prize, and appeared in the April 1834 issue as "A New England Sketch," by Miss Harriet E. Beecher.

No longer were Catharine's name and reputation necessary to lend authority to her quiet sister's writing. Harriet had, in her family's eyes, lived up to Lyman's prediction that she was a genius. Of course, that was only what was expected of a Beecher.

Soon Harriet was working on another character sketch, this time about Roxana. She found she had few factual memories of her mother, only the legends, but the legends were enough. Soon she had another piece to be read aloud and greeted with delight. Actually this one was less successful than the first, for she was dealing with the stuff of dreams, and Roxana (called "Aunt Mary") emerged as more saint than human woman. Nonetheless, Judge Hall bought the sketch for publication in his magazine.

Harriet was now a "real" writer. And fiction was no longer prohibited—or suspect—in the Beecher household.

While Harriet's dreams were coming true, Lyman's dreams for Lane Seminary were running headlong toward disaster. The issue that triggered this was slavery.

Lyman, in one of his optimistic highs, had allowed Theodore Weld to get out of hand. He had known Weld was antislavery; Lyman was himself. Any decent person, any real Christian would be, in his opinion. Slavery was moral evil and spiritual sin. He himself had been saying so for years.

Lyman had not considered seriously enough several things, in addition to Theodore Weld's charisma. One was that a large segment of the Presbyterian church was located in the South. Another that there were factions within the antislavery movement. Some were for gradual emancipation. Some believed that since the slaves had been wrenched against their will from their true homeland, Africa—like the Jews dispersed from their homeland Israel—the blacks in America desired and deserved to be repatriated to Africa. Some—the orator William Lloyd Garrison among them—were agitating for immediate abolition of slavery throughout the United States, and the immediate freeing of all slaves. Theodore Weld was one of these "Abolitionists," and Lyman knew it. He may or may not have known that Arthur Tappan, Lane Seminary's benefactor, was also a disciple of William Lloyd Garrison.

Unbeknownst to Lyman, Theodore Weld had met with Tappan before coming west, and had won Tappan's permission to agitate against slavery at the seminary. Lyman, happily occupied with all the different threads of his ministries, did not know what was going on when students talked to students.

By midwinter Weld was reporting to Tappan that there was only one black—or Negro, as the respectful term then was—student at Lane Seminary, and that he had not been present at a levee at the Beecher home. Was Lane Seminary—and its president—discriminating against blacks? Lyman had to write a lengthy letter to Tappan, explaining that *all* students had been invited, and that had he, Lyman, known Mr. James Bradley, the former slave, had reservations about attending the levee, he would have personally made sure he came.

Soon after this, Theodore Weld informed Lyman that he intended to turn the seminary into a center of Abolitionist activity. As a courtesy only, Weld was requesting permission to hold a public debate.

Lyman, controlling his explosive temper, counseled caution. A debate on slavery at this point in time would be unwise. Cincinnati was a river port, a gateway to the South, complete with drunken transients in the bottoms who could become a mob, and a good-sized community of free blacks who could become their victims if things turned violent. Anyway, abolition wasn't the only—or even the best—solution to the slavery evil. He, Lyman, believed in colonization. The debate should be put off until it could be held with safety.

Lyman was under the impression that Weld had agreed. Behind his back, Weld was proceeding with his plans. According to legend, when Lyman found out, he decided there was only one way to prevent a riot—to keep both the students and the city, in control. *He* would debate Weld himself, arguing for gradual colonization, not immediate emancipation.

Evening after evening the debate flamed on. Lyman brought out all his ammunition—his charm, his passion, his eloquence and ability to cajole. He was the old orator playing his greatest role.

He was Goliath, up against a younger David. Weld had all Lyman's gifts, and one thing more—he had *facts*. He *knew* that repatriation did not work. It had been tried—by the American Colonization Society. The slave population in the United States was simply too large for repatriation to be practical, and it kept growing larger. Besides, few of the slaves now alive were Africans by birth. They were *Americans*—and were entitled to be "free."

After eighteen evenings during which the city listened uneasily, the students' resolution for immediate emancipation passed almost unanimously. The only vote for colonization came from Lyman.

Lyman decided to give his students enough rope to hang themselves. They came close to hanging his career instead. Left alone, they formed the Lane Seminary Anti-Slavery Society, drew up and published a declaration of principles, and proceeded to put those principles in action while Lyman watched and waited.

Soon Lane students were meeting publicly with groups of blacks, both men and women. They were visiting Cincinnati's black families, even boarding with them. They established a lyceum, or cultural center, for the black community; started literacy classes. They gave a picnic for a group of young black women.

Suddenly Cincinnati discovered how close to being a southern city it really was.

Lyman realized belatedly that it was time he issued some wise warnings. He doled them out to his seminarians first, preaching the virtues of going slowly and not offending. Then he decided to reassure Cincinnati, and preached a rousing sermon on colonization from his church pulpit. Calvin Stowe gave a lecture on the same subject, which Harriet attended with Eliza.

Harriet was troubled by what was going on, more troubled even than her father. In many ways it was she who could see more clearly. She saw the angry glances Cincinnati citizens gave to mixed-race groups on the city streets. She heard the muttered comments. She had seen slavery firsthand in Kentucky, and squirmed at the condescension even the kindliest whites there had toward the blacks they owned. But she did nothing. Papa must be right; after the dual eloquence of himself and Professor Stowe, things would surely calm down for a while. Besides, the seminary was soon to close for summer vacation.

Henry Ward Beecher was about to graduate from Amherst, and Harriet was determined to be there to see it. Mary Dutton traveled with her. The first lap of the journey was by stagecoach across Ohio, in the company of three other women and two men. Mr. Mitchell, "the most gentlemanly man that ever changed seats forty times a day to oblige a lady," was quiet and correct. Harriet soon witnessed him "roused to talk with both hands and a dozen words in a breath. He fell into a little talk about abolition and slavery with our good Mr. Jones"—Harriet was being sarcastic—"who was finally convinced that negroes were black, used it as an irrefragable argument to all that could be said, and at last began to deduce from it that they might just as well be slaves as anything else, and so he proceeded till all the philanthropy of our friend was roused, and he sprung up all lively and oratorical and gesticulatory and indignant to my heart's content. I like to see a man that can be roused."

From Toledo, Ohio, Harriet and Mary Dutton journeyed by steamboat to Buffalo and visited Niagara Falls, at the sight of which Harriet's "mind whirled off, it seemed to me, in a new, strange world. It seemed unearthly." From there by stagecoach again to Albany, New York, and then to Amherst.

Harriet's reunion with Henry Ward was joyous, and the bond between them was as strong as ever. Henry was wonderfully improved—by working hard, he had managed to overcome the "thickness of speech" that had plagued him as a child. He was very handsome, very popular, and though not tall he towered over his tiny sister. Harriet reveled in her week with him at Amherst.

News trickled east from Cincinnati. The seminary had closed for the summer, to Lyman's relief. He was sure that by autumn the antislavery brouhaha would have calmed down. He was coming east himself on a round of personal appearances and fund-raising, and Catharine was coming, too, to recruit more teachers. The bad news was that cholera had broken out for the third straight year. Not so bad as in that first summer, but bad enough; some Cincinnatians had become convinced the place was a plague town and were putting their houses on the market.

Harriet went on enjoying Henry's company; they planned to travel to New York together and from there back to Cincinnati, after the danger from cholera was over. Lyman and Catharine started on their journey east.

In Lyman's absence, the Abolitionist seminarians staying on in Cincinnati for the summer devoted themselves to what they deemed "elevating their Negro brethren." And "sistern"—there was another picnic held *by* white seminarians *for* young black women. The resulting uproar made the Lane board of trustees hastily convene. They passed a resolution abolishing Weld's Lane Anti-Slavery Society. They passed another outlawing any discussion of slavery at the seminary.

These resolutions, which the trustees deliberately had published in the Cincinnati papers, were reprinted all across the country. Lane Seminary was rapidly becoming notorious. When Arthur Tappan read the resolutions, he was immediately convinced that the seminary he had funded had become a proslavery den of iniquitous oppression.

Weld and his followers walked out, accompanied by two likeminded and disgruntled Lane professors. Lyman hurried back to Cincinnati to attempt damage control. The cholera epidemic wore itself out. A traumatized city tried to heal itself.

On the sixth of August, 1834, gentle Eliza Stowe died. According to the obituary that her dazed husband wrote in final tribute, she died of a "scrofulous disease" that had apparently been eating away at her for months. Actually, the cause of her death was cholera, which struck her when she was already weakened from other illness. Toward the end she had been unable to eat without suffering great stomach pain. She left behind her, as Roxana had, a memory of an angelic being who had touched those who loved her with her physical and spiritual beauty, and a husband who was half-mad with grief.

XII

Religion and Slavery

1834–1835

HARRIET WAS DEVASTATED by the news of Eliza's death. Word reached her while she and Henry were still in the East. Eliza Stowe had been ailing, yes, but no one had had any idea she was in real danger. The fierce heat of that turbulent summer had destroyed the last of her resistance. Harriet Porter had visited her regularly during her worsening illness. Aunt Esther Beecher had moved into the Stowe house to nurse Eliza through her final days and to look after the numbed and helpless professor.

Eliza Stowe had been only the second close friend in Harriet's life. Now she was gone—not separated from Harriet by distance, like Georgiana, but gone forever.

The light had gone out of what had been Harriet's happiest year.

September came. Lyman, who had been galloping around the Northeast rallying souls against suspected Papist conspiracy, once again went back to his decimated seminary and tried to pick up the pieces. He was too late. By their actions, the trustees had broken his authority, and Lyman's power would never be quite the same again. Neither would the seminary, which had begun a slow descent into oblivion.

Harriet returned to Cincinnati, bringing Henry Ward, who started theological studies at Lane. He was joined there by Charles, the last of Roxana's children. Charles, an undergraduate at Bowdoin, had missed his family terribly. Lyman managed to get William called to a church in Putnam, Ohio. The great Beecher migration was complete, except for Mary, who had put down her roots in Hartford.

Catharine did not make the return journey west. She had hired Mary Dutton to be principal of the Western Female Institute; Catharine had launched it, now let Mary run it. Catharine was through with classrooms forever. She had found her cause—missionary for female higher education. From now on she would "ride the circuit" of relatives and friends, speaking, badgering, and lecturing. When she did come to Cincinnati, she would stay at her father's home. She would no longer be sharing room in the boardinghouse with Harriet.

Harriet found room and board in the E. F. Tucker home on Plum Street, at the western edge of Cincinnati. The Western Female Institute moved also, to the corner of Plum and Third. The one good thing to come for Harriet out of that sad autumn was the closeness that sprang up between her and her brother Charles, four years her junior. Charles was a true child of Roxana—gentle, sensitive, passionately musical. He played violin, loved religious music, and introduced congregational singing into the worship services at Lyman's church. This was still quite an innovation in Calvinist circles.

That October the Cincinnati Synod (the regional governing body) of the Presbyterian Church held its meeting at Ripley, Ohio, some sixty miles southeast of Cincinnati and diagonally across the river from Maysville, Kentucky, where Harriet had first set foot into plantation country. Harriet accompanied her father to Synod, and they and Professor Stowe were invited to be houseguests of the Rev. John Rankin, the good-looking, quiet young pastor of the Ripley Presbyterian Church.

His parsonage was a modest brick cottage, one story plus garret, scarcely large enough for the Rankins and their young sons. It faced south, its narrow front porch looking across the narrow lawn to the picket fence from which the cliff dropped sharply to the riverbank. A steep goat path provided the Rankins with faster access than by road to the church and community hundreds of feet below. Majestic trees shaded house and lawns, and the view was magnificent—up and down the bending river; across it to Kentucky's trees and hills.

The weather was gentle during that Indian summer, and in the evenings the Synod visitors and their host, brain-tired from meetings, would sit on the porch as moonlight turned the world to black and silver. During these hours, Harriet and Eliza's husband were brought together by their shared grief. Harriet, maternal since girlhood, could comfort Calvin, and he her, and both were comforted by sharing memories of their beloved Eliza.

Occasionally a light, tiny as a firefly, would flicker on the far Kentucky shore. Each evening at dusk the Rankins would place a lantern in one of the windows that faced the river. *Why?* someone asked at last. There was a pause. Then slowly, quietly, Rankin began to tell a story.

One bitter cold March not long before, a young slave mother had made the desperate decision to run away from a cruel mistress in backwoods Kentucky. Her baby at her breast, she had fled in late-afternoon dusk to attempt an escape across the river. It had been a terrible winter, and the Ohio River was still frozen.

It was after dark when she reached the riverbank and saw on the far shore the tiny flicker of light from the Rankins' window. The lantern was a sign, Rankin explained, that the parsonage was a "station" on the "Underground Railroad" along which slaves fled to the North and freedom. Every slave along the river knew the meaning of such lights.

The ice the young woman stepped onto was treacherously wet and beginning to thaw. She had slipped and fallen; struggled up, picked her way a few steps, and fallen again.

The story unrolled like a scroll for the rapt listeners, made more hypnotic, more terrifying, by the quiet way in which it was told. The words embedded themselves in Harriet's blood and bone and stirred unconscious memories and old legends. Aunt Mary, dying of sorrow and consumption, destroyed by slavery's dark, unnamed evils. An oddly beautiful young woman Harriet had glimpsed in a church pew during her Kentucky visit, her dark hair and olive skin evoking memories of Uncle Sam's tales of faraway isles. The girl was a quadroon, the whispered explanation had come; she had one-quarter black blood and was therefore legally a Negro and a slave.

As Rankin's story of the woman on the ice went on, Harriet not only *saw* the scenes but *lived* them. She heard the crackling of branches under the feet of the pursuers; heard the dogs baying— surely there had been dogs! She felt the icy water seeping into the woman's clothes; her heart pounded as that woman's heart. Suppose the baby cried out! Suppose she dropped it! Suppose the light beyond the river were not a haven, but a trap. . . .

No. Rankin was saying the terrified woman had reached the Ohio shore. She had labored up the goat path to the parsonage. Mrs. Rankin had warmed and dried mother and child, given them food and clothing, while her husband hurriedly harnessed up to drive them into hiding at the next stop on the Underground Railroad.

The miracle of it all, Rankin said thoughtfully, was that even as he was harnessing up he had heard the thunder of river ice cracking in the great spring break-up. Another day, another hour, and crossing would have been impossible.

When pursuers sent by the woman's owner reached the river, they had found only floating ice and a sodden garment dropped by one of the slaves. They had given up the search, assuming the runaways to be drowned. A few weeks later the woman's husband had made his own escape, and with Rankin's help been reunited with his family and gone on with them to Canada.

The story bound the Beechers and Professor Stowe with the Rankins in a dangerous secret. Only knowledge that Lyman

Beecher *was,* despite rumors to the contrary, antislavery, could have persuaded Pastor Rankin to reveal it. His listeners could well believe a miracle had been involved. But Harriet was a storyteller, and inevitably questions would crowd into her mind. What had caused the young mother, on that particular night and not before, to attempt escape? Why had her husband not gone with her? What had become of them? She asked no questions. The story, and the magic of the night, kept all the listeners silent.

In some nameless way the night forged a bond between Harriet and Calvin Stowe. Both had been, and continued to be, deeply moved. The story had affected Harriet profoundly, and Calvin had been a witness as it did so.

They never saw each other in quite the same way—Eliza's husband, Eliza's friend—again.

Synod ended. Lyman, Harriet, and Calvin Stowe returned to Cincinnati. Through the autumn their paths kept crossing—at church, at the seminary, at the Beecher house, at the Semi-Colon Club. And as winter set in Harriet had occasion to see even more facets of this surprising Calvin Stowe.

The serpent of politics that had caught Lane Seminary in its coils the previous summer suddenly reared its head again. It was clear by now that, with Arthur Tappan's blessing, Theodore Weld had come to Lane not as a theological student but as a missionary of abolition. When he had led his band of followers out of Lane—severely decimating its student body—he had delivered them to the new Oberlin College in Oberlin, Ohio. It turned out that he had pulled the same stunt earlier, leading some twenty-six students to transfer from New York's Oneida Institute to Lane. Now Weld, outraged at what he considered incorrect beliefs in the aging Dr. Beecher, was unleashing a deliberate campaign to destroy both Lyman Beecher and his seminary.

Weld had a powerful supporter—the fiery young founder-editor of the antislavery journal *The Liberator,* William Lloyd Garrison. Years before, Garrison had joined Lyman's church in Boston, and had pressured Lyman to join in a crusade for immediate abolition. Lyman had listened and then, with humorous condescension, pointed out that great political and economic issues could not be solved overnight. Being *right* was not enough; to succeed a reformer must also act at the *right time*. Indignant, Garrison had stormed away and bided his time.

Now he saw his chance to avenge that condescension and strike a blow for abolition at the same time. In January 1835 *The Liberator* published statements from Lane's seceding students and faculty members that branded Lane—and by extension, Lyman—as pro-slavery. Garrison's editorial comment labeled the seminary as "a Bastille of oppression—a spiritual Inquisition." The statements were reprinted in a pamphlet that was circulated by Arthur Tappan and New York Abolitionists. Enrollment at Lane dropped still further.

In February Dr. John C. Young, president of Danville, Kentucky's, Centre College, turned down an invitation to fill the Chair of Sacred Rhetoric at Lane. Now even a southerner, a believer like Lyman in gradual abolition, had turned against him. Next the Rev. John Rankin, forsaking his usual reserve, wrote a letter to the Cincinnati *Journal* that weighed all the evidence thus far and concluded that the Lane faculty had taken an unwise attitude during the student strike.

Worse was to come. Arthur Tappan turned his financial back on Lane and endowed Oberlin with a department of theology that he specified would be open to students "irrespective of color." An abolitionist professor whom the Lane trustees had fired became an Oberlin professor; a Lane trustee who had resigned in protest became Oberlin's president. Lyman Beecher's dream of making Lane the great seminary of the West was over.

He was an aging King Arthur, his vision still strong but his followers gone, the circle broken by betrayals, over-confidence, and internal strife. Only one knight picked up the gauntlet and rode out to do battle for the fallen hero's honor, and that was a most unlikely one—Calvin Ellis Stowe.

By defending Lyman, he was seriously damaging his own reputation and career, but that did not stop him. He responded to Rankin's charges, courteously but firmly, in a follow-up letter to the Cincinnati *Journal*. Rankin replied; Calvin Stowe replied again. For months the debate between the two men—both antislavery, both ordained Presbyterian ministers—went on in the paper's columns.

Suddenly Harriet was seeing Calvin Stowe—her friend's widower, who was becoming her friend—in another and very flattering light. No longer only a distinguished religious and scientific scholar, he was a crusader against injustice, in defense of the cruelly wronged, and despite the cost. Beneath the plump and prosaic exterior beat the heart of a hero out of a novel by Sir Walter Scott. And at some point during that disorienting winter something else occurred that revealed the inner man to her even more profoundly.

It happened at a meeting of the Semi-Colon Club. Calvin Stowe never made any claim to creativity or imagination. His writing—in sermons, lectures, and articles—inclined to be dry and heavy. Yet on this night, prompted by who knew what, this down-to-earth, scientific-minded scholar had turned in to be read aloud a signed essay that was nothing more nor less than his psychic autobiography.

Calvin Stowe saw visions and heard voices. He couldn't remember a time when he hadn't; they had begun so far back that he'd been a half-grown boy before he'd found out they weren't the everyday experience of everyone. He did know that he had been four when a very friendly figure began to materialize each night in his bedroom of the family's home in Natick, Massachusetts. Other visions there had been of hell, and a band of ashy-blue devils, shining and hairless. That recurring vision had finally frightened little Calvin into fleeing to his parents' room for comfort—but he had never told them why.

He saw tiny fairy figures, sinister or kindly. He saw ordinary human figures in rooms with him, by night or day, absolutely real and normal—except that if he went to touch them, they weren't there. He heard voices, and he had premonitions. They were all perfectly clear, and they were as much a part of him as breathing.

All of this he set out in his paper in a perfectly detached and matter-of-fact manner, rather as though he were making a scientific report. Actually, his fascinated listeners accepted it as such. Psychic phenomena was a promising field of study in this new scientific era of the nineteenth century. But for Harriet, Calvin's revelations meant something more. She herself was more of a mystic than she admitted or perhaps even realized. When she read . . . when she had heard the story of the slave woman on the ice . . . above all when she wrote, she saw visions. She could hear voices, feel the cold wind or the warm, smell the scent of flowers. She, like Calvin, was given to strange bouts of melancholy, and of being almost outside of one's own body.

She wasn't alone anymore. She and Calvin were kindred souls. More, beneath the exterior the world saw, he now stood revealed to her as a romantic figure, straight out of all the old stories.

Harriet had found her Byron, and had fallen in love.

XIII

"... And change to nobody knows who"

1835–1836

HARRIET AND CALVIN WERE thrown together a great deal as 1835 went on. Lyman and Calvin conceived of a grand series of Sunday-evening lecture-sermons to be given at Lyman's church by Calvin, drawing on his special Old Testament scholarship. The series ran for twelve weeks and was followed by another in which Calvin and Lyman alternated in speaking about inspiration, miracles, and prophecy.

Of course, these important lectures deserved to be reported on at length in the Cincinnati *Journal*, and by someone who had listened closely, who understood both the subject matter and the speaker. By now editor Thomas Brainerd, who had written the eloquent editorial about the slave ship at Cincinnati's dock, was also a pastoral assistant at Second Church. He was practically a member of the Beecher family. Lyman's sermons appeared in the *Journal*'s pages; so did Catharine's poetry and sometimes Letters to the Editor; Charles was planning a set of articles on church music. Who better than a Beecher to report on Professor Stowe's lectures? The articles appeared throughout the late winter and spring, and were signed by the initial *H*.

Harriet Porter Beecher died of consumption that spring. She left a thirteen-year-old daughter, eleven- and seven-year-old sons, a flock of stepchildren who felt no grief, and a husband whose mourning was perfunctory.

Roxana was gone. Harriet Porter Beecher was gone. Eliza Tyler Stowe was gone but not forgotten, still loved and mourned by her husband and her dearest friend. Harriet and Calvin were in love, but nothing could be spoken of it, nothing done, until the proper year of mourning for Eliza Stowe was over.

Lane Seminary lingered only as a living ghost. Lyman's power was diminished, and the rock of his Calvinist theology had been riven. The nation, too, was changed. It was no longer "new." The matters left in dispute when the Constitution was written were still in dispute, and the voices raised in protest were growing steadily more raucous.

Chief among them were the voices of the abolitionists. The term—uncapitalized—was coming to be a generic term applied to all who were antislavery, no matter which method of eliminating slavery they preferred. America was steadily pushing westward, and America—particularly in the South—was still an agricultural economy. New territories in the South clamored for the right to slavery. Voices in the North—other than those who profited from the South's cotton—were raised against it. No longer could anyone simply avert the eyes from slavery. Suddenly, it was in the public eye if not in the public's face. Suddenly, hard data on its uses and abuses were appearing in public print.

In Ohio, Theodore Weld was set upon by a mob. In Tennessee, another Lane dropout was flogged by a mob for handing out pamphlets demanding immediate abolition. In July Cincinnati's free black community held a demonstration that included a float of Liberty striking off the shackles of a slave. The Cincinnati *Gazette* published an account of a Tennessee lawsuit: An overseer had beaten a slave boy to death because of a misdemeanor. The plantation owner sued his overseer and recovered the value of his "destroyed property." The overseer faced no criminal charges. Seven thousand slaves had been sold at the New Orleans market during the previous winter; Virginia sent nearly that many "down the river" every year; in twenty years 300,000 slaves had been sold south by the combined states of North Carolina and Virginia.

Rumors spread that the Abolitionists (those demanding *immediate* abolition) were stirring up a great slave rebellion. Race riots broke out even in the North; Abolitionists caught by mobs in the South were hanged or tortured; slaves caught trying to escape met even worse fates. "In the frenzied excitement now abroad," the *Journal* stated, it was no longer safe even to be "calm and candid."

In that summer of 1835 there was, for once, no cholera in Cincinnati. When September came, the Beecher family was caught up in a weekend of great family joy. Catharine, her detested stepmother gone, was back for the moment under her father's roof. When Edward returned from his annual summer tour of the East he brought sister Mary Perkins with him. William and George both came from their respective parishes. There they all were together, for the first time ever: Catharine, Edward, William, Mary, George, Harriet, Henry Ward, and Charles; Isabella, Thomas, and James; Lyman the patriarch, and elderly Aunt Esther. Some of them were total strangers to each other; some had known each other only briefly. But the Beecher blood ran strong, and the Beecher looks, and the Beecher temperament.

Lyman wept; then made a ritual of the weekend. They joined in a family circle of prayer and singing. Edward preached from Lyman's pulpit on Sunday morning, William in the afternoon, George in the evening. The house was filled with visitors, flowers, presents. When the family was at last alone on Monday evening, a Beecher "disputation" took place. Lyman, being Lyman, analyzed each son and daughter's character, with wit that occasionally drew blood. On Tuesday morning a much-moved Lyman lined his Beecher Christian soldiers up for inspection—from Catharine, thirty-four, in curls and the current fashion of top-heavy sleeves, slightly raised waist and belling skirts down to little James, also in curls. There was one last prayer circle, one last hymn, and the family dispersed.

The weekend strengthened Lyman for what was to come.

Enrollment at Lane Seminary for fall semester was devastatingly low. In October, Lyman was to stand trial for heresy for a second time—on this occasion before Synod, to which Dr. Wilson, defeated at Presbytery, had taken his charge. Wilson fully expected to win this time, since ultraconservatives controlled the majority of Synod votes, but he did not. Lyman again was cleared, on a vote of ten to one.

That autumn Calvin's series of lectures appeared in book form. The *Journal* gave it a cool review. In November a notice appeared announcing that the Misses Catharine and Harriet Beecher were withdrawing from further responsibility for the now well-established Western Female Institute.

On January 6, 1836, a flustered and happy Harriet sat down at her desk in a spare minute to dash off a letter to Georgiana May.

> Well, my dear G., about half an hour more and your old friend, companion, schoolmate, sister, etc., will cease to be Hatty Beecher, and change to nobody knows who. My dear, you are engaged, and pledged in a year or two to encounter the same fate, and do you wish to know how you shall feel? Well, my dear, I have been dreading and dreading the time, and lying awake wondering how I shall live through this overwhelming crisis, and lo! it has come, and I feel *nothing at all.*

XIV

"Slave Women Cannot Help Themselves"

1836-1837

HARRIET'S WEDDING WAS small and private, with only her family and Mary Dutton as witnesses. Even Catharine was not there, and none of the friends who had for some time been playing Cupid even knew when the ceremony was taking place. There was, as Harriet told Georgiana, "a sufficiency of the ministry" within the family, so they had not even had to bring in an outside pastor to perform the ceremony.

Three weeks passed before Harriet continued her letter. "My husband and myself are now quietly seated by our own fireside, as domestic as any pair of tame fowl you ever saw." Two days after the wedding they had taken what Harriet called "a wedding excursion" they would gladly have skipped had not "necessity required Mr. Stowe to visit Columbus, and I had too much adhesiveness not to go too. Ohio roads are no joke at this season, I can tell you."

The "wisp of nerve" that was Harriet did not have her professor to herself for long. For some time, plans had been under way that would take Calvin to Europe for a long period of study and research. Lane had an endowment for a library, but as yet no books. With his scholarly specialties, Calvin was the logical person to select those books. He spoke fluent German as well as many other languages. Germany was the center of Protestant thought, and the books the seminary required could be obtained nowhere else. Lane, of course, had no funds to pay for Calvin's trip. However, William Henry Harrison, "General Tippecanoe," former territorial governor, member of Congress and U.S. senator, thought highly of Calvin and had great influence with the state government. Strings were pulled. The State of Ohio passed a resolution commissioning Calvin to collect data on European means and methods of public education that would be useful in setting up a state school system in Ohio. The expense money allotted to him was enough to cover his own modest expenses only.

There was no way that Harriet could go along, but she and Calvin planned that she would travel with him to "Boston, New York, and other places and . . . stop finally in Hartford, whence, as soon as he is gone, it is my intention to return westward." Harriet never made this honeymoon journey. By April, when Calvin had to start east, she had found out she was pregnant. It was not safe for her to jolt east over the corduroy roads. Calvin sailed for Europe on the first of May, 1836. Their first anniversary would have come and gone before he would see his bride again.

Both were desolate over the separation. Harriet, knowing the depth of Calvin's melancholy moods, wrote him a letter of wifely advice to read as soon as the ship had sailed. "Now, my dear, that you are gone where you are out of the reach of my care, advice, and good management, it is fitting that you should have something under my hand and seal for your comfort and furtherance in the new world you are going to. First, I must caution you to set your face as a flint against the 'cultivation of indigo,' as Elizabeth calls it." (Elizabeth was Uncle Sam Foote's wife; she was referring to Calvin's long-drawn-out blue moods.)

"[S]eriously, dear one, you must give more way to hope than to memory. You are going to a new scene now, and one that I hope will be full of enjoyment to you. . . ."

Harriet went back to her father's house, to wait out her pregnancy and to write. She was kept busy with columns and articles for the *Journal*. Henry Ward, still a seminarian, was serving as the paper's pro-tem editor that summer, for Lyman and Thomas Brainerd were off to Pittsburgh for the Presbyterians' General Assembly and the final round in the heresy war between Lyman and his nemesis, Dr. Wilson. The Old-School forces were outnumbered, and Dr. Wilson dropped his charges once and for all. Triumphantly Lyman and Brainerd went on to tour the East. Henry Ward was left in charge of the *Journal* until winter, and he relished it.

The heresy issue had burned itself out. The fires of the slavery issue burned ever higher all through that turbulent year, and Cincinnati was at the center of the conflagration. There were many reasons for this: its geographical position; its settled, prosperous free black community; its bustling river port (doorway to the South); its Underground Railway stations (doorway to the North); the notoriety of Lane Seminary.

In the summer of 1836 James G. Birney, publisher of the antislavery paper *Philanthropist,* arrived in Cincinnati. He was a lawyer, a former southern planter who had believed in Colonization but been converted to Abolitionism by Theodore Weld. He planned to publish the *Philanthropist* weekly in Cincinnati.

He had misjudged his market. Cincinnatians held a mass meeting that condemned Abolitionism and all who proclaimed it. A few years earlier, Cincinnati had been more open-minded, and many southerners had themselves felt slavery was gradually on its way out, the only question being *when* and *how*. That had been before the invention of the cotton gin (which made slave-produced cotton a hugely profitable crop) . . . before Theodore Weld . . . before Nat Turner's Rebellion.

Nat Turner had been a charismatic, highly intelligent Virginia slave who, believing himself called by God to free his people, had with six of his followers developed a plan for a great slave rebellion. One night in 1831 the first blows of this revolution were struck. Within forty-eight hours, the slave army had increased to sixty and fifty-five whites had been murdered. Turner was captured and hanged; seventeen of his co-conspirators were hanged; many more blacks, some of whom were wrongly suspected, were tortured, mutilated, shot, and burned. A terrible fear of blacks, magnified by all the nightmare demons out of legend, grew and multiplied like virus in the whites of America. By the hot summer of 1836 the explosion point was reached.

Birney and his associate Gamaliel Bailey kept churning out the *Philanthropist,* despite Cincinnati's anger, despite a ruling from Washington forbidding the mailing of "incendiary publications." On the night of July 12 a mob of young men, some of them from Kentucky, broke into the printing house and wrecked the presses. Having been chided mildly by the mayor, they went on to burn down the printer's home, headed for the hotel where Birney lived—to be turned away by Salmon P. Chase—and from there went "nigger-hunting" in the Cincinnati slums. A few shots scared the mob into a nearby bar.

No lives were lost that night, but for two more days and nights the city trembled. Panic set in. Some Cincinnatians in high places preferred to close their eyes to what was happening. Others talked of taking the law into their own hands to prevent the paper's being reestablished. Out in Walnut Hills, Harriet found Henry Ward at the kitchen stove, melting lead and making bullets.

"What are you making those for, Henry?" she demanded.

"To kill men with, Hattie!" he replied.

The mayor, fearing for the city, had put out a call for volunteer policemen to patrol the streets at night and keep the peace. Henry Ward was one of the first to be sworn in. He packed pistols for several days.

By now, the Beecher blood was up. Henry wrote editorials, condemning both slavery and the actions of the Abolitionists. Harriet, by now heavy with child, wrote a long article for the *Journal.* It was in dialogue form, supposedly an actual conversation between "Franklin" (her pseudonym) and a friend about the riots. Writing in the naturalistic style that had proved so successful, she was nonetheless preaching a sermon. Her message: Even well-intentioned ends do not justify the means, and *words in print*—such as in Letters to the Editor—were a better way of debating different points of view than violence. It was her first published writing on the slavery issue. The riots had confirmed Salmon P. Chase, Henry Ward Beecher, and Harriet Beecher Stowe as Abolitionists.

The "mobocracy," as Harriet called it, faded away. In the hot days of August the city slumbered. Lyman came home from the East. Apparently unable to do without a woman, he had managed between the trial and fund-raising to find himself another wife. Her name was Lydia Jackson. She was a widow with several children, the youngest of whom—Joseph and Margaret—she had brought with her to the Walnut Hills parsonage. Lyman's own children, at least publicly, maintained a tight silence on the subject.

Near the end of September, earlier than expected and frightening, Harriet's labor pains set in. On September 29, exhausted and astonished, Harriet delivered not one baby but two! Little Hattie Beecher Stowe was the mother of twin girls. In Calvin's absence, she chose the names. One must be named Eliza Tyler Stowe, in honor of her dearest friend. The other she named for Isabella Beecher.

Calvin sailed for home November 19, having gloriously completed all his overseas missions. He had written a series of travel articles, which Henry Ward had published in the *Journal,* he had purchased $3,500 worth of books for the seminary library, he had visited universities in Scotland and England, he had talked with the mighty (or near enough) and become cosmopolitan. The voluminous letters that he and Harriet had been sending back and forth to each other had been delayed that autumn by storms over the Atlantic, and the storms continued, battering and slowing down his crossing. It was not until he docked in New York on January 20, 1837, that the new father heard the astounding news. He hurried west to see his instant family, arriving during the second week of February.

He found his bride weary but triumphant, with much to tell him. The twins were adorable, at four and a half months already developing personalities that proved they were not identical. Installed under his own roof, his womenfolk were everything a proud husband and father could desire—with one exception. The *names*. Certainly Harriet could name one baby for his first wife if she so wished. But the other *must* be named for his second bride. The twins became Hattie and Eliza.

Other changes were taking place. The Cincinnati *Journal* was sold and the new owner was not hospitable to Beechers. The *Chronicle,* where their Litchfield friend E. D. Mansfield was now editor, became the "Beecher paper." Charles had already been writing music articles for it; now the others contributed pieces when time permitted and finances required. The *Chronicle* published a New England story that Harriet titled "Cousin William." Catharine, now back in Cincinnati and financially strapped, wrote Letters to the Editor under the pseudonym "Charitus," and ghostwrote McGuffey's *Fourth Reader* for Dr. William McGuffey, who was now tied up with duties as president of Cincinnati College.

In March 1837 a financial panic shook the nation. Arthur Tappan's New York bank failed, and since he personally had underwritten Lyman's salary as Lane president, that salary for the school year 1836–1837 could not be honored. Lyman was reduced to supporting his wife and younger children on the small amount the Second Presbyterian Church could pay him. Fortunately, Calvin's salary at Lane was not affected. Only fifteen students were attending Lane that year. The Western Female Institute, shorn of the luster of the Beecher name, was similarly affected. Both Lyman's dream and Catharine's were failing. Even wealthy, generous Uncle Sam went bankrupt. He sold his house on the heights to pay off debts, created housing for his family in a row of stores he owned in town, and began to make his second fortune. Without his big house to meet in, the Semi-Colon Club dissolved.

Harriet became pregnant again. Keeping house with two babies under a year old and another on the way was more than even a strong woman could manage alone, and Harriet was far from strong. The endless washing (water heated on the stove) and ironing (irons also heated on the stove), the scrubbing floors with lye soap, the pickling and preserving and preparation of food, the sewing of clothes demanded at least one extra set of hands. The well-to-do had real servants. In other homes the hands belonged to daughters, unmarried sisters or aunts or (if that failed) the untrained help of girls and women who, if they "lived in," had to be paid little beyond board and clothing.

Harriet and Calvin were fortunate to secure the services of a gentle, refined young woman who had been a slave. She was the daughter of a slave mother and a white father, and had with her two small daughters who were even lighterskinned than she. She referred to their absent father as her husband; what had become of him the Stowes did not know. She had been raised "in a good family as a nurse and seamstress," making her exactly the sort of help beleaguered Harriet needed.

"She has often told me," Harriet wrote, "how, without any warning, she was suddenly forced into a carriage, and saw her little mistress screaming and stretching her arms from the window towards her as she was driven away." She had been sold down the river. "She has told me of scenes on the Louisiana plantation, and she has often been out at night by stealth ministering to poor slaves who had been mangled and lacerated by the lash. Hence she was sold into Kentucky."

That was not the end of the story. Eventually it came out that the man she had called her husband had been her white owner. "You know, Mrs. Stowe," she said quietly, "slave women cannot help themselves."

Slave women cannot help themselves. The words burned themselves into Harriet's memory, along with the memory of the slave mother on the ice. She, too, had come from Kentucky. . . . The questions that had swirled in Harriet's mind that unforgettable night swirled again, and with them wild surmise. And then more memories, equally dark but older. Exquisite Mary Foote Hubbard, fleeing horror and a nameless evil in the islands. . . . Harriet the young child had not understood the shocked whispers passing over her head, but Harriet the wife and mother could. New-married Mary had arrived at her husband's plantation to find it populated not just by black slaves but by a troop of mixed-race children, sired by her husband on the bodies of black women whom he owned and who did not dare refuse. It was perfectly right and customary, her husband had assured her blandly. He had not been married; he had needed women; he had needed more slaves, and what better bloodline for them than his own?

Aunt Mary had borne it until she could bear no more, and then had fled back to Connecticut to die. Harriet's servant had—what? Harriet was too delicate to ask. But she had to have told Calvin—how could she not have?

One evening Harriet's servant arrived back from her afternoon off in a state of terror. The story tumbled out. She was *not* free, but a fugitive slave like the woman on the ice, and she had just heard that her former owner was in Cincinnati. Please, the Stowes *must* help her! . . .

The Stowes were galvanized into action, drawing on their memories of what they had learned at the Rankin home. Harriet's brother Charles, who was at Lyman's house, came hurrying over. Calvin, for all his wisdom and knowledge, was helpless in a crisis. Charles was not. He knew a John Van Zandt whose country farm was an Underground Railway station.

In the small hours of the night the two men, both armed, hid the terrified young woman in a wagon and drove off in the blackness over the corduroy roads. Back in the Stowe house Harriet watched and waited, listening for her babies' cries, listening for her men's return. In her mind she could hear the crack of ice breaking and the baying of the hounds.

XV

"My Dear, You Must be a Literary Woman"

1837–1842

THE TROUBLES—for the country and for the Beecher clan—continued. In November 1837, Edward Beecher's friend the Rev. Elijah Lovejoy was murdered when a St. Louis mob burned down a warehouse housing the printing press for his Abolitionist newspaper. Briefly, there were rumors that Edward had been murdered also. In April 1838 the locally built steamboat *Moselle* blew up at her Cincinnati pier, killing 136 and setting off a scandal that reached to Washington and back to the Cincinnati city hall.

The financial panic that gripped the nation was turning Cincinnati into a boomtown as thousands of unemployed easterners migrated west. This brought about a building boom that was built on barter and borrowed money.

In May fires burned in Philadelphia, and the Presbyterian Church was split asunder. Not a building—though many of those burned, too—but the very denomination itself. The spark was slavery; the fuel a mixture of doctrinal conflict, business, and politics.

Out in Cincinnati, the Western Female Institute closed its doors. Lane was in a state of terminal illness, kept alive only by

Lyman's incurable optimism, Calvin Stowe's loyalty, and the funds Lyman always managed to raise just in the nick of time. Henry Ward had been ordained (an ordeal at which he, like Edward, was raked over the coals by Lyman's enemies), married his New England sweetheart, Eunice Bullard, and become pastor of a tiny church (congregation: nineteen women; one man). Charles had dropped out of the ministry to work in, of all things, a New Orleans brokerage house.

Harriet was engulfed in domesticity. On January 14, 1838, she had given birth to a son, christened Henry Ellis Stowe. On June 21 she wrote Georgiana May a description of her life.

> My dear, dear Georgiana,—Only think how long it is since I have written to you, and how changed I am since then,—the mother of three children! [Today] I waked about half after four and thought, 'Bless me, how light it is! . . .' Up I jump, and up wakes baby. 'Now, little boy, be good and let mother dress, because she is in a hurry.' I get my frock half on, and baby by that time has kicked himself down off his pillow, and is fisting the bed-clothes in great order. I stop with one sleeve off and one on to settle matters with him. Having planted him bolt upright and gone all up and down the chamber barefoot to get pillows and blankets to prop him up, I finish putting my frock on and hurry down. . . . I apply myself vigorously to sweeping, dusting, and the setting-to-rights so necessary where there are three little mischiefs always pulling down as fast as one can put up.
>
> Then there are Miss H— and Miss E— . . . who are chattering, hallooing, or singing at the top of their voices, as may suit their various states of mind. . . . [Breakfast] being cleared away, Mr. Stowe dispatched to market with memoranda for various provisions, etc., and baby being washed and dressed, I begin to . . . cut out some little dresses, have just calculated the length and

got one breadth cut off, when Master Henry makes a doleful lip and falls to crying with might and main. I catch him up and, turning round, see one of his sisters flourishing the things out of my workbox in fine style . . . a second little mischief seated by the hearth chewing coals and scraping up ashes with great apparent relish. Grandmother lays hold upon her and charitably offers to quiet baby while I go on with my work.

"Grandmother" was Calvin's long-widowed mother, whom he had brought west to lend much-needed help. The comedy of errors went on.

Number one pushes number two over. Number two screams: that frightens baby, and he joins in. I call number one a naughty girl, take the persecuted one in my arms and endeavor to comfort her. . . . Meanwhile number one makes her way to the slop-jar and forthwith proceeds to wash her apron in it. . . . [O]f such details are all my days made up. . . . I suppose I am a dolefully uninteresting person at present, but I hope I shall grow young again one of these days, for it seems to me that matters cannot always stand exactly as they do now.

Well, Georgy, this marriage is—yes, I will speak well of it, after all; for when I can stop and think long enough to discriminate my head from my heels, I must say that I think myself a fortunate woman.

Her husband was feeling himself, by that time, most unfortunate in his "Beecher connection." Not with Harriet, whom he dearly loved. The thorn in his life was Lyman. By now Calvin knew, too well, that the once-brilliant future predicted for him while at Bowdoin College and Andover Seminary was being destroyed by his ties to the fallen colossus that was his father-in-law. Every time it looked as though Lane would finally have to close and he would be free, Lyman would somehow, somewhere, find just enough money and just enough students to go on. Calvin's strengths were his intelligence and humor, his vast knowledge in his field, and his wisdom; his weaknesses were his indecision, the way he went to pieces in a crisis, and his impracticality. He wasn't "handy"; he was the classic "absent-minded professor." Harriet realized early on that in practical matters she would have to be the strong one; in other ways far more important to her, he was her rock to lean on. At the seminary he carried on valiantly; at home he either roared against fate or was prostrated with the indeterminate ailments that were continually to fell both him and Harriet.

During most of the late 1830s and early 1840s it was Calvin who took to their bed and Harriet who brought him tea, sympathy, and determined encouragement. She was discovering a strength she hadn't known was in her, one that would always take over and see her through when all about were dissolving into pieces. God and her Calvinist backbone saw her through the crises; she didn't fall apart till they were over.

She was writing again. Not out of inspiration, but out of need. Another thing Harriet had realized was that she must gird herself to be the family breadwinner, at least until Calvin was finally free from Lane Seminary. There were huge numbers of magazines and newspapers being published, most of them having only a small in-house staff and requiring a constant supply of fresh materials. There were also the fashionable "annuals," intended as keepsakes and gifts for special occasions and filled with poetry, essays, and short stories full of sentiment, uplift, and romance. And there were numerous religious publications that would snap up anything written by a Beecher.

In bits and pieces, between housekeeping and babies and wifery, Harriet wrote this and that and sent it out. In bits and pieces, money began trickling in. Soon Harriet was able to report triumphantly to Mary Dutton, who had gone back east, that she was earning enough by her writing to hire a German girl named Mina to do the housework, while a young Englishwoman named Anna took care of the children. Both "lived in" and so did not require much pay.

I have about three hours per day in writing: and if you see my name coming out everywhere, you may be sure of one thing—that I do it for *the pay*. . . . I have determined not to be a mere domestic slave, without even the leisure to excel in my duties. I mean to have money enough to have my house kept in the best manner and yet to have time for reflection and that preparation for the education of my children which every mother needs.

It sounded easier than it was. More than once she was writing at the kitchen table while supervising the cooking and cleaning and being constantly interrupted by childhood crises. Somehow she managed to laugh about it and go on.

Eighteen thirty-nine was a better year, in spite of some embarrassing financial complications. Catharine had never actually paid out to Harriet her teaching salary; when her needs were pressing Harriet had simply drawn what she needed, "against money owed," out of the school's general funds. Now neither the school nor Catharine and Harriet's careers in it still existed. Catharine had to wind up its affairs once and for all, and she presented Harriet with the unpleasant news that she had overdrawn her account by $114. Harriet, humiliated, repaid the sum out of the writing earnings she had been putting aside to buy some decent furniture.

The summer brought happiness. Calvin was invited to deliver the Phi Beta Kappa address at Dartmouth. Leaving the baby and little Eliza in their nurse's care, Harriet and Hattie traveled east with Calvin, stopping off in Hartford while Calvin visited his Natick, Massachusetts, relatives and took care of his address. Then they had a glorious vacation in the White Mountains. Inspired by the local color Calvin related to her about his Natick stay, Harriet concocted another New England story for the *Chronicle*.

They returned to Cincinnati to find another weight on the chain that bound them there. The "new house," promised to Calvin when he accepted his Lane faculty appointment, had been completed. But by now Harriet and Calvin longed to move back east. Henry Ward had been called to the new New School Presbyterian Church in Indianapolis, at a salary of $800 a year. He and Edward were now the most successful of the Beechers. It was high time that Calvin was free to find his own place in the sun.

In May 1840 Harriet's second son was born and named Frederick William after the old king of Prussia, one of Calvin's idols. The birth was difficult, and in addition Harriet developed what she called a "neuralgic complaint" and was probably iritis, a painful rheumatic affliction of the eyes. Harriet had to remain in a dark room for two months, and for a long time more her eyes could not focus enough for her to read. At last she was able to take over the household—and write—again. Her family needed her, and as she wrote to Georgiana, when everything was weighted in the balance she considered herself greatly blessed.

She was developing a style of writing that would serve her all her days. *Two* kinds of writing, actually. One was what came out of her unconscious, out of her visions, out of passion—when the words or visions came so all-consumingly that all she could do was surrender to them and write them down. The other was like her writing in the Uncle Lot story—naturalistic, conversational, as if she were writing a letter, as if she were talking to a relative or to Georgiana. Either way, she neither planned far ahead nor thought nor polished. She simply "wrote it down." It was the only thing she had time for, and it worked.

Around this time someone—Catharine? Harriet herself?—wrote a hilarious sketch depicting Harriet's efforts to complete a touching story at the kitchen table amid constant interruptions from children and household help.

> Harriet [dictating to a "friend"]: *"I know my duty to my children. I see the hour must come. You must take them, Henry; they are my last earthly comfort."*
>
> "Ma'am, what shall I do with those egg-shells and all this truck here?" interrupts Mina.
>
> "Put them in the pail by you," answered Harriet.

118

" 'They are my last earthly comfort,'" said [friend]. "What next?"

"... You must take them away. It may be—perhaps it must be—that I shall soon follow, but the breaking heart of a wife still pleads, 'a little longer, a little longer.'"

"How much longer must the gingerbread stay in?" inquired Mina.

"Five minutes," said Harriet.

" 'A little longer, a little longer,'" [friend] repeated in a dolorous tone, and we burst into a laugh.

In the summer of 1841 Harriet celebrated her thirtieth birthday, nineteen-year-old Belle married Thomas Hooker, a law clerk in her brother-in-law's law office, and the streets of Cincinnati again ran with blood. In June an Abolitionist named Burnett assaulted a Kentucky slaveowner who came, with a Cincinnati constable, to reclaim a fugitive slave Burnett was concealing. A mob came after Burnett, but by then he and his sons were safe in jail. In August a German farmer was murdered by some blacks who were stealing his berries. A white woman was raped in Cincinnati. In September a race war broke out. After a week of terror the state militia, personally commanded by the governor, put down the riots, but not until after the mob had inflicted much bloodshed in the black community. In January 1842 the Bank of Cincinnati failed; a mob wrecked its banking establishment while the same mayor who had let the 1836 riots proceed looked on and did nothing. Cincinnati's anger forced the city council to formally censure the mayor, who died a few days later.

Cincinnati had become a city under mob rule, and the whole country knew it.

In April 1842 a party of nine escaping slaves making their way cautiously through Walnut Hills encountered John Van Zandt on his way to Cincinnati. Van Zandt did not dare transport this "contraband" in daylight; he hid them in his covered wagon for the trip to his farm with one of their number, a boy named Andrew, at the reins. He himself walked on to Cincinnati. Two whites flagged down the wagon to ask a question. Andrew panicked and ran. The whites, scenting reward money, drove wagon and occupants back into Kentucky. Salmon P. Chase sued the whites for kidnapping, but was defeated. The Kentucky slaveowner sued Van Zandt for the loss of his "property," Andrew, and won. Chase, representing Van Zandt, appealed the case all the way up to the Supreme Court, to no avail. Although Chase charged no fee for all his services, the fines and court costs drove Van Zandt into bankruptcy.

Harriet escaped to the East, again taking little Hattie with her. She had saved up enough money from her writing to go consult personally with Harpers, the New York publishing firm that Catharine had interested in a volume of Harriet's New England stories. Aunt Esther Beecher moved into the Stowe house to look after Calvin.

Harriet's stay in New York was eye-opening. The editors of the great New York publishing house were gracious and complimentary to Lyman Beecher's daughter. They accepted Harriet's manuscript, and expressed interest in seeing more. They also drove a hard bargain, but Harriet was too inexperienced to know that yet. She was, suddenly, filled with Beecher ambition and—for once—with absolute confidence in her own abilities and future.

From Mary Perkins's gracious home in Hartford, Harriet sent the good news back to Calvin. She had arranged to do some writing for the *Evangelist,* and did Calvin know anything about the editor of the *Boston Miscellany*? He had offered "twenty dollars for three pages, not very close print." Did Calvin think this liberal offer could be trusted? Harpers was not offering her much money, but they had hinted that they would take a second volume at better terms.

Calvin replied, "My dear, you must be a literary woman. It is so ordered in the book of fate. Make all your calculations accordingly. Get a good stock of health and brush up your mind. . . . [Y]our husband will lift up his head in the gate, and your children will rise up and call you blessed."

Calvin *believed* in her. Calvin understood. Calvin had faith in her, even when she did not herself. Calvin admired her mind. Calvin, as he went on to write, could not live without her. Calvin *loved* her—as she was, with all her strengths and weaknesses and doubts. It was why she loved him deeply—despite his hypochondria, his inability to cope with crises or to earn much money—and why she always would.

XVI

"I Must Have a Room to Myself"

1842–1850

The letters flew back and forth between Hartford and Walnut Hills, letters in which Harriet and Calvin poured their hearts out to each other . . . about themselves, their marriage, and their future.

"If I am to write," Harriet wrote, "I must have a room to myself, which shall be *my* room. . . . I can put a stove in it. I have bought a cheap carpet for it, and I have furniture enough at home to furnish it comfortably. . . . All last winter I felt the need of some place where I could go and be quiet. . . . If I came into the parlor where you were, I felt as if I was interrupting you, and you know you sometimes thought so, too. . . . You can study by the parlor fire, and I and my plants, etc., can take the other room."

The room she had in mind was the one they had been renting out above the kitchen. She meant it for office and study—and the children's schoolroom—*not* a separate bedroom. "God has written it in his book that you must be a literary woman," Calvin replied, "and who are we that we should contend against God? You must therefore make all your calculations to spend the rest of your life with your pen."

Alas, for best-laid plans and good intentions! When Harriet returned to Cincinnati, reality descended on her with a heavy thud. Calvin had meant every word he said in support of Harriet's literary career, but he was simply unable to do without his wife's presence, her attention to all the details of daily life at which he was fundamentally inept. And the children had needs, the house-keeping had needs. The worst interruption of all was the deterioration of both parents' health. The flames of Harriet's and Calvin's minds always burned so brightly that their bodies suffered.

The family limped along on little money. Calvin was still trapped at Lane. Harriet continued to sell her writing, but she wrote hurriedly and often poorly. The slavery struggles went on. In 1843 Cincinnati was gripped by "Millenium fever." A prophet named Miller was preaching that the world would end on the thirty-first of December. Harriet was pregnant again.

A month before the baby was due, George Beecher, perhaps the most brilliant of all the Beechers, accidentally shot and killed himself in the garden of his home in Rochester, New York. The news shook Harriet "like an earthquake."

The dark years had set in. The baby, born in August and named Georgiana May, was fragile. Harriet was in physical and mental anguish for months, and sank into a profound depression that she could not shake off. She was in a constant state of indistinct terror. Millenium fever provoked typical Cincinnati mob violence in October. Charles Beecher returned to Cincinnati and the ministry, bringing with him accounts of how Louisiana planters found it more profitable to work their slaves to death and then replace them, than to treat them fairly. So much for the pro-slavery argument that slaves were well treated because no owner would risk damaging his own "property." And the world did not end on December 31.

Eighteen forty-four dragged its way along, and 1845. Calvin was deeply worried about Harriet's health. He managed to take her with him when he went east that June on business. Harriet was "sick of the smell of sour milk, and sour meat, and sour everything." Even the joy of Hartford and Boston visits did not restore her health.

That winter Calvin, alarmed, rallied to her aid. In March 1846 she was writing, "My husband has developed wonderfully as housefather and nurse. You would laugh to see him in his spectacles gravely marching the little troop in their nightgowns up to bed, tagging after them, as he says, like an old hen after a flock of ducks."

At that time "water cures," half health spa, half hotel stay, were becoming wildly popular in America. Patients "took the waters" of the mineral springs, both internally and externally via baths and water packs. Water-cure houses also provided healthy meals, fresh mountain air and walks in the woods, mild exercise, and a pleasant social life. Dr. Conrad Wesselhoeft, a celebrated homeopathic physician, had opened one at Brattleboro, Vermont. The Stowes determined that one way or another, Harriet should go there for rest and treatment in 1846. She remained there for nearly a year.

Again the letters went back and forth between Harriet and Calvin—long, loving, thoughtful letters. They were able to talk to each other on paper more satisfactorily than they were ever able to at home, with daily cares, children's interruptions, and Puritan inhibitions. Harriet was happy at Brattleboro despite the cold baths. There were interesting, charming, and wealthy people among her fellow guests. Evenings brought dancing cotillions, and when white winter came there were outdoor sports. What fun it would have been, Harriet thought, to have Calvin with her for the sleighriding, the skating, the moonlight snowball fights! And how much *good* it would do Calvin!

She returned home in March 1847 and promptly became pregnant again. Her neuralgia of the eyes recurred, forcing Harriet back into darkness for months. Calvin's own health was also failing. Fortunately, after the birth of baby Samuel Charles in January 1848, Harriet's vitality returned. Dr. Wesselhoeft's water cure had done her a world of good. Now it was, as Harriet put it, Calvin's turn.

Calvin left in June for a stay that would last well over a year. Harriet was on her own, except for occasional visits from the constantly traveling Catharine. Harriet was the only one of Lyman's children still in Cincinnati, and Cincinnati had become notorious for mobs and crime. Eighteen forty-nine was known as its Murder Year. But gold had been discovered in California, gas lines provided lighting in Cincinnati's unsafe streets, and horse-drawn omnibuses now traveled regularly between the city and Walnut Hills.

In May 1849 cholera struck again. By mid-June new cases averaged thirty a day. The death rate climbed; eighty-four people died on June 25 alone. All those who could do so fled the city. Steamboats shunned the Cincinnati port, and the bars in the bottoms did an enormous business. Smudge fires, gingered up with sulphur, burned on every corner to fumigate the air, and greasy soot covered everything with its black pall. The plague peaked the week of the Fourth of July, but the usual festivities went on.

The greatest horror was that cholera killed so *quickly*. Newspapers reported five, six, seven members of single families dying during the same day between dawn and noon. Seemingly healthy persons would visit sick friends, be taken sick themselves, and die in the streets on their way home. One elderly black "root and herb" doctor spoke out, urging people to boil all water before using, but white Cincinnati laughed at this "Negro superstition."

Cholera spread beyond Cincinnati. President Zachary Taylor appointed a day of national fasting and prayer. Harriet kept on going. So far they were all safe, she reported by mail to Calvin; he *must not* think of coming home.

On July 10 little Charlie became slightly ill. The following day eleven-year-old Henry began vomiting. Charlie was enough better to act decidedly cross. By Sunday Harriet and the nursemaid Anna were ailing. The next day the Stowes' little dog Daisy went into spasms and died within half an hour. The twins, Anna, and Harriet spent the rest of that day making a shroud for the Stowes' old black washerwoman.

On July 23 Harriet, with heavy heart, took up her pen to tell Calvin, "At last, my dear, the hand of the Lord has touched us." Charlie, who had been in recovery, was sinking, and there was no chance he would survive the night. On the twenty-sixth Harriet was writing, "My dear husband,—At last it is over, and our dear little one is gone from us. He is now among the blessed. . . . I write as though there were no sorrow like my sorrow, yet there has been in this city, as in the land of Egypt, scarce a household without its dead. This heart-break, this anguish, has been everywhere, and when it will end God alone knows."

It was time for Calvin the indecisive to act, and he did. In September 1849 he returned to Cincinnati, rejuvenated by his water cure, to tell Harriet they were moving back east. He had accepted the new Collins Professorship of Natural and Revealed Religion at his alma mater, Bowdoin College. It paid less than any other teaching post at Bowdoin, even less than he was earning at Lane; he was letting down his still-optimistic father-in-law; but he had done it. Technically, he still had to break his contract with Lane, but with money so short there the Stowes foresaw no problem.

To their astonishment, the Lane trustees turned around and offered Calvin a $1,500-a-year raise if he would fulfill his contract. The Stowes were stunned. All their penny-pinching and doing without, all the stories poorly and hastily written to pay the bills, all the boarders Harriet had taken in and the children she had taught in her study along with her own children—and the Lane trustees had had money all along! Calvin and Harriet lost their last traces of financial innocence.

Calvin used the Lane offer as leverage with Bowdoin, and succeeded in obtaining a $500 contract-signing bonus from that college. He informed Lane that he would be leaving. His long-drawn-out loyalty to Lyman Beecher was at an end.

Harriet began writing again. She was full of hope, and any extra cash she could pull in would make the move easier. Besides, the Collins Professorship did not include free faculty housing. The Stowes would have to pay their rent themselves. Calvin had to finish out the 1850 spring term at Lane, to his disgust, but Harriet could not bear the thought of spending one more summer in Cincinnati's fetid, cholera-laden air. She was expecting another baby in July. Harriet and Calvin decided that she and the two youngest children should go east in April, while she could still travel. Harriet could buy furniture for the house that had been rented for them, and get everything settled before the baby was born and Calvin, the twins, and Henry arrived.

It meant much work and responsibility on the shoulders of one small and pregnant woman, but Harriet didn't care. Secretly she knew the house-settling would be easier without Calvin present; Calvin would get so flustered. She could not bear to stay in Cincinnati, with its painful memories, one moment longer than necessary. No one was left there now but Lyman, and he, seventy-five and growing senile, would soon retire and move east also.

One thing was certain. One way or another, in Brunswick, Maine, she *would* have that room of her own!

At last the trunks were packed and Harriet, ten-year-old Freddie, and Georgiana, at seven a tomboy called Georgie, were waiting at the Cincinnati pier in their shabby but bravely darned traveling clothes. They would go by steamboat to Pittsburgh; from there by canalboat across the Alleghenies through a series of canal locks called The Slides. Then by a 2 A.M. train to Philadelphia, and by boat and train to New York City where they would board a ferry and cross to Brooklyn and the home of that brilliant and celebrated orator-preacher, Henry Ward Beecher!

Behind them on the notice board, as they waited at the pier, flapped a handbill announcing that one Wm. F. Talbott, with offices in Lexington, Kentucky, was offering $1,200–$1,250 for #1-grade Negro males, and $850–$1,000 for #1-grade young Negro females, for the Louisiana market.

XVII

"I Will Write Something . . . if I Live"

1850–1851

HARRIET AND THE CHILDREN looked so bedraggled on the journey that at one point an officious petty railroad clerk, suspecting them of being destitute immigrants, had cross-examined them at length before allowing them to go on their way. But in spite of that, in spite of being six months pregnant, in spite of the jouncing of the railroad cars and the middle-of-the-night travel connections, Harriet's spirits rose with every mile. She was on her way to her native New England and her own people. She was going home!

First, though, there was the excitement of New York City and the splendors of Henry Ward's new church and home. Preaching at the new Plymouth Church in Brooklyn Heights, New York, he was covering himself with glory. His huge congregation adored him; they had given him a horse and carriage and salary of $3,300 a year. His purse was enriched by other "emoluments" for things like editing and writing, especially for the *Independent,* which had become practically "his" paper. The church sanctuary seated over 2,000 and was usually filled. Henry's wife, Eunice, had aged, and was growing tight-lipped and firm of manner, but that could be exactly what impulsive, bombastic Henry needed.

Harriet and Henry had much to talk of, especially the alarming developments in Washington—the California Compromise and the Fugitive Slave Act. The compromise, patched together by Henry Clay, now old from fighting the "slave wars" in Washington, would admit California to the Union as a free state, organize the New Mexico and Utah territories with no specification as to slavery, and—as an evidence of good faith to the South—enact a tough new law to prevent slaves from becoming free just by crossing the border into free territory. There would be punishment, harsh punishment, for those who tried it; those who had crossed into freedom must be returned to their owners, and bounty hunters paid to make this happen; there would be harsh punishment for any whites who aided and abetted such escapes.

To the Abolitionists, the proposal was absolute betrayal on the part of Henry Clay. To John C. Calhoun, champion of southern slavery, it was an insult. The South demanded equal claim to all new territory, a balance of power between South and North, and the North's absolute abstinence from any agitation against slavery. Late into the night, Henry Ward raged to Harriet how the Fugitive Slave Act was an evil act, how if passed it would be a law that *should* and *must* be disobeyed. Harriet, with memories of Cincinnati's bloodbaths and slave sufferings vivid in her mind, agreed.

From Brooklyn it was on to Hartford, to visit Belle and Mary and their families, to be reunited with Harriet's dear Georgiana May, now Georgiana Sykes, and introduce her to her young namesake. From there to Boston, where Harriet had to buy furniture—as cheaply as possible. The energy that had been propelling Harriet was running low. After fifteen years of loving marriage, she was well aware that Calvin, wise and learned as he was, had no "faculty" for coping with the everyday business of life and that she, surprisingly, *did*. But really, enough was enough! She wound up a report of her travels to Calvin with, "And now, lastly, my dear husband, you have never been wanting . . . in kindness, consideration, and justice, and I want you to reflect calmly how great a work has been imposed upon me in a time when my situation particularly calls for rest, repose, and quiet. To come alone such a distance with the whole charge of children, accounts, and baggage; to push my way through hurrying crowds, looking out for trunks, and bargaining with hackmen, has been a very severe trial of my strength. . . ." Her baby was expected in two months.

Edward Beecher and his wife, Isabella, were as flamingly angry over the slavery question as was Henry Ward, so there was more ardent political discussion with them. In Boston, too, Harriet met one of the leaders of Boston's black community, the Methodist preacher "Father" Josiah Henson. She "heard his story of his escape from slavery. He remembered seeing his own father lying on the ground, bruised, bloody, and dying from the blows of a white overseer, because, mere slave and 'nigger' that he was, he had pretended that the mother of his children was his wife, and had tried to defend her from the indecent assault that this same overseer had attempted on her person." She was chilled again at the horrors that whites, especially white men, could inflict on these people helpless in their hands, and struck by Henson's ability to endure and to forgive.

Then, at last, Harriet and her children were in Brunswick, Maine.

They arrived in the middle of one of Maine's signature nor'easters, a storm so relentless that the Stowes' furniture and baggage were indefinitely delayed. It did not matter. Their house was not ready for occupancy, and Professor and Mrs. Thomas Upham were prepared to take Harriet and the children in. Professor Upham was tall, stooped, and shy; his wife was maternal; both were shocked at the forlorn shabbiness of Professor Stowe's family. And she in her condition! The college community immediately rallied round.

Once the storm stopped, Harriet's spirits rose. The house they were to live in stood on Federal Street, one of the two best residential streets in this civilized little city. It was a classically simple white Federal house, two stories plus attic, with a wing to the rear

Harriet Beecher Stowe's home, Brunswick, Maine,
where *Uncle Tom's Cabin* was written

and a distinguished front portico. Harriet, who had grown up among just such houses and now longed for Gothic excess, was not impressed. But she went diligently to work, turning it into a home before the baby came, dealing with Yankee "characters" who simply cried out to be put in stories, upholstering furniture, getting someone to take apart the hogsheads she had bought for cisterns and reassemble them down in the cellar. Her new Maine friends admired her strength of character.

Early in July, Calvin, the twins, and Henry arrived. So did the baby. Just as Harriet's own parents had done thirty-nine years earlier, she and Calvin gave the new arrival the name of a child who had died. Little lost Charlie had been Samuel Charles; this one became Charles Edward.

Harriet stayed in bed for two weeks with the novels of Sir Walter Scott. Then she rose and enjoyed the enchantments of a Maine shore summer. There was swimming and fishing and picnicking. Harriet's face was soft with happiness and she had grown thin. The slope-shouldered, full-skirted dresses of 1850, with their tiny pointed waists and soft flounces, suited Harriet's small figure. Sitting on the rocks, her hair blowing in the breeze, she looked scarcely older than the twins, who were now fourteen.

Soon after Calvin arrived in Brunswick he had a real dilemma on his hands. Andover Theological Seminary had offered him a position, far more important and more financially rewarding than the one at Bowdoin. In addition, no replacement had been found for Calvin at Lane; he was obliged to return there for the 1850–1851 winter term. He asked the Bowdoin trustees to release him from his contract with them.

Bowdoin, which had already granted special favors, including that now-spent $500 bonus, was not inclined to be sympathetic. However, Calvin had been one of Bowdoin's own most distinguished graduates. College and alumnus crafted a compromise. Calvin could return to Lane for the winter term. After that he belonged to Bowdoin for two years. Andover agreed to wait until then for him.

Calvin Ellis Stowe, c. 1850s?
(Stowe-Day Foundation, Hartford, Connecticut)

Harriet foresaw a need for money. She began to write. She also, as autumn came, started a small school in her home, just as Roxana before her had done.

That September the Fugitive Slave Act became law, and all the North's worst fears began coming true.

Letter after letter arrived from Edward's wife, Isabella, flaming with indignation over the heartrending consequences of the Fugitive Slave Law. The city government of Boston, that so-called Cradle of Liberty, was not only cooperating with the slave-catchers but was actually assisting them.

In December Calvin had to return to Cincinnati, where he could see firsthand the consequences of the Fugitive Slave Law in the border states. In Maine Harriet struggled through her daily drudgery, dealing with children, dealing with servants, dealing with the defections of this shabby house. Inwardly, involuntarily, she was in Boston with the desperate black community that her sister-in-law was writing about.

All the scenes of Harriet's old visions, her worst waking nightmares were coming true there. Former slaves were hiding out in cellars and attics, as persecuted Christians had once hid in the catacombs of Rome. Black families, many of them settled in Boston for some time, were being wrenched apart, for escaped slaves had married into Boston's long-established "free black" community. Worst of all, men, women, and children who were genuinely free—having been granted freedom, bought their freedom, or been born so—were being seized and, under the pretext that they were escapees, sold down the river. In the process tortures, murders, and mutilations were taking place.

Some well-to-do blacks fled to Europe. The less well-off tried desperately to reach Canada. One Boston merchant, not daring to risk being spotted on public transportation, attempted to *walk* to Canada in midwinter. He succeeded, but his feet had become so frozen that they had to be amputated.

"Hattie, if I could use a pen as you can," her sister-in-law wrote, "I would write something that would make this whole nation feel what an accursed thing slavery is!"

Poster offering reward for runaway slaves, St. Louis, Missouri, 1853
(Stowe-Day Foundation, Hartford, Connecticut)

Feel. That gift was Harriet's blessing and her curse. She felt everything so deeply, and through her writing could make her readers feel as well. But to write was, for her, to walk with eyes wide open into the whirlwind of the very experiences she wrote of. It was devastating, it was draining, it was exhausting. It was haunting. She was so busy; she was so weary; she was not well. In this isolated village she had managed to avoid facing the slavery issue, but Isabella's letter tore at her.

Involuntarily she crumpled it in her hand and rose, her eyes seeing into her dark buried visions. "God helping me," she exclaimed, "I *will* write something. I will if I live."

In January 1851 Henry Ward was on the lecture trail. In his high collar and fine black satin stock, his hair waving off his noble brow and curling forward over his ears, he looked resolute, godlike, Byronesque. His orations were much less scholarly than his father's, but he outdid even Lyman in charismatic pyrotechnics. On January 8, Henry lectured before the Mercantile Library Association of Boston. He went from there by train to Maine to visit sister Hattie. A blizzard was whipping Brunswick on the night that he arrived, well after midnight. Winds tore at the shuddering trees, whistled down the chimney, piled the drifts high against the drafty walls.

He found Harriet waiting up for him in the sleeping house, looking tense and drawn. She packed wood in the stove, and she and Henry talked till dawn. About the Fugitive Slave Law; about the "peculiar institution" itself; about the "call" each of them felt to combat slavery; about what each could do.

Despite how much their beliefs had diverged from the old fire-and-brimstone theology, they were nonetheless Calvinists in their very bones. The doctrine of the "calling," of surrendering one's gifts and talents to God for God's purposes, was deep within them. Henry knew his gift was oratory, and that the main mission of his ministry would be Abolition. God had brought him to Brooklyn for just that purpose. Henry was committed to fighting slavery from the pulpit of Plymouth Church. He was the darling of his congregation, and he could get away there with almost anything. As for Harriet, she should take up her pen and write.

Then Henry was gone, leaving Harriet alone with her children and the harsh winter. In the intensity of Henry's enthusiasm, she had been set on fire. Now the letdown came. How was she to shake America, North and South, into a realization of what it *felt like* to be enslaved? Of how horrible, immoral, unchristian, the "peculiar institution" was, even at its best?

Sunday morning came. Harriet sat in the chilly church, surrounded by her children, and drifted, as she often did, into a kind of trance. This was a Communion Sunday, an occasion that always affected her profoundly. The order of the ritual went on; the words grew faint and her vision dim. Suddenly a picture flashed before her eyes. An old slave was being beaten to death, by two of his own race. A white man—overseer? master?—lounged nearby, face twisted with hate as he urged the killers on.

The old man never made a sound. He was, as the old Puritans would have put it, "standing mute"—until he could stand no more and sank, bleeding, to the ground. *Why* was he being tortured? Harriet didn't know. Because he had refused to *do* something, *say* something, beg for mercy? The one thing clear to her was that he had done no wrong; rather, he was *refusing* to do something that was a moral or mortal sin. His face was noble, full of pity even for his tormentors.

The vision passed, leaving her weak and shaken. When the service was over Harriet, still in a daze, gathered her children together and walked back home. Dinner would have to wait. She sat down at her desk and began to write—automatically, the words pouring out of her head and through her pen onto the paper. Then there was no more paper left. She found some leftover brown grocery wrapping and kept on writing. At last, having exorcised her vision, she corked her ink bottle and went to see about her children's dinner.

After the meal Harriet herded them all back into the sitting room and read the scene aloud. By the time she finished, she was not the only one in tears. "Oh, Ma," one of the boys gulped, "slavery is the most cruel thing in the world!" Harriet looked at him and nodded, unable to speak.

When she reread her own words the next day, she was shocked. Where had it come from, all the violence and all the blood? *This* wasn't the portrayal of slavery she had vowed to write—this was about escape from slavery; escape through death. She put the scene away and tried not to think about it.

In the days that followed, as she kept house and cooked, taught school in the parlor and supervised the twins' piano practice, visions and memories kept thronging in her mind. The night she and Calvin had sat on the Ohio riverbank, watching the lantern signals like fireflies on the far Kentucky shore. Faces of free blacks and escaped slaves she had met in Cincinnati; the sounds of their voices and the stories they had told. There were dozens of scenes, hundreds of scenes, all out of order.

The one thing she was certain of was the character of the slave she called "Uncle Tom." He was the Suffering Servant figure from the writings of the Prophet Isaiah, brought forward into the American South. Harriet was Calvin's wife and Lyman's daughter; she knew the passage well.

> *He hath no form nor comeliness; there is no beauty that men should desire him. He is despised and rejected of men; a man of sorrows, and acquainted with grief: and we hid as it were our faces from him; he was despised, and we esteemed him not. Surely he hath borne our griefs, and carried our sorrows. . . . [H]e was wounded for our transgressions, he was bruised by our iniquities: the chastisement of our peace was upon him; and with his stripes we are healed. All we like sheep have gone astray; we have turned every one to his own way; and the Lord hath laid on him the iniquity of us all. He was oppressed, and he was afflicted, yet he opened not his mouth: he is brought as a lamb to the slaughter, and as a sheep before her shearers is dumb, so he openeth not his mouth.*

It was a passage often read during the Communion service, long taken by Christians as both a description of Christ and a model of what Christians ought to be. She had recreated it in the person of that most "despised and rejected" of human beings, a black slave.

Even she did not know where the vision and the words had come from, unless it was from God. That was it; *God* had written the scene! *She* had not chosen the words, not thought it out. She had only provided the hand through which God had put the words on paper!

Obviously God had a use for this bit of writing, but Harriet did not yet know what. She set the pages aside and went on about her daily routine. In her mind the visions kept crowding. What was she, one small white woman, to do with them? None of the pieces fit together.

XVIII

A Slave Story of Three or Four Installments

1851

AT THE BEGINNING of March 1851 Calvin Stowe, free at last of Lane Seminary, came home to Maine, bringing with him the notes and papers of his own writing. Every parent knows the safest place to keep things from little hands is in the master bedroom. He emerged from this unpacking to face Harriet, tears running down his face. Harriet's close-written pieces of brown butcher's paper were in his hand.

"Hattie," he exclaimed, "this is the climax of the slavery story you promised to write!"

Of course! The scene wasn't the *beginning* of a story, but the *end*—or near enough! What Harriet had been seeing in her brain during those past chaotic weeks had been not *one* story line but *two*. Both of them were journeys—"picaresque tales," as they were called in literary circles.

One was the journey of the old man, Tom, a man much like Father Henson's father. That was a tragic journey that would take him from life on one of the "best" plantations with a kindly master through the breakup of his family, the dreadful slave auction, descent into the worst conditions of slavery, and ultimately death—

a death in which Tom, like Christ on the cross and true to his Christian beliefs, actually prayed for and forgave his murderers.

The other story would be of a loving slave family—the "woman on the ice" who had haunted Harriet's mind, her husband, and their child—and their escape to Canada via the Underground Railway. Already Harriet's brain was churning. If the couple could not travel together, she could work in even more scenes and character portrayals, white and black, South and North. She could show the various ways slaves achieved, or failed to achieve, their freedom; the various ways they were treated by whites—from deliberate cruelty to ignorant, kindly condescension. Harriet had seen and heard enough in almost forty years of parsonage living to know that often the worst prejudice was unconscious and insidious.

The main elements of the story lines came tumbling into Harriet's mind. They *weren't* parallel lines, but separate strands that had a common link on one "good" plantation. And the strands were not two, but *three:* the story of Tom, the suffering servant; the story of the wronged slave wife and mother; the story of her daring and heroic husband.

She named the young woman Eliza . . . the name of her dearest friend. Eliza what? Eliza Harris. That was a good English name, not uncommon in the South. Harriet knew by now that on the plantations African names, African tribal identities, had been lost or deliberately wiped out. If slaves *had* last names, they were the names of owners whose white blood probably ran in their veins. The young quadroon, disturbingly beautiful, whom Harriet had seen in the Kentucky church . . . *that* was what Eliza looked like. She would run away without her husband because . . . because she had married "off the plantation," a man with a different owner . . . a secret wedding because, as Father Henson had said, slaves weren't allowed to really marry.

So Eliza and George Harris had been married in secret by a black slave preacher. Kindly owners liked their slaves to have just enough Christianity to keep them docile, in hope of a better life in the world to come, even though the best "scientific" logic assured the owners that blacks didn't really have souls. Slaves weren't allowed to learn to read; in some states anyone teaching blacks to read received harsh punishment. But Harriet knew that black Christians, like she herself, had long passages of Scriptures locked in their memories just from having heard them read aloud. She herself had taken children from Cincinnati's black families into the small school she ran there in her home.

Why Eliza fled when she did, with no chance to send a secret message to her husband, was becoming clear. She was in danger of being sold down the river, and so was Uncle Tom. Why? Because their owner was in debt and had no choice. *That* was why he was being forced to part with Uncle Tom. And Eliza—

Not Eliza. Her little son. Back to Harriet came the memory of the slaves on that Kentucky plantation being made to "cut capers" for white visitors. The little boy would dance a jig, or something, before the slave trader, and the slave trader would want to buy him, too. He would want to own Eliza also, for darker reasons. All the viciousness of white males toward black slave women, all the buried memories of Aunt Mary, and the facts told Harriet by her servant in Cincinnati, all the grief and horror of losing a dearly loved child, welled up in her.

Eliza would overhear the sale of Uncle Tom and her baby, and she would run into the night, stopping only to warn Uncle Tom, to send out word on the slave grapevine to her husband. Uncle Tom would *not* run. *Why?* Because his Christianity was the "predestination" kind that Lyman used to preach. One's fate was in the hands of the Lord, and it was the Christian's duty to submit. *Harriet* no longer believed God would destine His people to terrible fates, but she knew many Christians still did.

Harriet had her characters and her setting. And how the story started: "Late in the afternoon of a chilly day in February, two gentlemen were sitting alone over their wine in a well-furnished dining parlor in the town of P—, in Kentucky." One was the debt-ridden plantation owner; the other was the slave trader Haley. Harriet knew a great deal about such men by now, just as she knew about the "camp-meeting" revival services (she established

Uncle Tom's conversion as having come at one), and the "good people" who preferred not to see what was going on, not to believe that blacks could have real human feelings. She unleashed the full sarcastic sting of her pen in portraying those who, like the priest and the Levite in the Parable of the Good Samaritan, "passed by on the other side."

She didn't have to *plan* any of this. She didn't know—other than Uncle Tom's death and Eliza's flight across the ice—what else would happen. No matter. All she had to do was sit and let the visions flood into her, the words ring in her ears and flow through her arm and hand and pen onto the paper. It would come. She hoped she could find a publisher to take it. She hoped it would do some good.

A thousand lives seemed to be concentrated in that one moment to Eliza. Her room opened by a side door to the river. She caught her child, and sprang down the steps towards it. The trader caught a full glimpse of her, just as she was disappearing down the bank; and throwing himself from his horse, and calling loudly on Sam and Andy, he was after her like a hound after a deer. In that dizzy moment her feet to her scarce seemed to touch the ground, and a moment brought her to the water's edge. Right on behind they came; and, nerved with strength such as God gives only to the desperate, with one wild cry and flying leap, she vaulted sheer over the turbid current by the shore, on to the raft of ice beyond. It was a desperate leap—impossible to anything but madness and despair; and Haley, Sam, and Andy, instinctively cried out, and lifted up their hands, as she did it.

The huge green fragment of ice on which she alighted pitched and creaked as her weight came on it, but she staid there not a moment. With wild cries and desperate energy she leaped to another and still another cake;—stumbling—leaping—slipping—springing upwards again! Her shoes are gone—her stockings cut from her feet—while blood marked every step; but she saw nothing, felt nothing, till dimly, as in a dream, she saw the Ohio side, and a man helping her up the bank.

Uncle Tom

The cabin of Uncle Tom was a small log building close
adjoining to "the house" — as the negro always par excellence
designates the master's dwelling — In front it had a neat
garden patch where strawberries raspberries & a variety of
fruits & vegetables flourished under careful tending — down The whole
front of the dwelling was covered with a large big scarlet
nonia & a native multiflora rose which entwisting
& interlacing left scarce a vestige of the building
to be seen & in the spring was redundant with
its clusters of roses & in summer as was balcond
with the scarlet tubes of the trumpet Various
gay brilliant annuals such as marigolds four
oclocks & petunias found here and there a thrifty
corner to expatiate unfold their glories & were the delight
& pride of aunt Chloe's heart

Let us enter the dwelling — The evening meal
at "the house" is over & Aunt Chloe who presides
over its preparation as head cook has left to inferior
officers in the kitchen the business of clearing away
& washing dishes & come out into her own snug
territory to "get her old man's supper" & therefore
doubt not that it is her you see by the
fire place presiding with anxious interest

Facsimile of manuscript page of *Uncle Tom's Cabin*

On March 9, 1851, she wrote to Dr. Gamaliel Bailey, who had been co-publisher of the Abolitionist paper *Philanthropist* in Cincinnati and was now the publisher of the *National Era*. She was, she told him, currently writing a series of sketches on life under the "peculiar institution" that would show it at its best and also at something near its worst. The sketches would be based on incidents of which she knew firsthand, or which had been reported to her by reliable relatives and friends. She would not be passing judgment or presuming to tell people what they should believe. She was simply painting word pictures of what she *knew*. Pictures could not be argued with. Pictures moved people, whether they wanted to be moved or not. The whole thing would be longer than her usual literary efforts—perhaps three or four installments. Would Dr. Bailey be interested?

Dr. Bailey would. He offered her, sight unseen, the generous first-publication fee of $300 for a slave story of three or four installments, the first of which would come out early in the summer.

Through the blossoming spring Harriet kept on writing. There was much to stoke the fire of her antislavery wrath. In April a runaway slave named Thomas Simms was apprehended in Boston. By law, the Boston police were obliged to assist the slave-catcher. Simms was tried in a courthouse guarded by two companies of militia; abolitionist Thomas Wentworth Higginson's Committee of Vigilance tried to rescue him by guerrilla tactics, but did not succeed. Three hundred Boston police marched Simms and his captor to Boston pier and the steamboat for Savannah. Church bells tolled throughout Massachusetts, but Dr. Edward Beecher was the only Boston pastor to publicly denounce Boston's official collaboration.

On May 15 the *Independent* reprinted a British paper's list of pro-slavery remarks made supposedly by well-known American clergymen. Britain had abolished slavery in 1833; in 1840 it had hosted a World Anti-Slavery Convention and been smugly condescending toward the upstart American Abolitionists who had attended. Now Britain was questioning the propriety of allowing American clergy to preach in British pulpits while attending the "May Anniversaries" (annual conventions of church and philanthropic societies) in London. Among the preachers quoted was Philadelphia pastor Dr. Joel Parker, a friend of Calvin, Lyman, and the Beecher brothers. His comment, meant to show that the evils of slavery lay not in the *institution* but in the depravity inherent in human nature, might have come out of the Calvinist doctrine of total depravity, but it sounded like a defense of the "peculiar institution." Harriet's blood, already steaming from the northern clergy's timidity about denouncing slavery from the pulpits, boiled over. To her, by now, they were (in biblical words) "hypocrites" and "whited sepulchres." She promptly inserted some of them into the ongoing saga of Uncle Tom and the Harris family.

Uncle Tom's Cabin had taken possession of her and was careening on like a railroad locomotive out of control. She had thought the tale would take two weeks to write, and then a month. Now two months had gone by and she was realizing she was only beginning. *Uncle Tom's Cabin* was turning into a novel, to the considerable surprise of both Harriet and her publisher.

Dr. Bailey had not bargained on publishing a serial quite this long. He had held back on running the opening installments, wanting the whole work "in hand" before it began. But week had followed week with no end in sight. On May 8 he had run a notice that in two weeks the *Era* would begin running a new story by Mrs. H. B. Stowe, titled "Uncle Tom's Cabin; or, The Man That Was A Thing." May 22 came and went. Harriet had still delivered only the first two chapters, but by then she knew that the story's focus was not only on Uncle Tom. A new subtitle would be needed.

The first installment of *Uncle Tom's Cabin or, Life among the Lowly* by Mrs. H. B. Stowe (copyright secured by the author) ran in the *National Era* on Thursday, June 5, 1851. It occupied three and a half columns on page one. The following week Dr. Bailey turned over only one column to Mrs. H. B. Stowe's new serial, for a short story by one of his regular contributors claimed the choice spot on page one, column one.

Neither Harriet nor her editor had realized yet what they had gotten themselves into.

XIX

Uncle Tom's Cabin

1851–1852

HARRIET WROTE ON. The flower-scented sweetness of a cool Maine summer unfolded, and the Stowe house was filled with interruptions. Lyman arrived, bringing his stepdaughter as a secretary. Now increasingly senile, he was determined to publish his sermons for posterity, and claimed the Stowes' kitchen table at which to work on them. Harriet, evicted, took her pen, ink pot, and manuscript portfolio out to the back steps and wrote there, the breeze ruffling her voluminous skirts and many layers of petticoats.

The summer was full of family doings. Calvin took the children fishing and wading while Harriet watched from the rocks, seeing visions and plotting further chapters. Calvin received an invitation to speak at the two-hundredth anniversary of his birthplace, Natick, Massachusetts, in October, and plunged into preparing his address. Catharine's book on the *True Remedy for the Wrongs of Woman*, her most important work so far, came out. It was her rebuttal to Elizabeth Cady Stanton and the 1848 Women's Rights Convention of Seneca Falls, New York, that demanded votes for women.

Catharine, not one to feel hampered by lack of the vote, considered *home* was the country in which a woman was queen, and that her great influence *there*—on her men, and through her children—would be diluted if she entered the public sphere. Catharine was having one of her ongoing arguments with brother Henry, who was toying with coming out for woman suffrage and also, in Catharine's opinion, influencing Lyman against her. Catharine thought Henry was becoming an opportunist and far too much of a popular celebrity. Henry thought Catharine was more peculiar and dictatorial than ever. Both poured their indignation out on paper to Harriet; neither, apparently, took seriously (probably because it was fiction) the tale she was so busy writing for an obscure paper. So much for Henry's promise on a snowbound night that if she wrote something against slavery, he would "scatter it thick as the leaves on Vallombrosa."

Harriet missed her deadline for the installment of August 12. It was chapter 12, "Select Incident of Lawful Trade," about slave trader Haley's marketing of his human cargo up and down the river. It told of the slave mother Lucy, tricked on board with her baby, her infant sold when she had her eyes off him for only minutes. This was some of Harriet's most powerful writing, for she avoided her usual emotional embellishments. Lucy did not even scream; she "stood mute"—until she threw herself overboard to drown.

Writing the scene had left Harriet drained. But not before she had unleashed her venom at "certain ministers of Christianity" who proclaimed the slave trade had *"no evils but such as are inseparable from any other relations in social and domestic life."* In a footnote she identified this direct quote from the *Independent* (and the *Bristol* [England] *Mercury*) as from "Dr. Joel Parker of Philadelphia."

Installment publication of *Uncle Tom's Cabin* resumed on August 28. By now it was attracting enormous notice—remarkable since the *Era* had a small circulation despite the hundreds of thousands that were weeping or ranting over the travails of Uncle Tom. A sort of underground lending library had sprung up—

everywhere a copy of Dr. Bailey's small print run went, it began to circulate from home to home. Readers were actually writing in to argue the slavery issue and to report how Mrs. Stowe's story moved them. People were clamoring to have *Uncle Tom's Cabin* published in book form.

By now Lyman had taken himself, sermons, and stepdaughter back to his rented house in Boston. But Catharine arrived at the Stowe house in the middle of the uproar and, observing all with a shrewd eye, sat down to read what sister Hattie had produced thus far. She recognized a phenomenon when she saw it, and promptly took charge of the household so that Harriet was free to write. Catharine also took it on herself to approach her own new publishers with the book rights to *Uncle Tom's Cabin*. After thinking it over, Phillips, Sampson & Co. refused on the grounds that the book would never sell—and if it did, would destroy their profitable southern market.

One of Harriet's Boston readers was a Mrs. John P. Jewett, whose husband owned a small publishing company. It rarely published fiction, but Mr. Jewett was swayed by his wife's enthusiasm to read her copies of the serial to date. On September 18, the *Era* announced that Messrs. Jewett & Co., of Boston, would be publishing the book version of *Uncle Tom's Cabin* "immediately after its close in the *Era*."

But it didn't close. The story raced on and on—through Harriet's whirling brain, through her arm and weary hand, and onto paper. The chapters poured out, scene after scene. The daring George Harris was boldly passing himself off as a Spanish gentleman as he made his way toward Canada. Other characters appeared—well-meaning New England spinster Miss Ophelia, more than a little like Aunt Harriet Foote in Nutplains; the mischievous Topsy who, never having known her parents, assumed she "never was born" and "'spect[ed]" she just "growed." *'Spect* was one of Calvin's favorite New Englandisms when he was telling his famous Natick stories. Harriet was trying earnestly to write regional dialects as they sounded to her, basing the speech of her slave characters on the voices of people she knew in

Cincinnati's and Boston's black communities. When she ran short, she improvised, using Calvin's Natickisms, and neither readers nor reviewers knew the difference.

September came. *Uncle Tom's Cabin* still wasn't finished. By now Calvin had a professor's office in Appleton Hall on the Bowdoin campus, and while he was in classes Harriet borrowed it as a quiet place to write, considerably startling the academic community. In October Calvin journeyed to Natick to give the anniversary oration. He had arranged a winter-term leave of absence from Bowdoin, during which he would teach a class at Andover, bringing the Stowes some much-needed money. The $300 that Dr. Bailey had agreed to pay for *Uncle Tom's Cabin* serialization, a magnificent sum for approximately four installments, was not magnificent when the installments had stretched to three or four times that many and showed no signs of stopping. Both Dr. Bailey and Mr. Jewett were discreetly inquiring how long the story would go on. Harriet would have been delighted to wind it up; she was exhausted, and the work was keeping her from other projects. But the words and pictures just kept coming.

Dr. Bailey, again discreetly, asked readers to indicate whether they wanted the serial to continue indefinitely. The response was a resounding *yes*. Mrs. Stowe should take as much time—and space—as her story needed.

The leaves on the trees of Federal Street turned to gold, to red, to brown. Harriet wrote on. She did not stop to proofread; she did not stop to edit. She was the handmaiden to God's dictation. Dr. Bailey could take care of the punctuation. Because of the financial situation, she was keeping school in the house again as usual. But when twilight fell, when classes were done and the ink pot corked, Harriet gathered husband, children, and sometimes students around her and read her day's batch of writing aloud. The same thing was happening all over America, Harriet knew from her mail. But *her* children heard the story from her own lips, and shared her tears.

On October 30 the *Era* again came out without an *Uncle Tom's Cabin* installment. She was becoming too exhausted to write. Mr.

Jewett, concerned that the book he had contracted for would now turn out to be *two* volumes, was begging her to wind things up. The great Mrs. Sarah Josepha Hale, editor of *Godey's Lady's Book*, wrote asking for a daguerreotype and biographical data, as she was writing a book on distinguished women writers of the world and wished to include Mrs. H. B. Stowe. Tired little Harriet was filled with a mixture of emotions. She—distinguished? As for a daguerreotype, those fashionable new "chemical pictures" cost at least fifteen dollars apiece—far too expensive for a professor's wife. She sent Mrs. Hale her apologies, suggesting sister Catharine as far more distinguished but giving a few lines of biographical information—teacher, wife, and mother—in case Mrs. Hale still wished to use them.

December came. Calvin left for Andover. Harriet had his Appleton Hall office all to herself. The week before Christmas she again missed an issue. She had been writing one of her most celebrated chapters—the death of Little Eva—and she was prostrated. All her grief over baby Charlie's death had come rushing back.

> *The child lay panting on her pillows, as one exhausted,—the large clear eyes rolled up and fixed, Ah, what said those eyes, that spoke so much of heaven? Earth was past, and earthly pain; but so solemn, so mysterious, was the triumphant brightness of that face, that it checked even the sobs of sorrow. They pressed around her, in breathless stillness.*
>
> *"Eva," said St. Clare, gently.*
>
> *She did not hear.*
>
> *"O, Eva, tell us what you see! What is it?" said her father.*
>
> *A bright, a glorious smile passed over her face, and she said, brokenly,—"O! love,—joy,—peace!" gave one sigh, and passed from death unto life!*
>
> *"Farewell, beloved child! the bright, eternal doors have closed after thee; we shall see thy sweet face no more. O, woe for them who watched thy entrance into heaven, when they shall wake and find only the cold gray sky of daily life, and thou gone forever!"*

The chapter appeared on Christmas Day, and even strong men wept.

A strange thing had happened in American Protestantism in the forty years since Harriet's birth. From being seen as possibly predestined to being "damned to the glory of God" or else untimely lost before conversion, children were now seen as filled with divine innocence, "angels in the house." It was a belief intensely comforting to mothers who, like Harriet, had lost children. This cult of the "divine child" was characteristic of the era, and so it seemed utterly believable to readers that the saintly soul and beautiful death of Little Eva could lead others to salvation. A generation that had grown up on Byronic excess never found an excess of sentimentality an inhibition to true feelings.

January 1852. It was now a year since Harriet's vision of the death of Uncle Tom. Snow battered Brunswick, and Harriet envisioned her villain of villains, the overseer Simon Legree. It was *he* who ordered the beating of Uncle Tom, who stood by watching as Tom was battered to death. The noble old man, the "suffering servant," died what Harriet knew readers would recognize as a "beautiful Christian death." He was "standing mute" in order to protect the whereabouts of other slaves who had escaped. Significantly, she had made her villains all northerners, and her "good people" all of the South—surely no one would be able to accuse her of prejudice against southerners after that!

Triumphantly she wound up the story, with the "morning star of liberty" shining over the Harris family—and all their friends and kin—in Canada, where for the moment at least it was still safe.

John P. Jewett of Boston now had the completed text of *Uncle Tom's Cabin* to ready for his press. It was forty-five chapters long, and would definitely require two-volume publication. Contract terms had not yet been arranged, so Calvin, as the man of the family, went hurrying down from Andover to attend to that detail for his wife. Jewett, alarmed about publication costs to his modest firm, offered the Stowes a remarkable deal: If they would "back" publication by putting up half the costs, he would assign to them half the profits.

Calvin consulted his friend Congressman Philip Greeley, who advised him not to take the gamble. *Uncle Tom's Cabin* was bound to be controversial, given the subject matter. Better to ask for a good 10-percent royalty on all sales. Calvin took his advice and asked for the 10 percent. He could not in any event have agreed to copublish; the Stowes simply didn't have the money.

Calvin did ask Jewett what, realistically, Harriet could expect to make from the transaction. Jewett wasn't sure. A great many people had read borrowed copies of *Uncle Tom's Cabin* in serial form, and a two-volume book would be expensive. He thought it would be safe for Calvin to tell his wife she would probably receive enough money to buy herself a good silk dress. Calvin was pleased. Harriet had never owned a silk dress, and had always wanted one.

On Saturday, March 13, Calvin made another trip to Boston to sign the completed contract, as was customary, on his wife's behalf. Publication date was set for March 20, but the presses were already running. While Calvin waited for the first books to be bound up, he stayed with Lyman who was quietly enjoying the publication of his own collected sermons.

The first copy of *Uncle Tom's Cabin* was bought by Calvin from the publisher (wholesale price fifty-six cents, clothbound) as a gift for Congressman Greeley, who read it on the night train to Washington. By the time the train reached Springfield, Massachusetts, Greeley was obliged to disembark and spend the night in a hotel—he had been publicly overcome by tears.

Calvin hurried north to deliver Harriet's own copies into her hands. Jewett had done her and Uncle Tom proud, for they were handsome volumes—two to a set, 312 pages and six illustrations each, in paper, black cloth (title-page illustration reproduced in gold on cover), or "cloth full gilt" (lavender cloth with heavy, elaborate gilt embossing everywhere).

Quiet little Mrs. Stowe, the professor's wife, was about to become notorious.

XX

Summer of Success

1852

THREE THOUSAND COPIES of *Uncle Tom's Cabin* were sold on its first day in the stores. Uncle Tom fever had broken out in America. Before it ran its course, both country and author would be forever changed.

In the first spring glow of the book's success, Calvin Stowe made a discovery that disturbed him. The footnote that identified Dr. Joel Parker as clergyman source of the "no evils in slavery" quote still remained. Hadn't Harriet meant to delete it? It was unfair to single out one minister when almost all of them waffled on the subject of slavery. Anyway, footnotes did not belong in a work of fiction. Harriet agreed, and dashed off a letter to her publisher.

Jewett's small publishing house was in ferment. The entire first printing had sold out on the second day, and large orders were arriving in every mail. Jewett rushed a second printing through so fast that he forgot to identify it *as* a second printing—or to remove the offending footnote.

Before reviews appeared, before a dazed Harriet comprehended what was happening, a third and fourth printing also sold out.

Jewett's presses ran night and day, six days a week. Unfilled orders reached into the thousands.

An enterprising young man at Putnam's, the New York publisher, secretly sent a two-volume set of *Uncle Tom's Cabin* to a British publisher, who paid him five pounds (approximately twenty-five dollars) for his thoughtfulness and rushed to publish a British edition without the permission of its author.

On April 15 the New York *Independent* published a glorious review of *Uncle Tom's Cabin*. This followed a sonnet it had published two weeks earlier, titled "To the Author of Uncle Tom's Cabin." Quaker poet John Greenleaf Whittier wrote Harriet a letter giving her ten thousand thanks, and also penned—at Jewett's request, as part of the promotion for *Uncle Tom's Cabin*—a memorial poem to Little Eva. It was certainly not one of his best, but his sentiments mirrored those of a multitude of readers.

Praise from the great and the general public poured in. Henry Wadsworth Longfellow considered *Uncle Tom's Cabin* a literary and a moral triumph. Then the politicians weighed in, realizing the propaganda power of the book. Abolitionist Senator Charles Sumner of Massachusetts sent his praise. New York's Senator Seward recommended the book to his southern colleagues. William Lloyd Garrison forgot his detestation of the Beechers in his joy. Jewett advertised *Uncle Tom's Cabin* as the greatest work of its kind ever issued by an American publisher.

In the middle of all the excitement Harriet thought about Canada, final destination of the Underground Railway. She thought about the dreaded slave-catchers, free by law to range throughout the United States and territories, and how easy it would be for them to slip across the northern border. Canada was a British colony, and British policy favored the American South. But English liberals were chastising America for not outlawing its "peculiar institution." Perhaps the great, the titled, and the literary among those liberals could use their influence. She began sending out lavender-and-gilt presentation copies of *Uncle Tom's Cabin*, each with a personal letter—to authors Charles Dickens, Thomas

Macaulay, Charles Kingsley; to the Duke of Argyll and the Earls of Shaftesbury and Carlisle; to the Prince Consort.

Then, Harriet corked her inkstand and relaxed. By mid-May fifty thousand copies of her novel had been sold, twice that many were in print, and she knew for a certainty that she could afford a good silk dress and a whole lot more. The Stowes' financial security was assured. Harriet, happily, set out as her menfolk always had, on a round of summer visits. Her excuse was a need to confer with her publishers. The truth was that for the first time in her life, she was doing something just for her own sheer pleasure.

First came Boston. Jewett, Harriet learned there, had actually been lobbying *Uncle Tom's Cabin* in person to the legislators in Washington! Then Harriet went to Hartford, to Mary and her family, in the newfound glow of her celebrity. Harriet had never been more radiant, and her sense of security was increased when Mary's husband, lawyer-financier Thomas Perkins, agreed to manage her money and investments for her.

Then it was on to New Haven, where she stayed with Mary Dutton's father. And from there, as the last stop of the triumphal tour, New York City! Henry Ward's wife, Eunice, had long made clear that their Brooklyn mansion was not one of the Beecher family's free-housing stops, but for Harriet an exception was made. She arrived there in time for the annual May Anniversary excitement.

Harriet had enough excitement of her own going on without this annual church celebration. She signed with the *Independent* to make irregular but frequent contributions of whatever she chose—essays, character sketches, stories, her New England tales. She had become one of the first women columnists in America. She was lionized everywhere—receptions, dinners, concerts, charitable affairs. She made lifelong friends in John and Susie Howard, members of Henry's church. Wealthy and religious, John T. Howard had been one of the men who had persuaded Henry Ward to come to Brooklyn. Now he and his wife took Henry's sister under their hospitable wing. The "Swedish

Nightingale," Jenny Lind, was completing her triumphal American tour, and the Howards insisted Harriet must hear her. Tickets were all sold out, but when Otto Goldschmidt, Lind's accompanist and husband, heard the tickets were being sought for the author of *Uncle Tom's Cabin,* he managed to find some that went to Harriet in an envelope addressed in Jenny Lind's own writing. The two women became correspondents.

One of the sweetest rewards of wealth for Harriet was being able at last to give to others. Catharine was starting an American Women's Educational Association to endow girls' schools in the West; Harriet gave money to the fund and her name to the board of managers as a drawing card. And she was able to do something, personally, to free three slaves.

Four years earlier, Henry Ward had scandalized and delighted his church by holding an actual slave auction—taking bids from the pulpit to free two beautiful young women from being sold down the river to New Orleans. Now their mother, Milly Edmondson, neither young nor beautiful, was back begging Henry to ransom her younger children also. Henry had no time for her, but Harriet stepped in. She wrote to Jenny Lind, and received back a donation of one hundred dollars. She organized a meeting of the ladies of Henry's church, and had Milly Edmondson plead her case to them. She contacted Edward's wife in Boston, and church connections elsewhere in New England; she took Milly Edmondson up to Dr. Dutton's New Haven church; she approached men of stature whom she had met in New York City. She had the pleasure of matching Jenny Lind's contribution with one hundred dollars of her own. Before she left Brooklyn she had raised enough money to buy the freedom of the two Edmondson girls and their mother, Milly.

Back in Andover, trouble had been brewing. Dr. Joel Parker had discovered the footnote that had *not* been removed yet from the *Uncle Tom's Cabin* typeplates. Parker had not bothered to challenge the serial publication, indignant as it had made him, because he considered the *Era*'s circulation too small to be a problem.

What had happened to *Uncle Tom's Cabin* since was another matter. A gentleman could not directly call a respectable woman a libelous liar. Instead Parker wrote fellow clergyman Calvin Stowe, asking in effect for him to keep his wife in line. He enclosed a letter to Harriet herself, demanding a public retraction. Calvin responded, placating Parker and forwarding Parker's letter to Harriet. Harriet wrote back, expressing herself as glad to hear Parker did not believe what he was said to have believed, and that if she had misunderstood or misquoted, she regretted, etc., etc. There, she thought, the matter rested.

It was time to go home. Harriet missed Calvin; she missed Brunswick. But she was going to have to move from Brunswick to Andover, and since there was no way out, she wanted to get it over with. During this summer of success an enormous change had taken place, subtly, imperceptibly, in herself—and by extension, in her family. *Harriet* was in charge. She had discovered executive skills, she had discovered her own power, she made the decisions.

It was fortunate she had found this strength within her, for the tide began to turn. Copies of *Uncle Tom's Cabin* were being banned in the South, which to her shock had risen up against her. Harriet was honestly bewildered. Didn't the good people of the South—she *knew* there were good people; they just hadn't grasped the evil they were perpetrating—realize she was condemning the "peculiar institution," not them? Why didn't they understand that God was holding out, through her book, a call for their salvation? And the hate mail wasn't all from the South. She received anonymous letters; threatening letters. She was being called obscene names; being accused of inciting another slave rebellion.

One day a small package arrived containing a black human ear, sliced off the head of a disobedient slave.

In England the unauthorized editions of *Uncle Tom's Cabin* began to appear. This piracy cost Harriet her English copyright and any hope of English royalties.

Harriet moved to Andover permanently in the beginning of July, returning to Brunswick occasionally to arrange the breaking-up of the Federal Street house and to see Calvin and the children. Andover was supposed to provide the Stowes with housing, but the only house available did not suit her. There was on campus a large stone building that had been the site of the college's "cottage industry"—coffin building. Harriet proposed that the college remodel the building into housing for the Stowes. There was no time to raise the necessary money? The now affluent Mrs. Stowe would loan it to them. *She* would design and supervise the renovation—leave everything in her hands. From then on it was Harriet, not Calvin, who made and managed the money in the household.

Harriet was in her element—renovating, decorating, making arrangements for her family. She begged off from professional demands on the old grounds of "poor health." Harriet had always been frail, but the days of drudgery, diapers, and depression were far behind her. At forty-one, with financial security now assured, she bloomed. She was a tiny dynamo on the Andover campus.

In all this satisfying whirl, a letter from Dr. Parker, accepting what he deemed to be Harriet's apology and asking only her permission to publish it, was never answered.

Jewett's first royalty check—for $10,300—arrived at the end of July. Harriet, blissfully engaged in decorating plans, was already "dreaming up" another novel. It would be called *Pearl of Orr's Island* and would draw on the New England sites and characters she loved, particularly those from Maine. She decided to enter the twins, now going on sixteen, and Georgie, nine, in Andover's famous Abbot Academy. She "sat for a daguerreotype." In August sales of *Uncle Tom's Cabin* hit 100,000, and gold miners in California charged twenty-five cents a head to share their copies. In England the pirated edition, after languishing for weeks, suddenly took off.

At the end of August the Stowe family—including Rover, the enormous and sedate Newfoundland dog—arrived in Andover, to stay in a boardinghouse until their house was finished.

In September the bubble of Harriet's happiness burst. The *New York Observer,* the only religious publication in direct national competition with the *Independent,* announced that Mrs. H. B. Stowe's retraction of a libelous statement against the Rev. Joel Parker (see June edition of the *Observer*) was actually a forgery penned by the famous Reverend Henry Ward Beecher.

XXI

Key to Uncle Tom's Cabin

1852–1853

THE UPROAR OVER Reverend Parker's accusations seemed to go on forever. Charges, countercharges, editorial comments, and interpretations of every possible extreme went on for months as press and public—especially southerners and enemies of the Beechers—had a field day. Henry Ward was by now America's most theatrical and adored preacher, and Harriet the country's most famous "lady authoress." With such a brother and such a sister involved, as well as other prominent divines and well-known lawyers, the "Parker case" was a most delicious scandal.

The whole thing rested on interpretation. What *had* Parker meant in those quoted words? It was quite a lesson, for writers and orators, in how words could be two-edged swords.

In the end no one really "won" or "lost." Even the "wronged" Parker couldn't be as wounded as he claimed, for he acquired in the process a pulpit in print for his point of view, and a reputation for having challenged the Goliath that was Henry Ward Beecher. Shy Harriet turned into a fighter—for her reputation, for her message, for her dear brother. She was more outraged than devastated. Calvin probably was the more stricken, hearing his loved wife termed a money-seeking liar, a coward, not a lady.

Harriet relieved her feelings by writing a hymn that began, "When winds are raging o'er the upper ocean . . ." Her point was that inner peace endured. Harriet *had* changed.

Eventually the deaths of Daniel Webster and the Duke of Wellington drove the Stowe-Parker brouhaha off the front pages. Popular sympathy remained with Harriet. And the footnote remained in *Uncle Tom's Cabin* for some time to come.

The phenomenon that was *Uncle Tom's Cabin* rolled on. America was singing songs about Uncle Tom, Little Eva, and Eliza on the ice, none of them by Harriet. Etchings and lithographs, some good, some bad, none authorized, appeared depicting the book's most famous scenes. Then the notorious "Tom Shows" started. Beginning as serious dramatizations, they turned into vaudeville revues having no connection to Harriet's antislavery novel other than character names and the bastardization of some famous scenes. Harriet never wrote them; she never authorized them; she never made a penny from them. And she had no power to prevent them—an author's book copyright at that time did not protect dramatic rights. Their portrayals of blacks—especially the way Uncle Tom was turned into a comic figure—were so counter to Harriet's viewpoint that they were truly terrible.

In August *Uncle Tom's Cabin* became an overseas phenomenon. The pirated English sales were skyrocketing. "Mrs. Beecher-Stowe" was now a British celebrity. Dickens reviewed *Uncle Tom's Cabin* and considered it noble but flawed, both of which were true. Lord Denman, the former lord chief justice, published an analysis of the book that practically told Dickens to "look who's talking." The recipients of Harriet's presentation copies read them, wrote her, and told others. *Uncle Tom's Cabin* was being translated for serialization in France, in Italy, in Sweden and Portugal and Germany—even in Russia. The notorious, gifted woman who called herself George Sand reviewed it favorably.

Up in the Massachusetts countryside, the dazed little "lady authoress" was still hard at work on the renovation and decoration of her family's new home. She was determined to write, as soon as possible, a response to those who called the evils of slavery described in *Uncle Tom's Cabin* unwarranted, undocumented, and just plain falsehoods. Harriet called this response to her critics *Key to Uncle Tom's Cabin,* and she began it the week she moved her family into their own Stone Cabin.

The Stone Cabin was far from a cabin in the usual sense. It was a distinguished, rectangular dwelling, three stories high counting the dormered, window-lit rooms beneath the roof. Three tall windows rose on either side of the pillared entryway, with a corresponding row of windows on the second story. There was a chimney at each end, with two windows on either side of it on the two main floors. Above all, it had *room*. Room for a long parlor with cozy, deep-cushioned window seats ideal for reading. Room for Harriet's quiet "room of her own" where she could write. Room for Calvin to have a proper scholar's study. Room for six children and one lovable large dog. And flowers, everywhere flowers—in vases, growing in pots, in Harriet's paintings hanging on the walls. Harriet adored flowers, craved flowers, had a gift for growing them. In her fingers, ivy twined its way up cords to frame the insides of her windows. Geraniums bloomed, and heliotrope, and calla lilies. She forced hyacinths and narcissus to bloom in winter. Andover had never seen anything like it.

In and around the pleasures of her new home, and the equally pleasurable but more demanding answering of voluminous mail, Harriet worked on her *Key to Uncle Tom's Cabin.* It was an enormous piece of scholarly work. Harriet had not "done research" when writing *Uncle Tom's Cabin;* she had *lived* her material and written about what she had seen and known—or heard of, as in the case of Eliza on the ice, from persons she absolutely trusted. Now she had to document such experiences. It was possible, but it took endless time.

When Harriet commenced the work early in December, she thought she would finish by the first of the year. She turned to all her sources—brothers, friends, acquaintances, the famous—asking for verification of slavery incidents they had related to her, or any other documentation that would be useful. Senator Sumner sent her the text of a wanted-dead-or-alive slave-catching flyer.

In December 1852 the Committee of the New Ladies' Anti-Slavery Society in Glasgow, and the Committee of the Glasgow New Association for the Abolition of Slavery wrote inviting "Mrs. and Professor Stowe" to visit the British Isles at the committees' expense. The "Women of Great Britain and Ireland"—spear-headed by Queen Victoria's close friend the Duchess of Sutherland, the Duchesses of Bedford and of Argyll, the Countess of Shaftesbury, and others of their position—were writing "An Affectionate and Christian Address . . . to Their Sisters, the Women of the United States of America," urging them to use their influence and prayers to sway America (through their men-folk) to abolish slavery. Unlike British men who had spoken out on the subject, the British women acknowledged "our share in this great sin. We acknowledge that our forefathers introduced, nay, compelled the adoption of slavery in these mighty colonies. . . . [I]t is because we so deeply feel and unfeignedly avow our own complicity, that we now venture to implore your aid to wipe away our common crime and our common dishonor." Thousands of signatures were being obtained. To whom could this remarkable document be presented? Whom else than Harriet Beecher Stowe? The Duchess of Sutherland wrote to Harriet about a visit.

Harriet began to dream dreams.

In February the famous Eliza Lee Cabot Follen of Boston, retired editor of *Child's Friend* magazine, wrote to Harriet from London where she was making a lengthy stay. There was much the outspoken Abolitionist widow wanted to know about this younger writer with Boston connections. Harriet, an admirer of Mrs. Follen's poetry, wrote back at length.

"I am a little bit of a woman,—somewhat more than forty, about as thin and dry as a pinch of snuff; never very much to look at in my best days, and looking like a used-up article now. . . ." This description was decidedly at odds with impressions of others who saw Harriet at the time. ". . . I am now writing a work which will contain . . . all the facts and documents on which [*Uncle Tom's Cabin*] was founded, and an immense body of facts, reports of trials, legal documents and testimony. . . . I had not begun to measure the depth of the abyss. The law records of courts and judicial proceedings are so incredible. . . . This horror! This nightmare abomination! Can it be in my country! It lies like lead on my heart. . . ."

Harriet concluded by saying that "If I live till spring [that old Puritan habit again, of not tempting fate] I shall hope to see Shakespeare's grave, and Milton's mulberry-tree, and the good land of my fathers—old, old England!"

The great arrangements had been made. The Stone Cabin would be closed up during the Stowes' Grand Tour. The twins would transfer to a boarding school in New Haven, where Mary Dutton's family could look after them. Georgie and little Charley would stay with relatives, and Henry and Freddie with Andover friends. So would Rover, displaced from his usual sleeping-place under Calvin and Harriet's bed.

Since Harriet's travels would be business-related, she needed a private secretary along whom she could trust. Her brother Charles took a leave of absence from his pulpit in Newark, New Jersey (where he had been ruffling feathers by urging disobedience to the Fugitive Slave Law) to fill that post. George Beecher's wealthy widow, Sarah, decided to come along, accompanied by her son George, an aspiring artist, and her brother William Buckingham.

On Wednesday, March 30, 1853, the party sailed out of Boston on the steamship *Niagara* on what was to turn into almost a royal progress.

XXII

The Lioness Abroad

1853

ALAS FOR HARRIET, she was seasick for most of the crossing. Early on the morning of April 10 the coast of Ireland came in sight. Soon after that the *Niagara* passed Kinsale Head, where the wreck of the *Albion* had taken place. Harriet made a sketch of it for her father. In late morning they dropped anchor near the Liverpool docks.

The Stowes had made no hotel reservations. To their surprise, a young man who had arrived aboard the customs tender sought them out. His mother was the daughter of former Lord Chief Justice Denman; his uncle, John Cropper, wished the Stowe party to be his guests at Dingle Bank.

Church bells were ringing as the tender ferried them in to shore. It was Sunday morning. The wharf was thronged with people, and more lined the roads. They gave way, silently, as Mr. Cropper shepherded his charges toward the waiting carriage. As Harriet passed on her husband's arm, as they drove off through the green countryside, the townspeople and country people lined the roads, and watched, smiled, and bowed, all keeping the Sunday silence. Gradually it dawned on Harriet—they had come to welcome *her.*

The "royal progress" had begun. The Cropper homes were mansions; the "breakfast" Mrs. Edward Cropper invited Harriet and Calvin to next morning turned out to be a formal collation with some three dozen guests. From then on it was one fine social affair after another. The Liverpool Negroes' Friend Society presented her with 130 gold sovereigns for her to put to use for blacks in the United States.

The trip to Glasgow was made by first-class railway carriage. Calvin was like a child in a candy store, watching out the windows with one finger in a guidebook. Carlisle . . . Solway Firth . . . Lockerbie . . . they were in the country of Sir Walter Scott. At every train stop people waited, through the day and through the night, to see and speak to "Mrs. Beecher-Stowe." Then they were in Glasgow, riding through the midnight streets.

Mountains of mail awaited them. Charles dealt with it: invitations, poetic tributes, deputations seeking visits from the famous author, gifts. For Harriet it was all a confused, overwhelming dream. She captured it all—the sights, the sounds, the smells, the wonder—in sketches and in letters home. The Lord Provost of Glasgow personally took the Stowes in his grand carriage to visit the cathedral. Thousands lined up to see Harriet see the sights. Harriet spent a day in bed to recover from exhaustion, then rose in the evening for a great public tea party in her honor at City Hall. Over two thousand people attended. A second tea party of the same size took place a few days later. This had been billed as a "workingmen's soiree," and Calvin outdid himself with a humorous speech, most of it in his best whimsical Yankee workingman's accent. The next afternoon and evening he preached in two of the leading Glasgow churches.

From there to Edinburgh, and even grander receptions. A wealthy Quaker, Mrs. Wigham, was the Stowes' hostess. Harriet was presented with the Scottish National Penny Offering (for the cause of American blacks) in the form of 1,000 gold sovereigns piled on a magnificent silver salver (a gift for Harriet) given by "A few ladies of Edinburgh" in testimony of the high esteem they

168

held her in as a woman, a Christian, and a friend of humanity. The Stowes were able to get in some private sight-seeing, and then were off to Dundee and Aberdeen, where similar events took place. Calvin, to Harriet's relief, made the acceptance speeches for her, and on occasion Charles did as well. One rainy day Harriet visited Scott's home and grave at Melrose Abbey while Calvin and Charles made public appearances on her behalf.

Harriet was discovering that celebrity had its drawbacks. She needed time to rest; she wanted time to go owling about, soaking in the sights in private. Charles began building such "offstage days" into Harriet's calendar.

Sarah Beecher, her son, and brother had already gone on to London. Harriet, Charles, and Calvin made their way there slowly, by way of Scott's Kenilworth, Warwick Castle, Coventry, and Shakespeare country. They arrived in London to learn Harriet was to be special guest that evening at the Lord Mayor's annual dinner for the English judiciary at the Mansion House. Charles Dickens and his wife had been invited to represent England's literary establishment.

This was only the beginning. Harriet and her party were staying with a clergyman in an unfashionable country part of London, but the titled and fashionable beat a path to her country retreat. The path ran both ways. The Stowes were guests of honor at a private family dinner party given by the Earl of Carlisle, the Duchess of Sutherland's brother. The next day Harriet appeared at the Anniversary of the British and Foreign Bible Society.

On Saturday the Duke and Duchess of Sutherland gave a levee in Harriet's honor at their London home, Stafford House, opposite Buckingham Palace. It was all becoming too much for Calvin. He feared his old homespun Hattie would be lost forever, and realized he would not get back to Andover in time to teach the summer term. He couldn't leave Harriet to deal with all of this.

But Harriet was loving every minute. And despite his grumbling, Calvin was so proud of her. Harriet had too much Puritan humility to have her head turned, and too much a sense of humor.

But all the same, London society was an eye-opener. The ladies all looked so *young*! They were considered heartbreakers in their forties. And their *homes*! What struck her most was the way they were arranged—the rooms each in a single color, the Oriental carpets in which patterns and shades blurred into a harmonious whole, the fabric-paneled walls, the way objects were composed like subjects for a painting. Harriet had an innate genius for decorating, but the rooms in the Stone Cabin would benefit from what she learned abroad.

The Sutherland levee marked the official presentation of the address from the "Ladies of Great Britain and Ireland." It began with what was called a "small luncheon." The lovely Duchess of Sutherland wore white muslin, with a tight basque bodice of drab-colored velvet and satin and a gold and diamond net on her hair. Other members of the Sutherlands' families were there—the Marquis and Marchioness of Stafford; Lord and Lady Shaftesbury; Lord and Lady Palmerston; the pro-abolition Marquis of Lansdowne—and government figures: Lord John Russell, Lord Grenville, Chancellor of the Exchequer Gladstone.

After lunch the party proceeded to the picture gallery with its magnificent paintings and colored-glass dome. And still the people kept coming. Lord Shaftesbury read aloud a welcome from the ladies of England. The Duchess of Sutherland gave Harriet privately a magnificent gold bracelet in the shape of a massive slave chain. It was engraved with the dates on which Great Britain outlawed the slave trade and freed slaves in her colonies, and with the words *We trust it is a memorial of a chain that is soon to be broken.*

The British and Foreign Anti-Slavery Society Anniversary Meeting was still to come. By this time Calvin's blood was boiling. He had been noticing that under all the adulation of his wife ran a strong current that was half British self-congratulation and half anti-American sentiment. This from a country in which whole families of laborers might live (if they were lucky) in tiny one-room-up-one-down dank cottages at their employers' pleasure, or (worse) in eight-foot-square windowless stone hovels too low to stand erect in! And as for the sweatshops of the great Industrial Revolution, and the disease-ridden filth of the East End! . . .

At the Anti-Slavery Anniversary Meeting, where four thousand people applauded Harriet so fiercely that the noise was like a blow, where speech following speech took speaking against slavery as a license to speak against America, Calvin's patience broke. Harriet was with the Duchess of Sutherland in a private gallery, and could not exert wifely control. In blunt New England speech Calvin informed his hearers that *England* was the primary (80 percent) customer for American cotton. England *liked* the financial advantage of buying slave-grown cotton. If *England* demanded free-grown cotton—and was willing to pay the price— American slavery would have ended years ago. It was *England* that kept the "peculiar institution" going.

It was Calvin Stowe's finest hour.

The Anti-Slavery Society still intended to hold a public soiree, which took place nine days later. In between the Stowe party did private sightseeing and visiting. Harriet sat for a portrait in crayon, by an artist named Richmond, that became one of her favorites. The Duke and Duchess of Argyll gave a dinner. Two other things occurred during the English visit that gave Harriet great quiet pleasure. One was her meeting with Miss Greenfield, a plain, plump young black woman, a freed slave from Alabama. She had a magnificent, double-range voice and, billed as the "Black Swan," had given concerts in the United States. She was trying in vain to establish herself in London. Could Harriet help? Harriet pulled strings. Soon the Queen's director of music agreed to launch the Black Swan on the concert platform, and Harriet provided funds for a concert gown of black moire silk, with bugle beading and white lace undersleeves. The Duchess of Sutherland introduced the Black Swan in a concert at Stafford House which Harriet attended. Harriet's other moment of private joy occurred at a luncheon in a home on Oxford Terrace: She was introduced to the lovely, fragile widow of Lord Byron.

Calvin was obliged to return to Andover. Harriet and the rest of her family party stayed on for a few more days in London. Then they traveled to the Continent as private tourists. Harriet reveled in art at the Louvre, bought fine silk gowns in Paris, went by boat to Lyons and by horse-drawn "diligence" to Geneva, along terrifying mountain roads through villages in the Alps. Then on by rail and boat through Calvin's beloved Germany; to Antwerp to see the Rubens paintings; back to Paris. There Sarah Beecher and her family decided to stay on. Harriet and brother Charles went to England for a last round of private visits and then sailed for home.

Only one thing had been lacking in the fairy-tale trip. The British government was finding America's North-South, abolitionist-slavery trauma a sticky subject, and so Queen Victoria had refused her good friend Lady Sutherland's entreaties that she give an audience to Mrs. Beecher-Stowe.

XXIII

First Lady of Abolition

1853–1857

A NEW WOMAN came home from Europe in September 1853—
poised, well dressed, accustomed to public appearances and adulation, accepting the role that had been thrust upon her. She
returned with huge sums of money for the Abolitionist cause, personal gifts and tributes that included the gold slave bracelet, an
enormous silver inkstand with allegorical figures, an Irish bog-oak
casket lined in gold, and the twenty-six volumes of signatures of
the ladies who had joined in the address to the ladies of the
United States. She was also a good deal wiser in the ways of the
world and politics.

She had known from the beginning that it wasn't the flesh-and-
blood New England wife and mother who was being given—
much less had earned—this tide of adoration. Having grown up
on the classics, she had to know she was not a literary giant. She
was a good storyteller with a desperately important story to tell.
Besides, "God wrote *Uncle Tom's Cabin.*"

That phrase, which time and repetition would make hackneyed,
was a metaphor for an experience Harriet knew all Calvinists
would understand—the doctrines of "gifts and talents" and of the

"calling"; the belief that God would use His children's talents if they were surrendered to Him. Harriet knew she hadn't "created" Uncle Tom; he and his story had come to her in visions and intuitions, the way such things had come to the biblical prophets. Yes, she had at times thought about the plot and characters. But when she took pen in hand to write *Uncle Tom's Cabin*, the words and pictures had simply "come." She hadn't weighed her words or edited her writing. Such literary skills as she possessed had likewise been pulled by God out of her unconscious. "To God be the glory," in the old religious words. She, Harriet, had been only the vehicle.

In the same way, people and politics were using her now as a focus for their attacks on slavery . . . or Abolition . . . or America. Calvin, that mixture of mystic and realist, had observed this first, during those hours as a bystander at the feasts. He had spoken out—magnificently. Harriet loved her new English friends, but she would not allow herself or her writing to be used. If she had, unwittingly, been made the First Lady of Abolition, it was time for Harriet the human being, not "Mrs. Beecher-Stowe," to become involved. She herself would use her celebrity status, her voice, the means at her disposal, for the cause.

The first thing she did was come to a kind of guarded alliance with William Lloyd Garrison. There were many differences, not the least of them religion, in their points of view. Garrison was, to Beecher eyes, too radical. That autumn he made the first move, inviting Harriet to be guest of honor at the American Anti-Slavery Society's twenty-fifth anniversary. It was an invitation she could not in conscience accept without discussion and public clarification. A series of letters between the two ensued, published by Garrison in *The Liberator.*

"What I fear," Harriet wrote, "is that 'The Liberator' will take from poor Uncle Tom his Bible and give him nothing in its place."

"Surely you would not have me disloyal to my conscience," Garrison replied. "How can you prove that you are not trammeled by education or traditional notions as to the entire sanctity of the Bible?"

Harriet's tart response was that she would not even attack the faith of a heathen unless she was sure she had a better one to put in its place.

Eventually Harriet invited Garrison to the Stone Cabin, for a meeting that ended in mutual respect and a sense that despite their differences they could work together. Garrison advised Harriet on the best uses of the British monetary contributions to the cause.

Harriet found time for a private life as well. She had been separated from Calvin for too long, and from her children for even longer. Hattie and Eliza were poised and pretty young ladies—Eliza had acquired a fashionable Italian greyhound named Giglio—and Georgie was an impish tomboy. And the boys were growing—Henry, especially, was turning into her heart's delight.

Harriet and Calvin commissioned a painting of Eliza Tyler Stowe from a Boston artist who had known the first Mrs. Stowe and could conjure her lovely likeness up from memory. She improved on the style and comforts of the Stone Cabin. Phillips, Sampson & Co., of Boston had bought out John P. Jewett's publishing house, but Harriet found the new publishers pleasing. She began work on her travel memoirs, to be called *Sunny Memories of Foreign Lands,* and planned another book on slavery. She resumed writing for the *Independent.*

Suddenly a new political move in the struggle between North and South erupted. The Missouri Compromise had fixed the northernmost limit of slavery forever. Now the "prairie schooners" (covered wagons) of the settlers were pushing into the area known as Kansas, and an even larger area of good farmland to the north would be next. In January 1854 Illinois Senator Stephen A. Douglas submitted a bill to carve the land into two territories, Kansas and Nebraska (in both of which Douglas owned land and planned a railroad). To win southern votes, Douglas proposed "popular sovereignty" for the territories, thereby wiping out the Missouri Compromise.

The Kansas-Nebraska Bill sent shock waves through the North. Harriet wrote a rousing "Appeal to the Women of the Free States of America," which was published in the *Independent,* and instigated a petition, drawn up by the clergy of Boston, that was signed by 3,050 pastors of the North. Despite this appeal, the Kansas-Nebraska Bill became law on May 31, 1854.

Slavery was suddenly an intense topic in every home in America and it was in the homes that Harriet hoped to defeat slavery completely. This was Harriet's peculiar genius—she spoke, and wrote, not as a politician nor even as a preacher, but as a *woman,* a wife, and mother. *Women* were the nurturers of America—including of American men. *Women* bore children in love and pain, felt most keenly the pain of losing a child to death, the traumas of homes and families being broken up. *Women* could best comprehend and ache with the traumas of the slaves. *Women could change the world.* This was her real message, and it struck something subliminal and deeply disturbing in all her readers.

But for the moment, life went along more or less peacefully. Life was good in America in the 1850s for all but the poor and the enslaved. Lyman Beecher descended on the Stone Cabin in the summer of 1854. No longer able to write or even to think coherently, he nonetheless wanted his memoirs written. Harriet, Catharine, and Charles rallied to the cause. It was an arduous affair. Lyman's memory had to be primed with questions, and his responses taken down word by word to keep the true Lyman Beecher flavor. Harriet, Catharine, and three of the Beecher brothers contributed chapters. Charles, busy collaborating with Henry Ward on the soon-to-be-famous *Plymouth Hymnal,* traveled back and forth from his New Jersey church. Catharine arranged for Harpers to publish the autobiography.

The Lyman Beecher autobiography collaboration wound up with a family reunion at Andover that November. The youngest Beecher, James, was a seminarian at Andover after several years at sea. Edward and his wife, Isabella, came up from Boston, and Henry arrived from a speaking engagement at Lynn. They planned another reunion on Lyman's eightieth birthday. That Christmas Harriet set up one of the newfangled Christmas trees and decked her halls with candles and holly. The Puritan strictures against celebrating Christmas were now forgotten.

In early 1855 the situation in Kansas grew dangerous. After spring elections, Kansas actually had two armed governments. The five sons of a New York Abolitionist named John Brown, who was plotting a slave rebellion and was considered by most to be half mad, moved into Kansas. Henry Ward's congregation was filling barrels with rifles, labeling them Bibles, and sending them out to Abolitionist settlers in Kansas, where the guns became known as "Beecher's Bibles." Henry's *Plymouth Hymnal* came out. Harriet wrote a letter of condolence to the Duchess of Sutherland, whose son had been killed in the Crimean War's tragic Charge of the Light Brigade. The duchess's loss made Harriet acutely conscious of how much she loved her own eldest son. Henry was her golden boy—tall, blond, athletic, handsome. He was sixteen, preparing to go to Dartmouth in another year.

On October 12, 1855, *all* the Beechers except James, who was in Hong Kong on missionary work, came together at the Stone Cabin to celebrate Lyman's eightieth birthday. They had a group family portrait taken at one of the new photographic studios by a soon-to-be-famous photographer named Matthew Brady.

In February 1856 Harriet began work on another slavery book. She wanted to show the degenerative effect of slavery on *all* society, black and white, rich and poor. Her plot revolved around two brothers, one the white plantation owner's son, the other his biracial slave half brother. She had a lot of new material, gleaned while researching *Key to Uncle Tom's Cabin,* that she could use.

Down in Washington, on May 19-20, 1856, pro-abolition Senator Charles Sumner took the floor for a long, impassioned speech on "The Crime against Kansas." On May 26, after Senate had just adjourned for the day, young Representative Preston Brooks of South Carolina came up behind Sumner, seated at his desk, and beat him severely on the head with a cane.

Blood streamed everywhere. Sumner lingered for days between life and death. Brooks was brought up on charges in the House for attempted murder and was acquitted; resigned his House seat and was promptly re-elected. Indignation meetings were held throughout the North. Calvin Stowe presided over the Boston meeting; Henry Ward gave the principal speech at the one in Brooklyn.

Out in Kansas blood was also flowing, as "Beecher's Bibles" and "border ruffians" clashed. On the first of June Henry Ward staged a publicity event guaranteed to incite national feeling still further. He held another slave auction in his church on Sunday morning, and this time he had the young, beautiful woman present on the platform. She had, Henry announced, been sold down the river by her white owner-father. Women wept, men blew their noses, the ushers passed the collection plates, and Sarah was set free.

Up in tranquil Andover, in the white heat of her rage over the attack on her friend Sumner, Harriet's slave novel abruptly changed. A new and very different black character strode onto the stage of her story and took it over. He was a fugitive, living in Virginia's Great Dismal Swamp, but not hiding out there—Dred was a violent black Byron, leading a slave rebellion like Nat Turner. Like William Lloyd Garrison, he saw violence as a necessary evil against the greater evil of slavery. He spoke in the language of the Hebrew prophets in the King James translation of the Bible. He became the first militant black hero in American literature, and he was guaranteed to inflame every reader in both North and South.

The first blood had been shed—in the Senate, in Kansas, on the printed page—in the conflict between the states.

Fueled by her research, Harriet's visions came faster than she could write them down. She drafted the twins as secretaries to take dictation. This time she meant to protect her overseas copyrights by being in Britain to file them as British law required, and booked passage on the July 30 *Niagara* crossing. She meant to have *Dred* finished by then—two volumes, 260 pages each—and was writing the equivalent of 10 printed pages a day.

Sailing day approached, and her work wasn't finished, although

Harriet was dictating far into the night. As a reward, Harriet took the twins along with her to Europe, along with Calvin, and Mary Perkins. And Henry, who would have a few weeks of travel before starting Dartmouth in the fall. And the greyhound Giglio. The sea was smooth as glass, and Harriet was able to write her way across it. On the thirteenth of August the final chapters of *Dred: A Tale of the Great Dismal Swamp* were put aboard ship for Boston. The British publisher, Sampson Low, was standing by to rush his edition of *Dred* through the presses in less than two weeks, with advance orders constantly coming in. The book came out—to poor British reviews—and sold fifty thousand copies within two weeks. The American reviews, too, were cool but, as in England, did not affect book sales.

This second visit to England was more a private visit than Harriet's first. London's social season ended in early summer, and the gentry were at their summer homes. The Duke and Duchess of Sutherland invited the Stowes to visit at Dunrobin Castle in northern Scotland; their son-in-law the Duke of Argyll invited them to Inverary Castle.

En route to Scotland an odd, and touching, interview took place. The Stowes were at King's Cross Station, London, when they were "informed" that Her Majesty, the Prince Consort, and the royal children were arriving there on their way to Balmoral. What Calvin referred to privately as "an accidental, done-on-purpose meeting" took place. A Colonel Grey—on his own or on Harriet's behalf, depending on whether one believes the public or the private version—presented the Queen with the two volumes of *Dred,* which Victoria and her consort accepted with pleased interest. The couples exchanged bows. Queen Victoria, who was rumored to have adored *Uncle Tom's Cabin,* who could not because of international relations have Mrs. Beecher-Stowe publicly presented to her, had just met privately with the First Lady of American Abolition. Only one person could have arranged that accidental meeting—Lady Sutherland, the Queen's good friend. Only one person could have authorized it—Victoria herself.

The other significant development of that summer was the intimate friendship that sprang up between Harriet and the reclusive Lady Byron. Sixty-four and frail, she was kept in London that summer by respiratory troubles. Harriet wrote, asking permission to call. By the same messenger the invitation came back, commencing, "My Dear Friend . . ." Through the summer and autumn, before and after Calvin and Henry returned home, the friendship deepened.

The Stowes toured Scotland, with cordial invitations extended everywhere. The Duke of Sutherland gave Henry a kilt in the Sutherland plaid. Word came to Harriet through the court grapevine that the Queen said she liked *Dred* even better than *Uncle Tom.*

October came. Calvin and Henry sailed for home. Harriet, Mary, and the twins traveled leisurely to Paris. In January Harriet and Mary went to Italy, leaving the twins in a Parisian boarding school to be "finished." The women returned to Paris in early May to find the twins longing to remain there. Harriet's brother-in-law Thomas Hooker, in Paris on business, was planning a tour of Switzerland, and Mary Perkins decided to accompany him. Harriet gave the twins permission to remain till autumn, but she herself was longing for home and husband. She went alone to England and booked passage on the *Europa,* sailing on the sixth of June.

In the meantime there was a last social flurry. Harriet met the celebrated writer-intellectual Harriet Martineau, who praised *Dred* highly . . . the art critic John Ruskin, who may have fallen a bit in love with her . . . Mrs. Gaskell, the well-loved English writer.

And Lady Byron. Something strange had occurred between Harriet and Lady Byron back in November. Harriet and Mary had been her guests, with two other close women friends invited in for lunch. While Mary and the other women visited in the drawing room, Lady Byron had taken Harriet into her boudoir for a private talk. The talk had lasted until night had fallen, and during it

Lady Byron had confided in Harriet a great secret, one so shattering that Harriet had emerged dazed and shaken and had sat up all night discussing it with sister Mary. Now, as she was to sail for home, Harriet sent Lady Byron "a cup made of primroses, a funny little pitcher, quite large enough for cream, and a little vase for violets and primroses. . . . When you use it think of me and that I love you more than words can say."

Harriet reached home to find Henry still at Dartmouth preparing for examinations. Georgie and young Charley were flourishing, but seventeen-year-old Freddie—who was always "undersized" like Harriet herself—looked peaked. She took him to a water-cure establishment in the New Hampshire mountains for two weeks, and then went down to Brooklyn for a visit with her friend from brother Henry's congregation, Susie Howard.

On the evening of Thursday, the ninth of July, a telegram arrived for Mrs. Howard, shattering her with news she would have to break to Harriet. Henry, Harriet's golden son, the love of her heart, was drowned.

XXIV

The Gathering Storm

1857–1861

HENRY THE ATHLETE, member of the Dartmouth crew, had drowned in the strong currents of the Connecticut River. His two companions had struggled to save him, at risk of their own lives. At the last moment, when his grip on them could have drowned them all, Henry had "let go."

Harriet was devastated, the more so because she had been wondering about the state of Henry's soul. Henry had never been "converted." Now all the long-buried ghosts of her past rose up to haunt her.

The Stowes owned no burial plot, but they bought one now in the Andover campus graveyard. Harriet planted it with pansies, petunias, and verbenas. She visited it daily, Calvin even more. Calvin said he was submissive but not reconciled. Harriet would not submit. How *could* this be God's will? She paced the house, where everything she saw reminded her of Henry; wrote to the twins for comfort; wrote Georgie at boarding school that she felt like "a tired, dead, leafless tree." And she began to investigate Spiritualism and go to séances. Gradually her heart eased, but it happened slowly.

The life of the world went on. In October the New York Stock Market collapsed, triggering another financial panic. Harriet began to write again for the *Independent,* and for the new *Atlantic Monthly*. A great religious revival swept the country. Out in Illinois orator-politician Stephen Douglas and an unknown lawyer named Abraham Lincoln were engaging in a series of political debates; Lincoln was a member of the new Republican party. Harriet began a serial for the *Atlantic* called *The Minister's Wooing,* based on Lyman's wooing of Roxana. In it she rattled the bones of Puritanism and the doctrines of conversion and predestination, and wrestled with her fears about the state of her lost son Henry's soul. This story came not out of visions, but out of her rational mind, and she wrote it with great care. It established her as a serious writer of the New England scene.

The twins had come home, but by spring of 1859 they were anxious to return to Paris. Harriet sent them back with Harriet Beecher, Henry Ward's daughter, and planned another foreign excursion for herself late that summer.

She finished *The Minister's Wooing;* then Harriet, Calvin, and Georgie sailed for England. After a few weeks of visits, reunions with Lady Sutherland and Lady Byron, came the channel crossing Harriet always dreaded. The Stowes joined the twins and Harriet Beecher in Paris, and together they traveled in Switzerland. In Geneva, John Ruskin immediately renewed his acquaintance. His marriage had recently been annulled, and his attraction to Harriet was warm—so warm, perhaps, that it explained why Harriet suddenly decided to accompany Calvin and Georgie back to England to see them off for home. After that she went directly to Lausanne, to join the twins for travel in Italy.

While they were enjoying the Italian autumn *The Minister's Wooing* was published in America. Boston's Ticknor & Fields publishing company bought the bankrupt *Atlantic Monthly*. On Sunday, October 16, at a small Virginia town called Harpers Ferry, John Brown and the two of his sons not killed in Kansas rioting captured the United States Arsenal and holed in to await

The Beecher family, c. 1859
(Stowe-Day Foundation, Hartford, Connecticut)

a great slave uprising. It didn't happen. Brown was captured, tried, sentenced to death, and hanged. The North had its first great martyr.

For Harriet, the troubles in the States seemed far away. She and the twins spent the Christmas holidays in Florence. Fred arrived, bringing friends; the Howards arrived, with their son and daughter. Harriet held a Christmas party, renewed acquaintance with Robert Browning and his poet wife Elizabeth Barrett, attended séances. She made new friends, including the visiting James T. Fields of Ticknor & Fields. His young second wife, Annie, became the closest friend Harriet had had since her beloved Eliza. The Stowes and the Fieldses traveled to Rome together, arriving in time for a Mardi Gras that turned into a riot.

William Wetmore Story, the renowned sculptor, gave a dinner in Harriet's honor. It was one of the nights when Harriet, splendidly dressed and fascinated by all around her, "came alive." She told the story of Sojourner Truth, the legendary African woman who held crowds spellbound at Abolitionist rallies. Harriet held her audience spellbound now, recreating the time Sojourner Truth, intent on meeting the author of *Uncle Tom's Cabin,* had interrupted Lyman's eightieth birthday party.

Harriet, the Howards, and their children moved on to southern Italy. While there Harriet found inspiration for her next novel, *Agnes of Sorrento,* which she "made up" aloud as they traveled. Back in the States, the radical Republicans selected Abraham Lincoln as their candidate in the upcoming presidential election. Slavery, everyone now knew, would be a major issue.

Harriet and her daughters went back to England to start their journey home. While there they were shocked by news that Hattie's friend, the Howards' daughter Annie, had died after a brief and sudden illness. Hattie was stricken with frightening fainting spells and panic attacks, but recovered enough for the voyage home on the *Europa.* The crossing was unexpectedly enjoyable, for James and Annie Fields, Nathaniel Hawthorne and his wife, Sophia Peabody Hawthorne, were all on board.

Harriet Beecher Stowe and twin daughters,
Eliza Tyler and Harriet Beecher Stowe, c. 1860
(Stowe-Day Foundation, Hartford, Connecticut)

That autumn Fred Stowe entered Harvard Medical School. The Howards brought their daughter's body home. After the funeral Susie Howard came to Harriet, in Andover, and in October Harriet returned with her to Brooklyn. The presidential campaigns were in their final weeks, and the young Prince of Wales was in New York on his first official visit. Henry Ward had appointed his young protégé, former secretary, and closest friend, Theodore Tilton, managing editor of the *Independent*. Tilton coaxed Harriet into writing something for him.

Election day was November 6. By midnight word was out that Lincoln had carried the North. The governor of South Carolina called the state legislature into emergency session.

Five days before Christmas, 1860, South Carolina seceded from the Union, and a week later sent out a call for all slaveholding states to follow its example and to meet in convention in Montgomery, Alabama, on February 4, 1861. Mississippi was the first to heed the call on January 9. Others followed swiftly: Florida on January 10, Alabama the next day, Georgia on January 19, Louisiana one week later. Texas seceded on the first of February. Virginia hung in the balance. It was a slave state, just across the narrow Potomac from Washington, D.C., and had a proud history as one of the Union's founders. Many Virginians, like Washington and Jefferson, owned slaves but had moral doubts about the institution.

A divided nation held its breath and waited. In North and South alike, people prayed and trembled, and some men lusted for battle. Everything rested on the head and hands of a lanky, regrettably folksy backwoods lawyer soon to be sworn in as the sixteenth president of the United States. He had been elected on an antislavery platform. His inauguration was scheduled for the fourth of March.

On February 4 the seceded states met to form their own confederation. The just-seceded Texas was the only one not represented. Jefferson Davis of Mississippi was elected president, Alexander Stephens of Georgia vice president; they were sworn in on February 18. Lincoln was in Philadelphia, preparing to participate in Washington's Birthday ceremonies there, when news reached him that an Illinois detective named Pinkerton had uncovered a plot to assassinate him as he passed through Baltimore. A plan was hastily devised to smuggle the president-elect into Washington under the guard of some of Pinkerton's operatives. This was the beginning of the American Secret Service.

Lincoln reached Washington unscathed, and took office. A bomb went off in Republican party headquarters that night. Rumors swirled in the city, and traveled from there south, north, and west. The Colt revolver factory in Hartford began turning out three hundred guns a day. And America waited as spring came in.

Up in New England the First Lady of Abolition was not at the moment focusing on politics. If Lincoln had been elected on an antislavery platform, could emancipation of the slaves be far behind? Hadn't Henry Ward had a mystic insight that the border states—Delaware, Maryland, Kentucky, and Missouri—would stay with the free-states North? With little conception of how fiercely the flames of sectional hatred now blazed, the author of *Uncle Tom's Cabin* went on writing columns on home beautification (a cause to which her European visits had awakened her), the Italian romance she had made up aloud on the European trains, and a Maine story called *Pearl of Orr's Island* that was currently running in the *Independent*.

The Confederacy was forming a volunteer army that was called "Rebels" or "Rebs" in the northern press. In March North Carolina and Tennessee voted against secession. Arkansas, Missouri, Kentucky, Maryland, and Delaware were holding off. But rumors were rampant. Gangs of thugs, like the Cincinnati mobs, hung around Baltimore hotels that northerners were known to frequent.

The rumors rose. Major Anderson, commander of the United States garrison at Fort Sumter in Charleston harbor, feared a Confederate takeover attempt. On April 11 Confederate troops demanded its surrender, which was refused. Shots rang out. For four days the siege went on. On Sunday, Anderson was forced to surrender. Bells clanged merrily in Charleston and tolled throughout the North. Henry Ward Beecher told a packed congregation at evening worship that it was ten thousand times better to have war than to have slavery; and President Lincoln called out the state militias.

The War Between the States had begun.

XXV

Terrible Swift Sword

1861–1863

THE NORTH MOBILIZED for war. Flags floated everywhere, and abolitionists were jubilant. Surely a proclamation abolishing slavery would come from the White House any day!

The Confederacy grew. Virginia seceded from the Union on April 17, to be followed by Arkansas on May 6, North Carolina on May 21, and Tennessee on June 8. The battle lines were now drawn.

At Harvard, young medical student Frederick William Stowe closed his textbooks and enlisted in what would soon be called his mother's war. In vain Harriet tried to persuade him he'd be more useful if he finished his medical studies first. "People shall never say, 'Harriet Beecher Stowe's son is a coward,'" he answered hotly.

The initial enlistments were for three months only; North and South alike assumed that the war would be over within ninety days. Fred became part of Company A of the First Massachusetts Infantry. They sailed south in June, by way of Jersey City. Harriet was visiting Henry Ward in Brooklyn at the time. She, Hattie, and Eunice Beecher took a ferry across the Hudson to see Fred off to war. "[My] first impulse was to wipe his face before I kissed him," Harriet wrote to Calvin. "He was in high spirits in spite of the weight of blue overcoat, knapsack, etc., etc. . . . I gave him my handkerchief and Eunice gave him hers, with a sheer motherly instinct that is so strong within her, and then filled his knapsack with oranges. . . . Now I am watching anxiously for the evening paper to tell me that the regiment has reached Washington in safety."

Through late spring and early summer North and South, two armed camps, waited for each other to make the first move. The three-month enlistments were running out. Lincoln still had not freed the slaves. Then came the confrontation at Manassas, a little Virginia town not far from Washington. From the capital, from the Virginia country, wagons and carriages of spectators drove out to watch as though going to a horse race, with parasols and picnic baskets. The sun glittered on gold braid on blue and gray. Shots rang out. Then suddenly—*panic!* A team of artillery horses bolted. A wagon fell over, blocking passage on the narrow bridge across Bull Run. After that, all was chaos—and a Confederate victory.

The news went to Europe, where the North was portrayed as far more debilitated than it really was. The Confederacy was working hard to be recognized in Europe as a new and independent nation. To Harriet's horror, Queen Victoria had proclaimed Britain's neutrality. Harriet wrote and wrote—to the Sutherlands, to the Duke of Argyll, to Lord Shaftesbury, begging her friends to make Britain speak out on the Union's side. Britain was antislavery; Britain was for abolition; Britain *must* be for the Union. In vain Calvin pointed out to her that Britain was also for southern cottons for its British mills. To Harriet's mind it was all so clear—this was a holy war to free the slaves.

But it wasn't. That was America's dirty little secret. Slavery was the South's great economic cause; abolition the North's great moral one. But underlying both festered factionalism that went back to the days of the Constitutional Convention and the great issue that had never yet been settled: "popular sovereignty"—

"states' rights"—or a strong *united* central government? That was what the war was really about—preserving the Union, or states' rights to separate from it. By oath of office, President Lincoln's first duty was to preserve the Union—to bring the South back, preferably with few lives lost. It was not politically feasible to consider abolition. And Britain did not respond to the pleas of the woman it had so idolized.

Fred Stowe achieved the rank of sergeant for his good conduct during the Bull Run debacle. All was quiet on the Potomac. Henry Ward added to his responsibilities by overhauling the *Independent* and appointing himself editor in chief, with his protégé Tilton continuing "in his old position." Harriet, trapped in literary deadlines, kept waiting for something to happen. Why were the Union army's successive commanders in chief doing nothing? It was a question to which President Lincoln also wanted an answer.

Horace Greeley's New York *Tribune* attacked the president for inaction on slavery. Lincoln responded, stating clearly that whatever he did or did not do about abolition would depend completely on which or what he believed would *save the Union*. Harriet struck back in print, using the very pattern of Lincoln's sentence structures to say that whatever *she* did was to free the oppressed, and whether that saved or destroyed the Union was unimportant. It was a far from wise statement; it made her look infatuated with her own importance, which she was not, and that phrase about destruction of the Union being unimportant gave the anti-abolitionists fuel for firing up the nation's worst fears.

To do Harriet justice, she had a great deal on her mind. Abolition was first—that was the Puritan sense of mission—but Fred off at the war had to come next. Calvin was nearing sixty and thinking of retiring. And Harriet herself was longing to move again. The Stone Cabin was beautiful, but the Stowes—Harriet— had never really "fit in" in Andover. She longed to be living nearer to her Beecher kin; *family* was the unifying principle, not just in her writing, but in her life. That life was easier now, for the slim,

Frederick William Stowe, 1862–1863
(Stowe-Day Foundation, Hartford, Connecticut)

elegant twins had become her executive secretaries and executive housekeepers. They were stylish, beautiful, and cultured, but they showed no interest in getting married.

In late 1862 word began to circulate that unless the South sought peace before the first of the year, Lincoln would indeed emancipate the slaves. *Here* was what Harriet needed to try once more to sway English public opinion, which was now overwhelmingly with the South. She had just the lever needed—the "Affectionate and Christian Address of Many Thousands of Women of Great Britain and Ireland to Their Sisters, the Women of the United States of America," all twenty-six volumes of it. For nearly ten years, since the address called for *America's* women to act against slavery, it had lain unanswered. What were the *British* ladies now doing? Encouraging British construction of gunboats for the Confederate navy—so romantic—in violation of the Queen's proclaimed neutrality! Lord Shaftesbury was calling the rumored Emancipation Proclamation a threat—to make the South hurry back into the Union with its "peculiar institution" still intact. *Now* Harriet would answer the "affectionate address"—turning it into an indictment of British hypocrisy—in an article for the *Atlantic*.

But first she had to make sure whether the emancipation rumors were real.

An opportunity came her way. Harriet, like many others, was invited to a great Thanksgiving Dinner being given for the Freedmen (escaped slaves) of Washington. Slaves had been escaping over the boarder for months; there were huge "squatters' camps" in the very shadow of the Capitol. Harriet would attend, and pull whatever strings were necessary to get a private audience with the president.

She left for Washington on November 14, taking Hattie and twelve-year-old Charley with her. They stayed with the Howards in Brooklyn for a week, during which Harriet composed the major part of her *Reply*. Her first thought in Washington was to find Fred, now a first lieutenant in the infantry and stationed nearby. "Filled out," bronzed by the sun, he was looking well. Harriet pulled strings and obtained for him a forty-eight-hour pass so he could stay with the family in a Washington hotel. Getting rooms there had to have involved string pulling also; wartime Washington was overcrowded. The Capitol's not-yet-completed dome sat on the ground of Capitol Hill. The Union Hotel had been turned into an army hospital.

Senator Henry Wilson of Massachusetts set up a meeting between President Lincoln and the First Lady of Abolition. Before it took place, Harriet attended the Freedmen's Thanksgiving Dinner. Over a thousand free black men and women were there. What moved Harriet most was the prayer of an aged, blind black preacher, given in a "strange rhythmical chant . . . the psalm of this modern exodus."

The day of the momentous presidential interview arrived raw and cold. Taking Charley with her, Harriet made her way to the White House through the streets crowded with soldiers, politicians, lobbyists, camp followers, and former slaves.

Neither Lincoln nor Harriet ever wrote or spoke publicly of the interview. As a result, speculation and "reconstructions" abounded from the moment the first news of it leaked out. The meeting took place in a small room Lincoln used as a private office-study. Harriet was escorted to the president by either Senator Wilson or a member of the Cabinet, depending on which version is to be believed. They found Lincoln sprawled in a chair before the fireplace, his big feet parked on the mantelpiece as he warmed himself before the flames of a small coal fire. He unfolded his awkward length and came to greet them, saying, "Why, Mrs. Stowe, right glad to see you!" Then, twinkling, he added (according to Stowe family legend), "So you're the little woman who wrote the book that made this great war!"

They made an incongruous pair, the "scarecrowlike," perpetually rumpled midwestern lawyer and the little New England woman whose enormous, spreading hoopskirts swayed girlishly as she walked. But it was a meeting of giants.

195

Wilson (or a member of the Cabinet) had the job of entertaining Charley while his mother and the president talked. Being twelve, fascinated by the war and Washington, and nobody's fool, Harriet's son listened in and remembered as much of the presidential conversation as he could.

Lincoln led the way back to the fire. "I do love an open fire," he remarked. "I s'pose it's because we always had one to home." He invited Harriet to sit down and did so himself, holding his great hands that critics called "apelike" out to the flames.

"Mr. Lincoln," said Harriet firmly, "I want to ask you about your views on emancipation."

According to Stowe family lore, the president spent some time explaining his controversial "border-state policy" and why it had been necessary to hold back on emancipation for fear those states—whose loyalty was none too certain—might have turned against the Union cause. Whatever he said, he convinced Harriet of his sincerity. He also convinced her that immediate emancipation *would* be proclaimed as of the first of January, 1863.

The first thing Charley asked after they left the presidential presence was why Lincoln said "to home" instead of "at home." Harriet had to give a swift lesson on grammar, dialect, *and* diplomacy.

She had one more errand to do, on behalf of Fred, before returning home. Fred wanted to get into real action. His mother, trained to stern duty, agreed. She persuaded General Buckingham to transfer Fred "from the infantry, where there seems to be no prospect of anything but garrison duty, to the cavalry, which is full of constant activity." In the process, Fred was promoted to the rank of captain. "General B.," Harriet wrote to Calvin, "seemed to think the prospect before us was, at best, a long war."

On New Year's Day Harriet was in Boston. That city, like many others in the North, had planned an Emancipation Jubilee. She was sitting in the balcony of the Boston Music Hall when the long-awaited telegram arrived during an intermission in the musical program. The whole place broke into an explosion of joy . . .

cheering, clapping, weeping. Tiny Harriet was almost crushed in the crowd, and her bonnet was knocked off-kilter. Then, little by little, a name began to be chanted through the uproar. It built in rhythm and crescendo. "Mrs. Stowe . . . *Mrs. Stowe* . . . MRS. STOWE! . . ."

People around her looked, smiled, nodded, spread out in a circle around her, guided her to the balcony rail. She stood there looking down into the hall, the lamplight glowing on the ladies' gowns, the radiant faces lifted up to hers.

The little woman who had started the great war could only bow, and wipe her eyes.

XXVI

Reconstructions

1863–1868

To Harriet, returning to Andover in the false spring of January 1863, it seemed as though the honorable but weary load she bore as author of "the book that made this great war" was over. Abolition had come. Soon, *soon* the South would be defeated, the slaves there would taste the fruits of freedom, and the boys would all come home.

But the war that had not ended within its first ninety days did not end with the Emancipation Proclamation. The Union navy blockaded southern ports; the flower of the South was dying on battlefields or prison stockades; the economy of the South was also dying. But the Confederate army, its ranks filled with old men and small boys, fought on.

At his home in Brooklyn old Lyman Beecher, a fragile shell in mind and body, teeth gone, speech all but gone, lay dying. "Do you know," Harriet had asked tenderly during one of her last visits, "that you are a very handsome old gentleman?" Lyman, eyes twinkling and faculties momentarily returning, had whispered back, "Oh, Hattie, tell me something new!" On Saturday, January 10, 1863, as Henry Ward put it, "the old oak finally fell." Lyman

Beecher was gone, along with all the other giants with whom he had fought the brave Calvinist fight. The family hurried to Brooklyn for the funeral. But his children and grandchildren had long since mourned his loss, and Harriet and the twins stopped off in Boston on their way home for shopping and concertgoing.

Harriet was planning a grand and Gothic new house in Hartford, on the very riverbank where long ago, with Georgiana May, she had dreamed just such a dream. The area was known as Nook Farm. Harriet's sisters Belle and Mary and their husbands already lived there; she herself had purchased four and a half Nook Farm acres in autumn 1862. As the war slogged on through cold of winter, sweltering sun, and mud, working on her new home gave Harriet momentary relief from worry.

"Who could write on stories that had a son sent to battle, with Washington beleaguered, and the whole country shaken as with an earthquake?" Harriet asked the *Independent*. But she forced herself to finish *Agnes of Sorrento* and *Pearl of Orr's Island*.

News came from England of reactions to Harriet's *Reply*. Infuriated Brits were sending letters to the British press, but a great meeting to express solidarity with the Union cause had been held in Liverpool, and the Emancipation Proclamation had been greeted with acclamation.

May came, and the bloody northern defeat of Chancellorsville. Confederate troops invaded the North, pushing into rolling farm country of Pennsylvania. The North shuddered, and rumors ran rampant. June came and went, the month of roses. Birds sang in the fields of Gettysburg, and Union troops settled in near a Lutheran seminary. Again a divided nation held its breath.

With the dawn of July 1, 1863, the fragile peace exploded. For three days the battle raged, and the sweet air was filled with the stench of dying, the fertile ground was soaked with blood, and the birds still sang.

Just over a week later a letter from an army chaplain reached Harriet.

DEAR MADAM,—Among the thousands of wounded and dying men on this war-scarred field, I have just met with your son, Captain Stowe. . . . He was struck by a fragment of a shell which entered his right ear. He is quiet and cheerful, and longs to see some member of his family. . . .

Calvin immediately started for Gettysburg. Soon Harriet had Fred home in the sun of the Stone Cabin's veranda. His cousin Fred Beecher, "literally shot to pieces," lay dying in Charles Beecher's parsonage while his father was undergoing, of all things, a heresy trial. New York City had draft riots, with violence against blacks who were being blamed for the whole bloody mess.

Chattanooga . . . Chickamauga . . . the Wilderness . . . Spotsylvania . . . now it was 1864, and the bloodbath still went on. Rumors of atrocities were rampant. Calvin had retired, but the Stowes stayed on in a rented Stone Cabin while the Hartford house, not yet completed, swallowed up huge quantities of money. Harriet, forced by finances to start writing again, began a column in the *Atlantic* called "The House and Home Papers." It was a composite of home decorating plans and instructions, advice on home management and mothering, and scientific instruction, and it blazed new trails.

Fred had had to report back to duty with his wound not healed. It *would* not heal. Harriet pulled strings and got him an honorable discharge. He settled in at the Stone Cabin, nursing a terrible depression and a terrible secret that his anxious parents soon discovered. He had become an alcoholic. The fact became one of those dark family truths that was known but never spoken.

Harriet was suffering from attacks of facial neuralgia and her old weaknesses. But she kept writing, for the new house, "Oakholm," was turning into a hungry octopus that sucked her blood. It was partly the design and details of the house, built largely from oaks and chestnuts on the property; partly all the glass (Harriet was preaching the virtues of conservatories, and

"Oakholm," Harriet Beecher Stowe's first Hartford house, c. 1865
(Stowe-Day Foundation, Hartford, Connecticut)

hers soared to the rooftops); partly the fact that she kept adding in new inspirations. Finally the Stowes were able to move in. Georgie, a fiery and beautiful twenty-one, added to the excitement by becoming engaged to the handsome and wealthy young pastor of the Stockbridge Episcopal Church, Henry Allen. They planned a wedding in the summer of 1865.

On April 9, 1865, the war at last was over. Five days later President Lincoln, attending a theatrical performance with his wife at Washington's Ford's Theatre, was shot by John Wilkes Booth, a fanatic Southern-sympathizer and member of a famous theatrical family. *"Sic semper tyrannis!"*—"Thus to all tyrants"— Booth shouted as he leaped from presidential box to stage and ran away, to be caught and killed later in a burning barn.

Lincoln died in the time of lilacs, the North mourned, and a terrible period of reconstruction began. With his death, Lincoln's plea of "With malice towards none, with charity for all, we must bind up the nation's wounds" was forgotten in a wave of political revenge. The South was destitute; the freed slaves were destitute and often exploited by northern "carpetbaggers," and a vicious pattern of "separate but unequal" was established. It was not the future Harriet had foreseen for the children of Uncle Tom.

Harriet, her war over, devoted herself professionally and personally to her other real mission—the creation of beautiful, nurturing, and happy homes in which the next generations could grow up well and strong. Beauty as essential was a given with her, and too many people she knew lived in houses that were not truly homes. She suggested expanding her *House and Home Papers* column into a whole household department in the *Atlantic;* Mr. Fields said no at the time, but doubled her current column rate to keep her exclusively with his paper. Ticknor & Fields started a juvenile magazine called *Our Young Folks* and signed Harriet as a regular contributor.

In Hartford Harriet followed her heart at last into the Episcopal Church. Lyman was gone now, daughter Georgie was about to "marry Episcopal," and the old Calvinist-Episcopal conflict seemed so far away. Her children were grown and following their own calls also. Young Charley, who at fourteen had gone to sea, had returned brown and muscular and ready to prepare himself for divinity study at Harvard. Georgie and her minister were married in a flurry of excitement. The Fieldses sent as their wedding present a complete set of Nathaniel Hawthorne's works, specially bound in bridal white. Harriet loved the idea, and from then on a similarly bound set of her own works became her standard wedding gift.

The postwar peace that was not quite a peace went on. Harriet and Henry Ward spoke out for conciliation with the reunited South, offending vengeance-seekers including Theodore Tilton, whom Henry had, under pressure, made editor of the *Independent* in his place. The magazine now bore a masthead proclaiming, THE SLAVE A MAN; THE MAN A CITIZEN; THE CITIZEN A VOTER. Harriet and Henry both had reservations—Harriet saw education as the blacks' first right and need; Henry, recalling that elections in the South were filled with mob violence already, foresaw a race war if universal suffrage was immediately granted. Harriet and Henry were called traitors by Abolitionist extremists.

Calvin had retired, but he had still not started writing his long-dreamed-of *Origin and History of the Books of the Bible*. He had the scholarship, he had the skill, he simply did not have the drive. Harriet and James T. Fields conspired together to push him into it. Harriet dredged for New England recollections, hers and Calvin's, to come up with more cash to throw into the bottomless pit of Oakholm. She took on a masculine pseudonym—Horace Holyoke—in order to write in a first-person male persona that was actually Calvin Stowe's.

Henry Ward was also writing New England stories, getting $25,000 advances to Harriet's $10,000. Rich and famous as Henry was, he never—though Harriet seemed not to realize it—equaled her in influence and celebrity. And he rarely read her writing.

Harriet had more important things to worry about. Fred was not getting well, in body or in mind, and his alcoholism was

Henry Ward Beecher, c. 1865
(Stowe-Day Foundation, Hartford, Connecticut)

growing worse. He needed safer surroundings, fresh air, and physical labor to build him up. Opportunity offered itself in, of all places, one of Fred's habitual barrooms. Two young army veterans who had been mustered out in Florida, had returned to Connecticut glowing with enthusiasm. They had rented a thousand-acre plot, full of possibilities, on the Saint Johns River, not far from Jacksonville. They needed cash and partners. Fred proposed to become one, if Harriet would put up the money.

Seeing possibilities not only for Fred but for newly freed slaves who were in need of jobs, Harriet bought an interest in Laurel Grove Plantation that included the superintendent's post for Fred. With Fred safely off for the South, and Calvin prodded and encouraged into writing, life was going well at last.

Calvin's book turned out to be so successful that a Hartford publishing house came after him for another—a "popular" book, made up out of his sermon and lecture barrels. The money offered was alluring. The same firm also approached Harriet, who offered them a collection of already-written biographical sketches. After getting her signature on a contract, the publishers demanded many more biographies as well, ones that would match up with eighteen engraved portraits they had on hand. The subjects included President Lincoln, all the current political celebrities, famed black abolitionist Frederick Douglass, and Henry Ward Beecher. The signed contract, and the money offered, put Harriet in a straitjacket. *Men of Our Times* was the result.

Glowing letters came from Fred in Florida. The sun was so warm. . . . He wore white linen suits. . . . The place was a paradise of birds and flowers. By February 1867, Harriet could bear to stay away no longer. In March she went south, traveling from New York by boat. She found Florida utterly captivating, and Fred seeming well. The first cotton crop had been planted. Across the river lay a village called Mandarin, settled mainly by English expatriates. The live oaks spread their branches more than 130 feet wide, their trunks had diameters of seven feet, the boardwalk along the river was foaming with Cherokee roses.

Harriet fell in love with a small house—a cottage or a hut, depending on to whom she was describing it—with a burgeoning orange grove in the back. Oakholm had already proved itself too much a financial responsibility, and she loathed the northern winters. Why not a smaller house in Hartford, and a second home—this one—in Mandarin? It would be so good for Calvin, too! Before the voice of reason could set in, she bought it.

Reassured that Fred was "reconstructing" his life, Harriet returned to Hartford with an easy heart. Her books were doing well; to their mutual joy, Calvin's were also; but expenses still were mounting. She forced herself to work on *Oldtown Folks* and the biographies. Fortunately, she had set some of her wealth aside in a trust, but Laurel Grove Plantation cost money to maintain and the Oakholm expenses went on. She returned to Mandarin in February 1868 (to Ticknor & Fields's annoyance; *Oldtown Folks* wasn't finished). The Stowe party went by train, and the trip was an eye-opener for Harriet, who for the first time met the southern "beasts" and found she could not hate them. The reconciliation that Lincoln had preached, that Harriet herself had preached but not accepted, had begun.

What awaited her in Florida was far worse. Laurel Grove Plantation was a wasteland. What little cotton the inept crew had managed to grow was rotting with mildew. The Yankees had not known how to grow cotton, run a plantation, or manage and train the newly freed slaves. Harriet's $10,000 investment was gone. Worst of all, Fred had become irrational, unbalanced, a stupefied drunken ruin.

XXVII

Fall from Grace

1868–1872

HARRIET RETURNED TO the North with Fred in tow. The only solution his distraught parents could come up with was a long sea voyage, with Calvin as his guide and keeper. In July the two men left on a Mediterranean cruise.

They were home again by Christmas, with Fred not improved. Harriet persuaded one of her Foote cousins, a Civil War veteran, to manage the plantation, and apparently Fred went back south with him.

Then it was 1869—Harriet was finally finishing up *Oldtown Folks*. It was the best work she had done since *Dred*. At fifty-eight she was at the pinnacle of her powers. She had also written, with sister Catharine, *The American Woman's Home,* a remarkable book that drew on and expanded the advice and information of her "House and Home" columns and Catharine's *Treatise on Domestic Economy.* Both Catharine and Harriet were far ahead of their time in their psychological and physiological advice. The home-science chapters were undoubtedly Catharine's; the rest was pure Harriet—right down to instruction on how to build and upholster chairs and sofas and how to train ivy up indoor windowframes.

Her finances were looking up. James Fields had taken one look at *Oldtown Folks* and wanted to buy U.S. and British serial rights, and all book rights for one year after publication, for a flat $6,000. Harriet had turned down the serial sale—what she hoped to preach through the story would be better said in a book, she thought—and let him have the book rights only. Now it occurred to her that she had more New England tales left to tell, lighter ones for which prebook serialization would be just fine, and she struck another excellent deal with the *Atlantic*. The Unitarians, Transcendentalists, and so on, could chuckle over droll tales in the *Atlantic* while she preached to the Puritan orthodoxy in the *Oldtown* book.

She went to Mandarin in March 1869, with a happy heart. Fred Stowe was doing well there in his cousin Spencer Foote's company, and the orange grove was flourishing. Ingenious Spencer Foote had had two bright ideas: Plant peaches, lemons, and grapes as well; advertise the fruit as from the lands of Harriet Beecher Stowe.

The "hut" had been slightly enlarged. Behind it the Freedmen's Bureau was employing a contractor to build a school for the neighborhood's black children. Harriet immediately constituted herself teacher and board of education. She also arranged for further enlargements to the cottage, planning to bring the whole family south next year. Then she headed north so as to be in Canada when *Oldtown Folks* was published there on May 15.

En route, she stopped off in Boston as was her custom, and went browsing for books to take along. Her eye was caught by a new offering from Harper & Bros., *My Recollections of Lord Byron,* by the Countess Guiccioli. She took it with her to Canada, and returned home in a mighty rage. And with a new mission: the vindication of her dear, and now departed, friend Lady Byron.

America might not know who the Countess Guiccioli was, but all Europe did, and so did Harriet. The old harridan, a notorious sight on the fashionable avenues of Paris, had been Lord Byron's last mistress. That was bad enough, but in her book this fallen woman had devoted herself, from first to last, to telling the world that the fall from grace and hope of heaven of that shining Lucifer, Lord Byron, had all been due to the vicious, unforgiving cold-heartedness of the wife who had so cruelly left him.

It was exactly what all the young ladies at Miss Pierce's school had whispered; exactly what Harriet had for years believed herself . . . *before* she had met the frail, maligned Lady Byron. Lady Byron, whom English society had ignored all through the long years, preferring to take the side of the fallen angel. And all, Harriet thought indignantly, because they did not know the truth about why Lady Byron had left her husband. *That* was the secret Lady Byron had confided to her. It had shaken Harriet to her shoetops, and she had advised Lady Byron that it should not be told—certainly not till all involved were dead.

But Lady Byron was dead now, and could not defend herself. It came to Harriet that she—perhaps she alone—had the power to clear Lady Byron's name. If she had that power, surely she had the duty to use it? The truth was shocking, but it would clear Lady Byron's reputation.

The truth was that the young Lady Byron had left her husband because she had discovered that he and his half sister Augusta Leigh had been lovers. *Incest*—that most terrible of sins. How *could* Lady Byron have stood by him after that, Harriet thought indignantly. It was no use saying that no woman could resist Byron and vice versa; nor that brother and sister had been raised separately and met as adults and strangers. If the world, if Lady Byron's detractors, only knew—

They would only know if Harriet told them.

Once she would have quailed to think about, let alone write about, such things. But Harriet was nearly sixty and a sophisticated woman.

"Leave all to some discreet friends," Harriet had advised Lady Byron. Wasn't that she? Wasn't that why the dear soul had confided in her? Harriet came home from Canada determined to tell Lady Byron's story in the *Atlantic Monthly*.

Calvin counseled against it, as did others. But Harriet was determined. The only person who might have stopped her was the publisher, James T. Fields, but Fields and his wife, Annie, were in Europe. So Harriet wrote her column—very carefully; never coming right out and saying Lady Byron had told her the story directly; never actually mentioning the name of Augusta Leigh. But anyone who knew anything at all about Byron's life could guess.

The column appeared in the *Atlantic* and the storm broke. The fanatical Byron-worship of Harriet's youth was over, but Byron was still a huge literary and romantic hero. Oliver Wendell Holmes wrote a friend that there were three storms over the Atlantic that year—the September gale, the gold crisis, and the Byron whirlwind. He was the only one to stand at Harriet's side, for the whole rest of the world attacked. Lady Byron was a demented, malicious woman; Harriet was a naive, gullible, mercenary ("she did it for the money") fool—these were the least of what was said. Mr. Fields was so angry about the column that Harriet dared not write directly to him for a long time.

Like a good journalist, she stood by her story. ("Mrs. Stowe felt her message from the Most High," was how Annie Fields put it.) But the Lady Byron column had become the target of everyone who loved Byron, hated his wife, or loathed any of the Beechers. No one but Dr. Holmes defended Harriet; her other friends turned against her. The negative reaction to *Uncle Tom's Cabin* and *Dred* had been as nothing compared to this. And she did not understand why.

The truth was that she had destroyed illusions. The truth was people wanted to believe the Byron legend. Harriet had committed the unspeakable sin: She had told the truth people didn't want to know. The sad irony was that all over Europe the aristocracy *did* know, had known for years, had laughed over it and over poor, naive Lady Byron. She hadn't "played the game" of upper-class moral hypocrisy. Now Harriet hadn't played the game.

When *Uncle Tom's Cabin* had been attacked, Harriet had backed up her charges by writing the *Key*. She would do the same thing now. After taking a breather by going with Catharine to visit a girls' reform school in Providence, Rhode Island, in September, Harriet embarked on *Lady Byron Vindicated*. It almost totally destroyed what reputation she had left.

The Beecher family rallied around. Harriet's two lawyer brothers-in-law checked the manuscript, as did a respected New York judge. James T. Fields advised Harriet to stay in New York during the final stages of publication; his contact with her was only through her editor, a Mr. Osgood. Ticknor & Fields could not let this explosive project go to another publisher, but they were extremely disturbed about it.

Eunice Beecher did not offer Harriet the hospitality of the Brooklyn parsonage. Harriet stayed instead with a Dr. Taylor in Manhattan. Calvin came down to write the press releases. Henry Ward, energized by it all, called every day to advise and soothe.

The final stages of editing were completed in time for the Stowes, gratefully, to go home for Christmas. The book came out in January 1870 and was for Harriet a major catastrophe. As a writer, as a role model, as a virtuous woman, her reputation would never be the same.

Soon after that Harriet closed her "dream home," Oakholm, forever. At least a year would go by before it found a buyer. Meanwhile Harriet took her family south to Mandarin. The house was large enough to house all the Stowes and also Spencer Foote and his wife and child. Her planned additions had been made, and more would come—Harriet could never let well enough alone on a house. Eventually verandas would encircle it, enclosing as well a magnificent live oak, dripping with Spanish moss, that grew near the house and, apparently, right through the roof.

Hattie and Eliza made a bargain, with Eliza serving as house-keeper in Hartford and Hattie in Mandarin. This gave each approximately half a year's vacation. Calvin took to the rocking chair on the veranda like a cat to cream. Always theatrical, he now looked much like Santa Claus with stout belly and white beard.

Harriet called him "my old rabbi," and he took to wearing a black skullcap over his bald patch to increase the effect. Harriet acquired a permanent Florida staff—former slaves Laura and Tesia Summerall and "Aunt" Felicia Zeigler, whom Harriet paid the then-fabulous wages of $12.50 a month.

A pleasant little social circle began to develop in Mandarin. The Howards came south for a visit, and John Howard made Harriet a business proposition. A religious weekly called the *Church Union* had gone bankrupt, and Howard and his sons were buying it. Henry Ward had agreed to be what might be called "executive editor," with Joe Howard as managing editor. John Howard wanted Harriet to buy in and edit. Harriet agreed. The paper was eventually rechristened *The Outlook*.

On the flower-fragrant veranda at Mandarin, talking with friends, the uproar over Lady Byron could be forgotten. Harriet was moving on to other projects. Fred was there, a physical and mental wreck, but *trying*—Harriet had to believe he was trying. He was a tragic by-product of the war. Secretly, he had made up his mind to try his fortunes elsewhere. Somehow, he got money from Harriet to board a boat around South America. Instead of disembarking in Chile as he had planned, he sailed on to San Francisco, went ashore to the rough waterfront, and disappeared forever.

XXVIII

Scandal

1872–1875

THERE WAS, in Harriet's philosophy, always sunlight after rain. Her daughter Georgie gave birth to a beautiful boy. Oakholm was sold, and Harriet began building what she called a "Gothic cottage" on a Nook Farm side street. Catharine Beecher, now old and weary, living (as Harriet teased her) "like a trunk without a label" in the home of one brother or sister after another, was asked to become principal of the Hartford Female Seminary she had founded nearly fifty years before. Harriet agreed to "aid," and Calvin to give biblical lectures. Life was growing mellow.

Harriet began writing another novel through a first-person male persona, Harry Henderson. It was called *My Wife and I* and in it—even in the order of words in the title—Harriet was taking potshots at the more rabid of the new militant feminists like Victoria Woodhull and Tennie Claflin.

Like Catharine, Harriet believed that with the world—and men—the way it was, woman could exercise more influence and power in the home than at the ballot box. She was thereby clashing head-on with Elizabeth Cady Stanton and Susan B. Anthony, who were eminently respectable, and the much less respectable

Harriet Beecher Stowe, c. 1870
(Stowe-Day Foundation, Hartford, Connecticut)

Woodhull-Claflin sisters. Victoria Woodhull was a believer in "free love"—by which she meant free, promiscuous sex without benefit of marriage. To the Beechers' chagrin, Belle Hooker had become a militant feminist, a believer in Spiritualism (and her own spiritual gifts), and a loyal partisan of the sisters. Harriet could not resist taking jibes at her younger sister in *My Wife and I,* and had no qualms at all about satirizing Woodhull and Claflin. It is a toss-up whether Harriet's character Victoria Dangyereyes (Danger-eyes and Dang-yer-eyes) is a cartoon of Victoria Woodhull or Belle Beecher Hooker.

Belle was furious, and a rift began within the Beecher family. Then, suddenly, a volcano erupted that split the family to its very foundations and made the Lady Byron scandal look tame. Theodore Tilton sued his mentor Henry Ward Beecher for alienation of his wife's affections (translation: adultery) in both the religious and the civil courts.

The roots of the scandal ran deep and far into the past, fertilized with jealousy, envy, and probably all the deadly sins. Tilton was a member of Henry's famous church. Tilton had hero-worshiped Henry, who had taken advantage of him by shoving him into assistant editorship on the *Independent.* When Henry had "slacked off"—by choice or pressure—Tilton had become senior editor "in name as well as in fact." At the same time, Henry had begun speaking conciliation toward the South, offending radical Republicans, including Tilton. The *Independent* had abruptly stopped publishing Henry's sermons. The reading public presumed Henry now felt himself too good for the *Independent,* and lambasted him accordingly.

Meanwhile Tilton was proving to have more brilliance as a writer than judgment as a newspaper editor. Specifically, he was speaking out on marriage and divorce in ways that conservative Christians identified with "socialism" and free love. His ideas, and "other difficulties of a more personal nature," drove the distraught and beautiful Mrs. Tilton to consult her pastor—Henry Ward Beecher himself. He advised patience. But Elizabeth Tilton's patience soon wore out and she "sought refuge at her mother's house," sending Henry Ward a request for advice as to her Christian duty.

Henry conferred with one of his church deacons, and with his own wife, Eunice; the three of them were unanimous in recommending a permanent separation for Elizabeth Tilton. This had not immediately taken place, but Theodore Tilton had found out enough about these pastoral counseling sessions to severely wound his self-respect and destroy all he had believed about the greatness of Henry Ward.

For nearly a decade Tilton had bided his time, playing loyal disciple to Henry Ward and sowing seeds of doubt among the congregation. There was a matter of an earlier deathbed confession, of intimacies with Henry Ward, supposedly made by a female parishioner to her husband. Recently Tilton had been confiding to fellow churchmen that Henry was an adulterer leading other men's wives into sin. That, supposedly, was the reason Elizabeth Tilton had temporarily fled her husband's bed and board. Now Tilton went before the church board to charge his friend and pastor Henry Ward Beecher with having made "improper proposals" to the pure and virtuous Elizabeth Tilton, thus tempting her to sin and ending the Tilton marriage.

Even this bombshell might have been kept within the confines of the church establishment had it not been for Victoria Woodhull. Somehow—the Beechers had their own suspicions how—she had gotten hold of the story and proclaimed it at a spiritualist convention in September 1872. Victoria Woodhull broadcast her version of the Beecher-Tilton story not as condemnation, but as proof that chastity and monogamous marriage were unnatural if even the devout like Dr. Beecher could not live up to the demands of those restrictions. Not one of the many reporters at the convention printed the sensational story, though the *Journal* hinted that prominent New York clergymen were being accused of hideous crimes. But people heard, and guessed. Frank Moulton, a mutual friend and go-between for Henry and Tilton, heard, and knew he could do nothing now to keep things quiet. Annie Fields heard, and knew she had to break the news to Harriet.

Victoria Woodhull, stalemated in her publicity tactic, published the whole thing—what Tilton had told her, and what her fertile imagination added—in *Woodhull & Claflin's Weekly*. Worse, she had somehow maneuvered Belle into believing the story was true, free love was natural, she should persuade her brother to speak out like a man and testify that this was the natural order of things.

The split in the Beecher family cut deep, directly between the children of Roxana and the children of Harriet Porter. Harriet could believe no wrong of Henry Ward. The nation rocked with the scandal, which dragged on for two years. Harriet, horrified, defended Henry, as did Mary and their full brothers. Catharine, old and dependent on living in her relatives' homes, kept remarkably quiet. But the family was terrified of what Belle might do. The only member famous enough, and daunting enough, to "handle" Belle was Harriet.

Sunday after Sunday Harriet was stationed in a front pew of Henry's church, in case Belle did, as rumored, appear to take over the pulpit. She never did. Ultimately the case was settled in both church and civil courts in Henry's favor, and he retained his Plymouth Church pulpit. But his reputation was never the same.

Harriet herself never doubted Henry. But Henry had always been what was called a "full-blooded man" with an eye for the ladies. Handsome in his youth, he had become, like his father before him, an aging lion—women still buzzed around him like bees at a honey pot. Even a breath of scandal could ruin a clergyman's career. It did *not* destroy Henry's career—only his reputation.

Were the charges false or true? Only Henry Ward Beecher and Elizabeth Tilton knew for sure—and they never told.

XXIX

"She Told the Story"

1875–1896

THE ENORMOUS HOOPS in which Harriet looked like a child in her mother's clothes had given way to the low bustles of the 1870s, that would soon be supplanted by the high bustles of the 1880s. Harriet sat for formal photographs in black silk with jet, but as time went by she clung to her bonnets and shawls, and velvet ribbons binding the curls that had now turned white.

Harriet and her world were becoming old-fashioned as America reached its hundredth birthday—one nation, no longer divided—and hurtled toward the twentieth century. Her books were considered too pious, too sentimental for modern tastes. The "Tom Shows" went on, but now Tom and the others were actually considered figures of mirth and were played for broad comedy. Harriet would have been horrified had she witnessed this. True to her upbringing, she did not attend theatrical performances, which to Puritans were on a par with naughty novels. She saw a dramatization of *Uncle Tom's Cabin* (not one of the worse ones) exactly once—when she was given two passes to a performance in Hartford. She asked a neighbor, author-editor Charles Dudley Warner, to escort her. While she wept over Tom and Eva and laughed over Topsy, just as she had done when she first saw them in visions, the play was so different from her book that she couldn't even follow the plot. And she never said what she thought of the performance. The one good thing that Tom Shows, however bad, accomplished was that they confronted hundreds of thousands of people with the evils and inhumanities of slavery.

For some time Harriet was busy editing for the *Christian Union* (formerly the *Church Union*), signing up, among others, Louisa May Alcott as a contributor. Harriet herself was busy writing *Poganuc People,* her last novel and considered one of her best—an affectionate, heart-true story of Connecticut people that drew long and lovingly on memories of Litchfield.

The "new house" in Nook Farm seemed quaint and old-fashioned, too, compared with the modern splendor of the Samuel Clemens (Mark Twain) house next door. Clemens had commissioned something up-to-the-minute, and there it was— orange-red brick, adorned with vermilion-and-black enameled designs like a Navajo blanket, every sort of carved wood and gilded leather ornament within. He had a huge billiard table on which he sorted manuscripts, and a private dressing room where he could cuss to his heart's content without his children hearing. Harriet wrote in a little flower-walled study where the white furniture was ornamented by her own hand with vines of ivy.

The Stowe house at 1 Forest Street, Hartford, was a "Gothic cottage"—foursquare, gabled, the mauve-taupe color of a mourning dove, with minimal gingerbread and much more room within than at first appeared. It was also much more modern than at first appeared, just as were Harriet's homemaking, cooking, and child-raising ideas. The house was, in fact, a life-sized model of all she and Catharine had written in *The American Woman's Home,* and it was perfectly charming. Eliza kept house there, but the style was all her mother's. Harriet's paintings were everywhere—the magnolia of Florida, dramatic on a black ground; woodland flowers; portraits. Everywhere, too, were photographs—of family; of the great who were her friends. Crystal twinkled in the sunlight that flooded the rooms and the house was ringed with flowers.

In May 1878 Catharine died of a stroke at her half-brother Thomas's home. The Beechers had more or less made up with Thomas and James, who had been on the "Porter side" of the Henry Ward scandal, but not with Isabella Hooker. She was becoming a great lady of the suffragist movement, but also increasingly strange. Always deeply into Spiritualism, she was beginning to believe that *she* was the matriarchal Christ of the Second Coming prophesied in Scriptures. Mary's husband had died suddenly in 1872, but Mary went on, as elegant and lovely as ever. There was joy for Harriet in 1879 as her last son, Charley, married Susie Munroe of Cambridge in a May wedding. The young couple went to Saco, Maine, where Charley had become pastor of the Congregational Church. It was a comfort to see them so happy, and to see grandson Freeman Allen thriving. Georgiana May Allen, Harriet's sparkling, volatile youngest daughter, had become a manic-depressive. Her doctor had prescribed morphine, the current miracle medicine, and within a short time she had become an addict. Another family secret not to be spoken of.

Harriet was seventy in 1881. The *Atlantic* had a tradition of holding seventieth-birthday celebrations for its original contributors, but somehow no one there knew exactly in what year Harriet's was. Characteristically, she did not tell them. Poet John Greenleaf Whittier's "day" had been honored with a stag dinner in 1877. (Harriet, Louisa May Alcott, and other *Atlantic* women writers had had a bit of fun with that. The party was "stag" since Whittier was a bachelor; each lady sent an unsolicited letter of regret, including a hint that the ladies were going to found an all-female competitor to the *Atlantic*.) Dr. Oliver Wendell Holmes had been honored with a breakfast in 1877. It had been years since Harriet had written anything for the *Atlantic*, but in 1882 it occurred to somebody that that was probably her "year." Tactfully, Harriet went along.

As the first woman recipient, Harriet was honored with a garden party. Her friend former Governor Claflin lent his summer home, "The Old Elms," for the occasion, and several hundred people were invited for the afternoon of June 14. At least two hundred came: Holmes, Whittier, Bronson Alcott, William Dean Howells, abolitionist and educator Frank Sanborn, President Alice Freeman of Wellesley College, a mass of Beechers. Others showed up out of curiosity—Harriet Beecher Stowe and *Uncle Tom's Cabin* seemed to them from another world.

Dr. Oliver Wendell Holmes wrote a poem to read, decided it was too solemn—and too good—for a picnic, and wrote a comic one instead, full of intellectual puns.

> *Her lever was the wand of art,*
> *Her fulcrum was the human heart,*
>
> *Whence all unfailing aid is.*
> *She moved the earth! Its thunders pealed;*
> *Its mountains shook, its temples reeled . . .*
> *All through the conflict, up and down,*
> *Marched Uncle Tom and Old John Brown—*
>
> *One ghost, one form ideal.*
> *And which was false, and which was true,*
> *And which was mightier of the two,*
> *The wisest sibyl never knew,*
>
> *For both alike were real.*

Whittier, another close friend, also honored her in verse:

> *. . . the unending years*
> *Shall tell her tale in unborn ears.*
> *And when with sins and follies past*
> *Are numbered color-hate and caste,*
> *White, black, and red shall own as one*
> *The noblest work by woman done.*

Henry Ward responded for Harriet to the *Atlantic* publisher's address of welcome.

The winter trips to Mandarin were becoming hard on Calvin. He was several years older than Harriet, and he was failing. After the 1883–1884 winter trip Harriet knew he could no longer travel. From now on her friends must come to her; she would not leave her husband.

"The girls," as the twins were always called, looked after the house and Harriet's literary matters, but Harriet herself looked after Calvin. They had married to love, honor, and cherish; *he* had always done that for her; so would she for him. But the physical strain became increasingly difficult for her frail body, and her mind sometimes seemed to slip away and run in flowery meadows.

Calvin died of a stroke in 1886. Henry Ward followed, struck down by the same illness, in 1887. Belle, distraught, tried to get in to see him as he lay dying, but Henry's wife, Eunice, held her off. In 1887, also, the tragic, mercurial Georgie was gone. But Charley and Susie—and in time their son Lyman—were in Hartford, where Charley was pastor of the Windsor Avenue Congregational Church. Having been "born and converted Presbyterian," and "confirmed Episcopalian," Harriet was back worshiping under a Calvinist roof again with her son in the pulpit.

Visitors came, among them Frances Willard, the educator and temperance leader. Florine Thayer McCray, new editor of Hartford's *City Mission Record* and a bold and sporty lady, asked permission to write a "life-sketch" of Harriet for publication. Harriet was an old hand herself at life-sketches; that was what those thumbnail biographies of Civil War noteworthies had been. She granted permission.

Mrs. McCray, wiser than Harriet in the ways of rough-and-tumble journalism, asked for the permission in writing, and for the opportunity to read through Harriet's papers. Harriet complied. She was already working on her own full-length autobiography—or rather, Charley was, with her collaboration. Harriet wrote reminiscences down daily for him to use. The work went slowly, and so did Mrs. McCray's life-sketch.

By 1889 the "authorized autobiography" was almost finished. In September Charley brought Harriet the final manuscript. Harriet herself wrote the preface, her handwriting clear and firm. "It is the true story of my life, told for the most part in my own words, and therefore has all the force of an autobiography." She ended with a quotation from *Pilgrim's Progress*, which she first had read so long ago:

> I am going to my Father's; and, though with great difficulty I am got hither, yet now I do not repent me of all the troubles I have been at to arrive where I am. My sword I give to him that shall succeed me in my pilgrimage, and my courage and skill to him that can get it.

A few weeks later Harriet was felled by a stroke. Her body recovered, but her mind was never the same. It was clear enough late that autumn to explode with rage when Florine McCray's "sketch" about her appeared. Mrs. McCray had written no brief article, but a full-length, unauthorized biography of 450 pages, titled *Life-Work of the Author of Uncle Tom's Cabin*. It was much more fascinating than the careful work Charley had produced. Worst of all, Mrs. McCray was flourishing that brief note Harriet had written her two years earlier, as proof that her book *had* been authorized.

Harriet, outraged, rushed to disavow the McCray book and banned it within her circle of family and friends.

The mists were closing in. By 1890 Hattie was obliged to tell interview-seekers that her mother now had the mind of a child of two or three. "My mind wanders like a running brook," Harriet wrote her old friend Susie Howard during one of her lucid moments. "I have written all my words and thought all my thoughts. . . ." She who had always been small shrank still further until she was like a tiny, fragile doll, her white hair still bound up in curls with a black velvet ribbon. Her teeth were gone; she could not, or would not, wear false ones, and her face had the fragile sculpting of a china figurine.

Her eightieth birthday came and went. An old Litchfield friend continued to send birthday flowers from Roxana's grave, and Oliver Wendell Holmes still sent her birthday letters. Dr. Holmes, himself two years older than she, wrote on January 31, 1893, to ask about her health. Harriet was lucid enough on February 5 to respond personally in a long, poignant letter. Her last letter, written the day after her eighty-second birthday, thanked Mrs. Seymour for a bunch of pansies from the Litchfield garden.

Then the mists enfolded her completely. She was a child again, running through meadows on the rolling Litchfield hills in the golden light. She still loved beauty; she still loved music; she still loved flowers. But the meadows she roamed were the green sweep of lawn between the Stowe house and the Clemenses'. She loved to pick flowers; the ones she usually picked were growing in the Clemens garden, and she "picked" them by pulling up the plants. In warm weather when doors stood open, she would escape from her daughters or the household help and wander into Mrs. Clemens's white-and-gold drawing room, to sit at the piano playing happily until word was sent for someone to please come take Mrs. Stowe back home.

In 1895 Edward died. So many of Harriet's generation were gone now—Catharine, William, Edward, George; James, dead by his own hand in a sanitarium. Mary was a beautiful old lady, determined to live to celebrate her hundredth birthday. Harriet knew none of this. In her own mind she was a young girl, not recognizing Hattie and Eliza as her daughters and sometimes mistaking one of them for her mother. One day, seeing a dignified middle-aged neighbor on his way to a Grand Army of the Republic meeting in full Civil War uniform, she ran out to embrace him. *Freddie!* It was her Freddie, home at last! The twins had great difficulty persuading her that it was not.

Her belief that Fred would soon be coming home intensified. She would be up, haphazardly dressed, and out before sunup, gathering armloads of wildflowers to deck the house for his return. Hattie and Eliza could no longer manage her. They hired a

Harriet Beecher Stowe, 1896
(Stowe-Day Foundation, Hartford, Connecticut)

sturdy, tenderhearted Irish girl to be her nurse and keeper. By her eighty-fifth birthday on June 14, 1896, Harriet was bedridden, living in her inner visions of long ago.

Just before midnight on Wednesday, the first of July, she opened her eyes. The bedroom she had shared with Calvin was in shadows, the young Irishwoman sitting quietly in the light of a shaded lamp. The flicker of life from the little figure beneath the white sheets brought the nurse forward, medicine in hand.

Harriet's face lit with the ghost of her old smile. "I love you," she whispered.

Then she was gone.

They buried her in the Andover Cemetery, between Calvin and her beloved firstborn son. They were all there, all who remained and still could come: Hattie and Eliza, who had made so much of her work and her later life possible. Charley, her youngest, with his wife and son. Brother Charles, with his daughter. Sister Belle with her doctor son. Georgie's son, the first grandchild, Freeman Allen. Annie Fields, and the author Sarah Orne Jewett. A sprinkling of others, including a representative of all the Stowe neighbors of Brunswick, Maine. They stood in a circle around the three graves banked with briar roses, and sang the hymns Harriet loved.

The wreath on her casket had been sent by the black community of Boston. The card bore the inscription: *The Children of Uncle Tom.*

Two years later the distinguished black poet Paul Laurence Dunbar, son of slaves, published his tribute to Harriet in the November 1898 issue of *Century Magazine.*

She told the story, and the whole world wept
At wrongs and cruelties it had not known
But for this fearless woman's voice alone.
She spoke to consciences that long had slept:
Her message, Freedom's clear reveille, swept
From heedless hovel to complacent throne.
Command and prophecy were in the tone,

And from its sheath the sword of justice leapt.
Around two peoples swelled a fiery wave,
And both came forth transfigured from the flame.
Blest be the hand that dared be strong to save,
And blest be she who in our weakness came—
Prophet and priestess! At one stroke she gave
A race to freedom, and herself to fame.

BOOKS FOR FURTHER READING

ABOUT HARRIET BEECHER STOWE AND HER WORLD

Abbott, Lyman. *Henry Ward Beecher.* New York: Chelsea House, 1980. A new edition of the "life of the celebrated preacher who inspired the heart and conscience of 19th-century America," first published in 1903; contains new introductions by Daniel Aaron (editor) and William G. McLoughlin.

Beecher, Charles, ed. *Autobiography, Correspondence, etc., of Lyman Beecher.* New York: Harper Brother, 1864–1865. Based on Lyman's oral reminiscences to his children Catharine, Charles, and Harriet, and edited by Charles; published the year after Lyman's death.

Boydston, Jeanne, Mary Kelley, and Anne Margolis. *The Limits of Sisterhood: The Beecher Sisters on Women's Rights and Woman's Sphere.* Chapel Hill/London: University of North Carolina Press, 1988. A fascinating study of the dynamics between Catharine Beecher, Harriet Beecher Stowe, and Isabella Beecher Hooker—as sisters, as women, as activists, as authors—told in large part in their own words.

Fields, Annie A. *The Life and Letters of Harriet Beecher Stowe.* Cambridge, MA: Riverside Press, 1897. Edited (in the nineteenth century the term meant coauthored) by a close friend who was both an author herself and the wife of one of Harriet's longtime publishers. The book draws extensively on the materials being prepared by Charles Stowe for his version of the *Life* that was published the following year—but there are many small, telling differences in both transcription and interpretation. If you want a real sense of eavesdropping on Harriet's private talks with friends, this is the book to read.

Hedrick, Joan D. *Harriet Beecher Stowe: A Life.* New York: Oxford University Press, 1993.

Johnston, Johanna. *Runaway to Heaven: The Story of Harriet Beecher Stowe.* New York: Doubleday & Co., Inc., 1963. The book that, when it was published shortly before I was to direct a production of the play *Harriet,* first fascinated me in the dynamics between Harriet, her religion, and her world. A wonderful, insightful portrayal of America in the first half of the nineteenth century. The author (no relation to me) and I differ on interpretation: She sees Harriet as a "little bundle of contradictions," an enigma that cannot be solved, who had a deep desire to run away from life as it was. *I* see her as a characteristically Calvinist paradox who juggled the real and the ideal as two parts of her earthly mission.

McPherson, James M. Introduction in *Uncle Tom's Cabin.* New York: Vintage Books/The Library of America, 1991.

Stowe, Charles Edward. *Life of Harriet Beecher Stowe* compiled from her letters and journals. Boston: Houghton Mifflin and Company, 1889. "It is the true story of my life," Harriet wrote in the book's foreword, "told for the most part in my own words, and therefore has all the force of an autobiography." She assisted her son Charles in his research. Filled with quotations from private family papers; since many of these were written years after the events they describe, it is not always accurate about names and dates. Harriet herself was notorious for this, and frequently didn't bother to date her letters.

————, and Lyman Beecher Stowe, eds. *Harriet Beecher Stowe: The Sotry of her Life.* Boston/New York: Houghton Mifflin and Company, 1911. An expanded version of the earlier *Life and Letters,* edited by her son and grandson and published as a "centennial edition" honoring her birth one hundred years before.

Stowe, Lyman Beecher. *Saints, Sinners and Beechers.* Bobbs-Merrill, 1934. Harriet's grandson's multiple biography of the great-grandfather for whom he was named, and *all* of Lyman Beecher's children. Told by a family member who had both access to private Beecher materials and the perspective lent by time, it is full of affection and humor and no illusions. The title comes from a close friend of the family who, at the time of Henry Ward Beecher's sensational trial, remarked that "this country is inhabited by saints, sinners and Beechers."

Wilson, Forrest. *Crusader in Crinoline.* Philadelphia: J. B. Lippincott Co., 1941. The great definitive Harriet Beecher Stowe biography of its time, fascinating reading and full of previously unpublished details.

THE BOOKS OF HARRIET BEECHER STOWE

Except for *Uncle Tom's Cabin,* most of Harriet Beecher Stowe's books—like the earlier biographies listed above—are out of print. All have outlived their copyrights and are now in public domain. Thanks to this, and to growing appreciation of the contribution of the "Beecher women" to women's history and feminist scholarship, some are now being reissued by scholarly presses. Your librarian can help you find out which are in print and from which publishers. The out-of-print books can sometimes be found in libraries—especially through interlibrary loan programs—and at secondhand or rare bookstores.

Books about Slavery

Uncle Tom's Cabin; or, Life among the Lowly (1851–1855)
Key to Uncle Tom's Cabin (1853)
Dred: A Tale of the Great Dismal Swamp (1856)

New England Stories

*The Mayflower; or, Sketches of Scenes and Characters
among the Descendants of the Pilgrims(1843)*
The Minister's Wooing (1859)
Pearl of Orr's Island (1862)
Oldtown Folks (1869)
Oldtown Fireside Stories (1872)
Poganuc People (1878)

Other Novels

Agnes of Sorrento (1862)
My Wife and I (1871)
Pink and White Tyranny(1871)
We and Our Neighbors (1875)

Nonfiction

Primary Geography (1833)
Sunny Memories of Foreign Lands (1854)
Our Charley and What to Do with Him (1858)
A Reply to the Women of England in Behalf of the Women of America (1863)
House and Home Papers (1865)
Little Foxes (1866)
Religious Poems (1867)
The Chimney Corner (1868)
Men of Our Times (1868)
(with Catharine Beecher) The American Woman's Home (1869)
Lady Byron Vindicated (1870)
Palmetto-Leaves (1873)
Women in Sacred History (1873)
Footsteps of the Master (1877)
Our Famous Women (1884)

For Young People

Queer Little People (1867)
Little Pussy Willow (1870)
Betty's Bright Idea (1876)
A Dog's Mission (1880)

ACKNOWLEDGMENTS

My thanks to the many Connecticut historians and curators who introduced me to "Harriet's Connecticut": women from the Litchfield Historical Society, the Litchfield Hills Travel Council, the Farmington Valley/West Hartford Visitors Bureau who took time from their busy professional schedules to steer me (sometimes quite literally) in the right directions and to the right sites; the staff of The Stowe-Day Foundation in Hartford, especially Diana Royce, Librarian, Suzanne Zack, Assistant Librarian, and Beverly J. Zell, Curator of Photographs, who shared with me the treasures of Harriet Beecher Stowe's last home and the Foundation's archives, and who answered innumerable questions in person, by mail, and by phone. My special gratitude and thanks to Dr. Joan D. Hedrick, director of women's studies and professor of history at Trinity College, Hartford, who not only checked my manuscript but also generously shared with me insights and then-unpublished facts about the Beechers and the Stowes that would otherwise have been unavailable to me until her own justly acclaimed *Harriet Beecher Stowe: A Life* was published.

—N.J.

INDEX

Page numbers in italics refer to illustrations.

Stowe, Calvin Ellis (husband), 74, 80, 99-100, *133*, 222. *See also* Writing, Calvin's
and Harriet, 97, 102, 169-170
and Harriet's writing, 120-121, 122-123, 153-154, 158-159, 162
at Lane Seminary, 82-83, 114, 123, 126-127
and Lyman, 68, 98-99, 101, 115-116
marriages of, 79, 92-93, 104-105, 129-130
as parent, 109-110, 124, 126, 148, 182, 200
positions of, 151, 152
retired, 192, 200, 211-212
and slavery, 90, 94-95, 170-171, 178
travel, 105-106, 109, 168, 169, 179-180, 183, 207
Stowe, Charles Edward (son), 132, 181, 220, 222, 226
childhood, 166, 194-196, 203
and Harriet, 175, 222-223
Stowe, Eliza Tyler (Calvin's first wife), 79-81, 82, 83-86, 92-93, 175
Stowe, Eliza Tyler (twin daughter), *186*, 226
childhood of, 109-110, 114-115, 160, 166, 175
in Europe, 179-181, 183-185
working with Harriet, 178, 192-194, 219, 222, 224-226
Stowe, Frederick William (son), 118, 175
in Army, 190-192, *193*, 194-195, 196
childhood of, 166
disappearance of, 212, 224
health of, 199-200, 203-205
travel, 185, 205-206, 207
Stowe, Grandmother (Calvin's mother), 115
Stowe, Harriet Beecher, *ii, 184, 186, 214, 225*
Stowe, Harriet Beecher (twin daughter), *186*, 190-191
childhood of, 109-110, 114-115, 160, 175
travel, 179-181, 183-185, 194
working with Harriet, 178, 192-194, 222, 223, 224-226
Stowe, Henry Ellis (son), 114-115, 166, 175, 177, 179-181, 181-182

Stowe, Lyman (Charley's son), 222
Stowe, Samuel Charles (son), 124
Stowe, Susie Munroe (Charley's wife), 220
Suffrage
for blacks, 203
for women, 148-149, 220
Sumner, Charles, 156, 164, 177-178
Sunny Memories of Foreign Lands, 175
Sutherland, Duchess of, 165, 169-170, 172, 179, 183, 191
Sykes, Georgiana May (friend), 57, 62, 70-71, 129
at school, 51, 52, 56

T
Tallmadge, Benjamin, 2, 13, 32
Tappan, Arthur
and abolitionists, 88-89, 92, 97-98
and Lyman, 69, 74, 110
Teaching, Harriet's, 56-57, 60, 78, 79
Theology
Catharine's, 43-44
Harriet's, 45-47, 59-60, 63-64
Lyman's, 24-25, 30, 55
Ticknor & Fields. *See* Fields, James T.
Tilton, Elizabeth, 215-217
Tilton, Theodore, 187, 192, 203, 215-217
"Tom Shows," 163, 218-219
Translations, of *Uncle Tom's Cabin,* 163
Travel, 90-92, 94-95, 205-206
and Calvin, 117, 207, 222
to Europe, 109, 166-172, 178-181
Harriet's, 79, 85, 120, 157
moving, 73-75, 127-132
Treatise on Domestic Economy (Catharine), 207
True Remedy for the Wrongs of Woman (Catharine), 148-149
Turner, Nat, 107-108

U
Uncle Tom, 137-139, 140-142
Uncle Tom's Cabin, 134-136, *144*
criticism of, x, 159, 163-164
dramatizations of, 163, 218-219
effects of, ix, xi, 174, 195
publication of, 145-147, 153-154
reactions to, 137-138, 140, 151, 156, 157, 163